Praise for *The Mind's Own Place*

The author's prose is always vivid and evocative, almost poetic. The dialogue, moral dilemmas and contradictions are all handled with equally exquisite expression. It's been a long time since I came to the end of a novel and immediately wanted to read it again to uncover more of its nuances. Ian Reid is a revelation, and deserves the widest recognition as a remarkable ambassador for Australian historical fiction. *Historical Novel Review (U.K.)*

A great gathering of personality, character after character, in irreducible and fully imagined life… In *The Mind's Own Place* Ian Reid gives us the 'life-surplus' of history: love and journeys and work and ideas, fear and purposeful action and sometimes failure, all playing out before us in this big and beautifully balanced novel of character. *Rochford Street Review*

Reid richly evokes the abandoned English worlds of those who travel to the antipodes, whose loss is therefore the more poignant. Turn by turn he engages us with his characters' untidy and unruly fates in an assured work of historical reconstruction and imagination. *The Australian*

A compelling portrait of Perth's beginnings… mastery of story-telling… ability to capture the machinations of the mind. *Have A Go*

Reid's vivid writing and attention to historical detail result in settings and characters that make for an enthralling and immersive reading experience. *Writing WA*

A captivating tale… incorporates a strong sense of place. *The Post*

Compelling fictional characters that leap off the page with all the veracity of their historical counterparts… It is historical detective fiction and social commentary rolled into one. The texture shimmers. *The West Australian*

Praise for *The End of Longing*

The End of Longing is a cleverly written piece of historical fiction … a complex story of mystery and intrigue… I was completely absorbed from the first page until the final scene. *Bookseller And Publisher*

The End of Longing is distinguished by its sense of place, which is ironic really, as one of the themes in this richly layered book is that of travel and the peripatetic lives of the married couple at the centre of the story. But wherever his characters go, be it Japan, Canada or Honolulu, Ian Reid places us vividly there. *The Age*

Reid scores a considerable success in recreating the hard-scrabble frontier towns of an age that is increasingly alien to our own. The reader encounters a pageant of nineteenth-century lives here…a realistic portrait of a bleak world. *Australian Book Review*

Reid's fine and unusual historical novel concerns a man who is a fugitive not only from the law and his past misdeeds but perhaps more essentially from his repressed better nature. Maybe – as Reid subtly suggests – it is the desire for revenge against the angels of his own nature that Hammond self-destructively seeks. *The Australian*

A tale rich in historical detail, creating two memorable and affecting main characters. *The West Australian*

Skilfully realised… How well does any person know the 'truth' of another? This question underpins much of the novel and keeps the reader turning the pages… The gradual revelation of clues allows the reader to become the detective in pursuit of truth. *Transnational Literature*

Compelling… intense… poetic… it stayed with me and has been hard to shake off. *Sydney Morning Herald*

Beautifully told. *Launceston Examiner*

Praise for *That Untravelled World*

It is beautifully written and eminently readable… I enjoyed the finely balanced structure of the story, its accuracy, restrained telling, and the way in which the era, age and physicality of the character, at various stages of his life, was so clearly evoked. *Iris Lavell Blogspot*

Perth comes alive in Reid's hands, and throughout the book Western Australia's regional towns are deftly depicted… We are persuaded to ask to what extent we can let unfair disadvantage dictate how we live the remainder of our lives. *The Australian*

Set predominantly in Perth's southern riverside suburbs in the early 1900s, *That Untravelled World* paints a vivid picture of the area at the time. Harry's tale of early confidence followed by recurrent disappointment is evocative of the period in which it is set. With its rapid technological change and economic ups and downs, it's a period that resonates with our own. *The West Australian*

This has everything – snippets of Perth's history, lots of philosophy, a little geography and marvellous descriptions… Ian Reid acquaints us with our own journey into the 'untravelled' world of our aspirations, and the life experiences that are encountered as we struggle with broken dreams and upheavals on our way to becoming older and wiser. Buy this book – you won't be disappointed. *Have A Go*

Reid has deftly woven some fascinating WA history into the narrative, giving a very vivid and familiar sense of Perth in days gone by. This history provides a fitting backdrop to a story that is compelling and satisfyingly unpredictable. *Writing WA*

This fine novel presents a story faithful to its period. *That Untravelled World* covers the gamut of human emotion, from passion to apathy, ecstasy to dysphoria, sacrifice to indulgence, and love to racism. *Bonzer*

That Untravelled World draws the reader into a walk through time… Dreams and disillusion, difficult and concealed family relationships, regional disenfranchisement, the tyranny of distance, as well as the pros and cons of technological advancement… They are themes that speak to our present society. *Trust News Australia*

Celebrated author Ian Reid's latest tale relates the incredible journey of a young man through the Great War, the Depression, and the years after. *World Literature Today*

ABOUT THE AUTHOR

Ian Reid is the author of more than a dozen books – fiction, poetry and several kinds of non-fiction. His writings have been translated into five languages and won international acclaim including the Antipodes prize for poetry. *A Thousand Tongues* is his fourth historical novel. He lives in Perth and is an Adjunct Professor in English and Cultural Studies at the University of Western Australia. His website is at www.ianreid-author.com

A Thousand Tongues

Ian Reid

First published in 2019 by
Framework Press
27 Cunningham Street, Ardross,
Western Australia 6153
www.frameworkpress.com.au

National Library of Australia
Cataloguing-in-Publication entry:

Reid, Ian
A Thousand Tongues/Ian Reid
ISBN: 978 0 648 52230 0 (pbk)
A823.4

Front cover image (Merrivale, Dartmoor): the author
Back cover image (Dartmoor Prison): W.R. Gay / David Worth
Cover and book design: All In One Book Design, Perth, Western Australia

For Gale

My conscience hath a thousand several tongues,
And every tongue brings in a several tale...

Shakespeare, *Richard III*

Now that he had seen more of life, and been deafened by the noise of time, he thought it likely that Shakespeare had been right, had been truthful: but only for his own times... Perhaps conscience no longer had an evolutionary function, and so had been bred out. Penetrate beneath the modern tyrant's skin, go down layer after layer, and you will find that the texture does not change, that granite encloses yet more granite; and there is no cave of conscience to be found.

Julian Barnes, *The Noise of Time*

THOUGH SHE HAD FELT IT MANY TIMES BEFORE, THIS particular kind of uncertainty still made her anxious. To be mildly reproached by an acquaintance she'd failed to recognise, or mistaken for someone else, was disconcerting enough; but how often had she remained quite unaware of seeming to snub people she ought to know? And there were awkward glancing encounters like the present one, where a person looked vaguely familiar yet she couldn't be sure who it was. Something about the demeanour of the young woman walking in her direction from the other side of the store rang a faint bell, but Valerie didn't like to stare. Besides, all the clothes racks, cosmetics counters and glittering reflective surfaces made it hard for her to focus on the effort of identification. There was brief eye contact now as they moved closer, symmetrically, towards one another. So Valerie ventured a hesitant smile, and at the same instant the approaching woman smiled in a tentative way too. It was going to be difficult: in a moment each would have to acknowledge the other, but who was this person? What on earth was her name? Then Valerie stopped abruptly, on the point of colliding with her own likeness in a tall mirror.

It's almost, she thought afterwards, as if I've been enacting some sort of parable. A burlesque parable of bewildered perception.

Talking to Tim that afternoon, she characterised the incident as just amusingly foolish. 'Well, I starred in another ignominious little farce today. A solo display of silliness.' With a forced chuckle she told him what had happened. He smiled sceptically.

'Your laugh isn't quite convincing, Valerie. Are you a bit upset?'

She frowned. 'Why would I be?'

'Well, when you told me recently how it's hard for you to recognise people, you mentioned the time you walked straight past your waiting parents at the airport, completely oblivious, and you said they made light of it but you were annoyed with yourself – despite pretending otherwise.'

'Look, OK. This morning's near-mishap did trouble me a bit. Almost bumping into an image of myself – it was weird, all right, but that didn't really bother me. No, it's more like it felt as if I was…I don't know…somehow absurdly performing a sense of being unsure who I am.'

'That's a big jump. From the ridiculous to the…what? Hardly sublime. To the grandiloquent?"

'Don't tease, Tim. I'm trying to be serious now. Perhaps this research project of mine is eroding my self-confidence. Even my identity, in a way. You know, I'm not convinced that the person enrolled under my name in the postgraduate program is really me.'

'A bit soon to be thinking like that, isn't it? You arrived here only a few months ago, so you can hardly expect your thesis work to be steaming along at this stage. Took me a while to get my own project under way, but it seems to be moving pretty well now. Persistence is the key.'

She shrugged. 'You may be right. I'll try to follow your example.'

Prelude

'Don't set me up as a model. For all I know, my line of research may take me down a track that goes nowhere.'

'But I suppose tracks always take us somewhere, don't they? Even if it's just back to the beginning.'

Dartmoor

1917

ONE

———

A LANKY STRANGER APPEARED AT THE DOORWAY, WATER dripping from his hair and sodden clothes. Although he held himself erect, chin raised, the men nearest to the entrance of the cavernous room could see a tremor in his limbs. Haggard he looked, and pale, despite an air of stoical defiance. The wind that had begun to swirl across the moorland as nightfall approached was fiercer now, and the inmates could hear rain being driven in groaning squalls against the thick stony stronghold that enclosed them. They knew how bone-chilled he must feel, this shivery newcomer; the train station was barely a mile away, but walking that distance under guard in such a drenching storm was more than enough to freeze anyone to the core. They watched as one of the warders muttered something to him with a perfunctory gesture towards the clustered tables and then led him off down the dark corridor.

Even before the late-afternoon tempest arrived, this had been another miserable day for most of the men. Forced to work unprotected out in the open, they were wet and weary. Nothing unusual about long hours of sporadic drizzle under leaden skies, or a bitter wind gusting from the southeast. The year's pattern around these parts, as local folk liked to say, was 'nine months winter and another three months foul weather.' But for the gangs toiling in quarries or loading huge granite blocks on tramway waggons or building that strange high wall, the constant cold made their labour utterly wretched. Chilblained fingers were stinging; backs and knees ached; empty bellies rumbled. The bleakness of the place was inescapable.

None of them at work on the wall knew the ultimate purpose of their daily task. The dark shape, partitioning a tract of empty land up beyond the river, had risen slowly during the previous months until it reached a man's height, and they were continuing to extend it in both directions. Too tall and elongated, surely, to be just another field boundary for enclosing livestock or crops.

'So what's all this for, then, Mr Higgins?' Not the first time they'd asked, and his answer was the same.

'Yours not to reason why.'

'How much higher is it to go?'

'Never you mind. Just get on with it.' The warder strode on, shoulders back, teeth clenched on a pipe, hands tightly gripping each other behind his beefy buttocks.

'Taciturn bugger, isn't he?'

'Don't expect him to change. Pointless to ask what we're doing here. If Higgins knows he won't bother to explain, you can be sure of that.'

'Then what do you reckon, Bertie? This thing we're constructing – what is it?'

'Could be they expect a big influx of additional conchies, I s'pose, and need new quarters for them. What are you grinning about, Scotty?'

'Och, your explanation's just a wee bit too rational to be

likely,' said Eric Duthie, raising his rust-red eyebrows to signal jocularity. 'Our crazy imperial warlords will have wilder plans than that, you can be sure. I'd say they're aiming to construct a grand barrier from coast to coast – a southern counterpart to Hadrian's Wall, ye ken? So high that no invading Hun can climb over it. And then they'll put all of us hapless COs beyond the pale, on the outer side of the rampart, and leave us to expire.'

His fellow workers chuckled. You could always rely on young Scotty to lighten the mood. At the sound of laughter the warder turned towards them and bellowed a reprimand. 'Enough cackling and slacking! Back to work!'

'Are ye getting paid a bonus for every yard of our wall, Mr Higgins?' Duthie called out.

'Very funny, carrot-top. You'll soon be sniggering on the other side of your cheeky face if you're put on reduced rations for impertinence!'

Giving him a mock salute, Duthie curtseyed theatrically.

The next day dawned sombre and damp. The evening's gale had subsided, and fog now clung to everything. Warming themselves with cigarette smoke, half a dozen men stood beneath the stone arch of the prison gateway. One of them, pointing to the Latin words inscribed above their heads, asked another, 'What's it say, Bertie?'

'Ah, that's from *The Aeneid*,' he replied in his usual schoolmasterly tone. 'Virgil's epic poem. *Parcere subjectis*: the phrase means "Spare the underdog." Strangely benign motto for a place like this.'

Higgins the warder called out to them. 'He's been assigned to your gang, that new fella,' he said, indicating with his pipe-stem the sallow rangy man who had arrived during the storm and was now standing apart from the group that clustered at the entrance. They ambled towards him, introducing themselves one by one. Expressionless, he nodded cursorily at each in turn. Then there was an expectant pause.

'Staines,' he said at last, as if the name was being prised from between his teeth. 'Gavin Staines.' He began to cough, and the catarrhal rattle turned into gusts of wheezing. He held a scrawny forearm over his face until the spasm subsided.

'Welcome to our splendid Princetown Work Centre,' said Duthie. 'Grandest of all the Home Office Scheme establishments in the country. Not to be confused, of course, with Dartmoor Prison – identical place but now quite transformed by a name change.'

The hint of a wry smile flickered briefly across Staines's pallid face but he made no comment.

'Time to get moving!' Higgins shouted. The men made their unhurried way down the road in a straggle, Staines at the rear. Dropping back to pad along beside him like a cocker spaniel, the small meek fellow called Doug Lindsay tried to strike up conversation.

'Last night's wind seems to have blown itself to a standstill,' said Lindsay. 'This fog will soon lift. I'd say the rain will probably hold off, too. So you'll be able to ease yourself into the work without a lot of aches and pains.'

Staines grunted. 'What's it involve, this work?'

'They've got us building a long high wall. Don't know what for. You'll see it soon – not far to walk before we're there. Anyway, the work will take a bit of getting used to. The stone slabs are massive. Even heavier than you'd think, and awkward to handle. So take it quietly. Just ignore Higgins if he yells at you. None of us'll expect you to go hard at it for the first few days.'

Staines's mouth became a thin flat line. 'No need to make allowances. I'll pull my weight.'

'But you shouldn't be doing work like this. That cough of yours sounds bad.'

'Ah, it's nothing much. I'll soon be on the mend.'

'Not if you push yourself too hard.'

Shaking his head, Staines fell silent again.

At casual intervals during the next few days, Doug Lindsay persevered in his cheerful attempt to get Staines talking more openly. Others, too, made occasional efforts as they laboured alongside the newcomer or walked together between the prison and the field beyond Blackabrook. Deferring to his reticence, they avoided direct questions. Instead they talked about recent news from Russia, where it seemed Lenin's Bolsheviks now had tight control of the revolution, and from the battlefields of Flanders, where the latest Ypres offensive was reportedly mired in futility, as well as from the home front, where their own confidence in the No-Conscription Fellowship was stronger since Bertrand Russell, its President, had visited them here in Dartmoor a couple of months ago to explain persuasively why it opposed illegal forms of protest. Staines cocked an ear to these scraps of conversation but didn't join in.

They told him about a few things that were happening in and around the town. About the muster of horses requisitioned from local farms by the army. About the long overhead ropeway carrying timber from the big plantation at Brimpts to the railhead at Princetown for onward transport across the channel to the battlefront. About the depot where women cleaned and dried the sphagnum moss that boy scouts and girl guides harvested from moorland bogs, to be stuffed into sacks for use by the Red Cross in surgical dressings because it was antiseptic, absorbent, and cheaper than cotton gauze. Staines seemed to show little interest in any of this.

For his benefit they described the arduous tasks that various gangs were engaged in. All the slow hewing and hauling of mighty chunks of stone at Foggin Tor and Swell Tor. The wielding of hammers, hour after hour, to pound smaller lumps into fragments for road construction. The harnessing of eight men like horses to a field roller. The digging of a deep long trench by the Mis Tor group on a high slope a few miles to the north-west – supposedly to lay a pipeline, though nobody knew for certain. Staines made no comment. During the working day he remained an impassive listener, aloof and unforthcoming. Most evenings he kept to his cell. After nearly a week of trying to wring more than a dozen words out of him, the men began to mutter among themselves.

'Odd bird, eh? Can't work him out.'

'You can see he's been ill. That may've deadened his feelings somehow. Shows as much emotion as a slab of rock.'

'Hard to guess what makes him tick.'

'Makes you wonder if there's something passionate under that hard surface.'

'Could be pride, do you think? Or shame, even. Perhaps he's hiding something?'

Before long, Wally Bryce passed the word around that he'd found out a few things about the silent stranger.

'Turns out my comrade Jim Nott has heard of Staines through a fellow socialist and reckons he deserves our respect. Been treated badly by the military system, so the story goes, because of his defiance. Uncompromising, to judge from what Jim's picked up. Refused to cooperate with authorities in any way, so for a start they put him in a punishment cell in that bloody big fortress at Harwich, the Redoubt there – heard of it, eh? Cruel place, people say. And that's not all. I'm told he was one of those absolutists got sent in irons from Harwich to France last year.

Front line exposure. Against the law, of course. God knows what would have happened to that group over there if the episode hadn't come to light so publicly. The questions in parliament, remember that? Big fuss, but exactly what the army brutes did to those men nobody'll say. Details kept hush hush. And since being brought back from France he's mouldered for months in Pentonville. Solitary confinement much of the time, got a touch of pleurisy. No wonder he's a bag of bones.'

'Shouldn't we ask him about it?'

'Best not to say anything, that's Jim's advice. Story is, Staines keeps everything to himself, and he's a touchy cove. No surprise there, eh? If people start probing he's likely to bite their heads off.'

'So whatever was done to him must be too painful to talk about.'

'Or he may have other reasons to stay mum. Who knows? A secret of some sort.'

Warily, speculatively, they continued to watch him. And he watched them.

TWO

———

AT THE END OF EACH DAY HE SOUGHT REFUGE IN reading, but it wasn't easy to fend off interruptions. Now, from the corner of his eye, he saw the stocky figure of Bertie Gregg approaching.

'A few of us are going to stroll into the town. Like to come?'

Eyebrows raised, Staines looked up from his book. 'They let you wander around out there after dusk? Without warders?'

'Oh yes,' Gregg nodded. 'Until half nine, if we want. There's a decent little pub. Wet our whistles with a pint or two.'

'Not really my kind of thing.'

'Oh, come on, man. Don't be standoffish.'

Staines suppressed a sigh. 'All right then, I'll get my coat.'

He was soon leaving the prison precinct with others from his work gang. Gregg fell into step beside him.

'Glad you've come along. Princetown doesn't have a lot to offer but a trot around the streets is better than the sheer monotony of being cooped up.'

Staines made no response. Already he was beginning to see why officialdom insisted that the term 'captivity,' recurrent in pacifist pamphlets, didn't reflect accurately the situation of conscientious objectors deployed at Work Centres like this one. Though constrained, they weren't imprisoned – not quite. No locks on their cell doors, for one thing, and there was this unanticipated freedom in choosing how to spend their time after finishing a day's work. When the evening weather was mild enough, some of the men would walk around the town. When wind or rain or chilling mist kept everyone indoors, the common room with its many tables and bench seats was large enough to accommodate a good number of them. Some played board games, wrote letters or made diary entries. Others liked to gather around an old piano at one end of the room, singing together. The socialists opted for political anthems while the pious favoured hymns, though most would join in for sentimental protest songs.

> Let nations arbitrate their future problems
> It's time to lay the sword and gun away
> There'd be no war today
> If mothers all would say
> 'I didn't raise my boy to be a soldier.'

Choral unison could be pleasant enough but didn't imply complete unanimity. These inmates were a motley assortment, Staines reflected, brought together only by a common refusal to fight. Their very different reasons for taking that stand tended to make them argumentative at times, though generally in a good-humoured spirit. The diversity was obvious, even within this affable little group he was now accompanying into the town. It hadn't taken him long to recognise each man's distinctive attitude – none quite matching his own.

Eric Duthie, the redhead they called Scotty, was just an irreverent high-spirited youth with broadly socialist leanings whose ideas seemed half-baked. Evidently not an absolutist, Staines could see, because Scotty declared he'd be willing to shoulder some duties that contributed indirectly to the war effort as long as they weren't under military control. More impetuous than rational in his opposition to combat, he probably couldn't explain with any clarity what he thought about war and peace.

Wally Bryce, in contrast, knew exactly where he stood. A big broad-shouldered man, bluff and vociferous, he contended vehemently that British workers should regard their German counterparts as comrades. 'We've no reason to fight them!' he'd shout, smacking his thigh with a fist. 'Mortal combat between countries belongs to the benighted past!' Wally made no secret of his anarchist sympathies and liked to hold forth loudly about the total wickedness of conscription as 'an authoritarian intrusion by the state into the life of an individual.' He scorned clergymen for their complicity with oppressive patriotism. 'Ministers of religion,' Bryce told Staines, 'show their true ugly colours when the nation goes to war. Instead of urging us to love our enemies they get up on recruiting platforms and preach bloody murder. The Bishop of Exeter even refuses to let us conchies into the prison chapel here, yet the vilest kinds of criminal have used it in the past.'

Oddly, firebrand Bryce got on quite well with doe-eyed Douglas Lindsay, the quiet little Quaker and founding member of the No-Conscription Fellowship, whose pacifism was pure and simple. 'I just can't picture Christ, in any circumstances, with a weapon in his hand' – that was how Lindsay put it, and his choice of words seemed apt because *picturing* things was his habitual mode of perception, and whenever possible what he held in his own hand was a pencil or a paintbrush. Much of the time he communed with his sketchbook.

As for Bertie Gregg, squat as a toad but squeaky as a cricket, he'd told Staines that his own opposition to enlistment was the logical result of his training as a historian. 'Every war in every age,' he declared with high-pitched fervor, 'has caused more misery than it alleviated. The only thing that's different about this one is the terrible scale of it. Many more people than ever before will suffer grievously – and for no palpable gain!'

Gregg shared with Humphrey Latimer the experience of having once been undergraduates at the same minor Cambridge college, but otherwise they seemed to have little in common. Latimer, known to all as Humph, proclaimed himself in stentorian tones to be a champion of personal freedom, by which he seemed to mean mainly the freedom to indulge a passion for the theatre as an autonomous realm of spectacle, larger than life, unfettered by social norms. In his libertarian view any restriction imposed on individuals – except perpetrators of vicious crimes – was abhorrent. 'Conscription,' he boomed at the dinner table, beating the air rhythmically with his knife to signal complete certitude, 'is hardly different from the coercive impressment of men by the British navy in times past. Today's military recruiters are just glorified press gangs.' It was ironical, he told anyone who'd listen, that Australia, once used by the British navy as a dumping ground for prisoners, was now the only country taking part in this war that didn't depend on conscription. Humph Latimer characterised himself as a thespian aesthete steeped in the rich language of Elizabethan drama. Staines thought his manner self-important but recognised a quick intelligence underneath the stagey preciosity.

As far as Staines could see, for all their differences these men were mutually tolerant. There was plenty of banter within the group but appeared to be no real truculence. Yet some, he'd heard, could be harshly critical of a certain minority of inmates, regarding them as a lazy and obstructive set that brought discredit on men of good intentions. 'Most of us in this place,' said Bryce, frowning, 'are here because we have a strong conscience. A few others, I must say, are not genuinely conscientious at all.'

'Ah, but it's a drab word, *conscientious*. We should ban all use of it here,' retorted Humph, flexing his eyebrows histrionically.

'Elsewhere people apply it in a patronising tone to dullards, don't they? It's a verdict that school housemasters like to deliver in end-of-year reports. Faint praise, signifying "uninspired but dutiful." Amusing that it's now being given a different sense altogether: a conscientious objector is someone who refuses to be dutiful in the way his nation requires, and claims to be inspired by a higher ideal than pugnacious patriotism.'

A ten-minute walk brought them to their destination. 'Incongruous name, eh?' Gregg pointed to a sign: the Plume of Feathers Inn. To Staines its dark granite frontage looked as if it had been hunkering at the street corner forever.

'Don't be surprised if we meet a bit of hostility in here,' Gregg murmured as they approached the entrance.

A reeking fug and a rumble of conversation confronted them, and then the room went suddenly quiet. Ignoring the taut silence, they ordered their ales and looked around for a table; but as there was nowhere for their group to sit together they remained standing at the counter.

A sneering voice came from one corner. 'So the coddled conscience men have crept out from their cosy club!' This merry piece of alliteration produced raucous guffaws.

Emboldened, someone else called out, 'Back to your funkhole, you poltroons!'

Staines turned to Gregg. 'Always like this?'

'Oh yes, we get plenty of abuse in the streets and public houses. I blame it on the newspapers. The churches, too. They fan local resentment.'

Facing the noisy rabble, staring at them coldly, Staines didn't hide his contempt. 'Riff-raff!' he said loudly with a curling lip, and turned back to his glass of ale.

A few moments later there was a large hand on his bony shoulder.

'I heard what you said.' The speaker was a great ruddy-jowled ox of a man, eyes streaked with red, as tall as Staines but about twice his bulk and age. 'Looking for a fight, are you?'

'I think you are,' Staines replied, slowly putting his glass down. A hush fell over the room.

'You take it back – what you called us.'

'No, I won't do that. Riff-raff is the right description for you and your nasty loud-mouth cronies."

The big man clenched his teeth and a vein in his forehead bulged. 'You've got a bloody hide, you lot, coming in here. Good brave men from our families suffer and perish in France fighting for our country, while you shirk your patriotic duty. Lily-livered, that's what you are! Malingerers!' He drew mucus into his mouth and spat on Staines's chest.

Staines, his mask of composure slipping, said scornfully, 'I know more about suffering on the French front than you could ever imagine.'

With a roar of rage, his adversary swung a fist and struck Staines full in the face, sending him backwards to the floor. Others, brimming with menace, leapt up from their tables and rushed towards those at the bar. A melee erupted. It took several minutes for the conchies to push their way to the door, half-carrying a dazed Staines, who seemed unaware of the blood running from his nose and lip.

'You're a fool, Staines,' the warder told him the next morning. 'And don't think your bent nose and black eye will earn you any respite from work.'

'I don't seek that or expect it.'

'You chose the wrong person to provoke last night. Got what you deserved.'

A shrug. 'Perhaps so.'

'The word's got around pretty quick. A sure way to get yourself thrashed, going into that pub and acting supercilious. He's not a man to cross, Albert Starkey. Used to work in the gaol here, like his old man the Duke before him. Little wonder it made him see red – a smart alec conchy like you, claiming to know what it's like in France. Starkey's had two sons in the trenches. One of them's dead, left a widow and baby. The other's a permanent invalid – mustard gas. So show a bit of respect around here.'

Staines said nothing. Thin fingers pushed back his untidy forelock, drawing a curtain of shadow across his face.

THREE

AFTER THE FRACAS IN THE PLUME OF FEATHERS INN, Gavin Staines spent the evenings indoors, sometimes in his cell but more often on his own in a corner of the big communal room, reading. It had been a pleasant surprise to find Stopford Brooke's tome on Shakespeare in the little library there – just his cup of tea! Yet although every page was full of interest he couldn't sit still for long. Small fidgets belied his pretence of a nonchalant temperament. He jiggled his foot, rubbed his chin, closed his book, got up and walked around the room for a few minutes, skirting the groups, pausing near the edge of conversations but not joining in.

'See how twitchy he is?' Latimer asked Bryce, nodding in Staines's direction.

'I suppose it'd make any of us a bundle of nerves,' said Bryce, 'if we'd been treated the way he was over there. The things he must've gone through…'

Latimer shrugged. 'Mmm. Perhaps it's no more than that. Wouldn't be surprised, though, if he's got something else on his mind. Looks troubled, to me.'

There were a few others who tended to keep to themselves much of the time, but none who seemed such an inveterate solitary, so plainly resistant to company. Most of the men, even the least gregarious, would occasionally be drawn into a game of cards or a singsong around the piano. Not Staines.

Standing behind Doug Lindsay, Bertie Gregg stretched out his stubby arm and pointed over Lindsay's shoulder at the pencil drawing of tiny human figures toiling in the quarry.

'You've scaled us down,' said Gregg. 'We look insignificant beside the rock face.'

'Well we are, aren't we? Puny latecomers. But those great hills of granite have been here almost forever. Primeval giants.' He flipped back a few pages of the sketchpad and held out one of the drawings. 'I'm pleased with this one.'

'A view from up near Foggin Tor, isn't it?"

Lindsay nodded absently, drifting into a reverie. To his eye the outcrops were like slumbering beasts. As if they'd begun to shoulder their way up through the surface of the moors and then fallen asleep, oblivious to the passage of time, indifferent to human comings and goings. He turned back to his drawing. Most evenings he would sit quietly like this at the end of one of the tables for an hour or two, sketching from memory an assortment of scenes. Quarries and hillsides in pencil and charcoal. Shadowy grey shapes that had imprinted themselves on his mind during the daylight hours.

A couple of minutes passed. Gregg coughed. 'Not distracting you, am I, if I just stand here and watch you at work?'

'Mmm? Oh – didn't know you were still here, Bertie. I get into a bit of a trance when I'm developing a sketch.'

'The artist as dreamer, eh? Mind's eye, and all that. I admire your skill, Doug, in conveying how you see what's around us. But for me, you know, the most interesting thing about this landscape is the mark that people have left on it. Dartmoor's human story over the centuries. It's what you'd expect from me, isn't it? A historian's view of the place. That's why your drawing of the abandoned corbels has such appeal for me. It implies so much. About ambition, futility...'

'Their mysterious quality is what I wanted to capture. Intended for London Bridge, I've heard, but nobody seems to know why they were just left there.'

'Well, it's obvious the Bridge was rebuilt without them, so perhaps someone simply miscalculated how many corbels they needed, and these are the leftovers. Or the design may have been modified at the last minute.'

'Anyhow there's something eloquent about the way they're just lying there. Like gigantic toppled tombstones.'

Gregg left Lindsay to his sketching and ambled towards the table where other members of their work gang had just finished a game of cards.

Staines stood in the background, beyond the lamplight, thin arms folded, observing the men at the table, silent except for his intermittent half-suppressed cough, unsure why he was lingering there. Not a companionable impulse, exactly; but did he feel – did he have any right to feel – even faintly wistful about the part he had played in society for a short while before the war, his irretrievably lost role?

Gregg approached the group, calling out in a tone of self-parody, 'Enough of those fruitless pursuits, you idlers! Put your cards away! High time you picked up a few books and learnt a thing or two.'

'Always the teacher, eh Bertie?' Wally Bryce's smile was indulgent. 'And we're your surrogate class. Every one of us a docile pupil, aren't we, lads?' Winking at the group that sat around the table, mugs of tea in hand, he made a gesture of deference and affected a fawning tone. 'So give us another little lesson, prithee, about bygone times.'

'Ah, you can mock,' said Bertie Gregg, with equal good humour, 'but you'll never make the transition from unlettered oafs to responsible citizens without acquiring a modicum of historical knowledge.'

'All right, venerable master, we're all ears, so tell us something more we ought to know about Dartmoor. We remember what you said yesterday about the local people being mostly moor farmers and tin miners for centuries back. So when did the quarrying start, eh?'

Needing no persuasion, Gregg held forth chirpily. From about 1820, he explained, scores of men worked in Haytor quarry several miles to the east of Princeton, splitting the moorstone and loading the horse tramway waggons with blocks intended for bridges and buildings in London and other cities. At one stage, he told them, about a hundred men lived in huts around Haytor. The granite for Nelson's Column came from nearby Foggin Tor. Their prison had been built earlier still, in the first decade of the previous century, with stone from near Yelverton, its purpose being to house French prisoners of war, then Americans; but that need passed after a few years and the place lay empty till about 1850, when it became a convict gaol.

'And stayed like that,' Gregg added, 'until the felons kindly made way for us.'

'You're a fount of knowledge, Bertie,' said Bryce. 'A talking textbook. The rest of us may be a motley lot of ignoramuses, but our saving grace is that we've got one classroom teacher here.'

'Two, actually,' said a low voice behind them. They looked around.

Staines was no less surprised than the others that he'd

spoken up. It had been an involuntary blurt and he wished he could retract it.

'What – you're a teacher too?' Gregg asked.

Staines gave a reluctant nod. 'Used to be.' He started to turn away.

'Where did you teach?' Gregg persisted.

'Queen's College, London. Visiting lecturer. But I left Queen's more than a year before the war began.'

'Not planning to go back there after it's over, then?'

'No chance of that.' Staines hesitated, but couldn't stop the words from welling up. 'There was a falling out. It's all water under the bridge. Or rather, the bridge got swept away.' He spoke quietly, and only to Gregg. The other men at the table, with raised eyebrows, left them to it and began another game of whist. Abruptly Staines moved off to roam around the large room. Gregg followed, intent on continuing their conversation.

'Queen's – I don't know much about the place,' he told Staines as he caught up with him. 'The only scholar I associate with it is the notorious Cramb. I've seen that bellicose book of his, *Germany and England*. Died before it appeared, didn't he? But it whipped up a lot of foolish jingoism. You'd have known him in person, I suppose. What was he like?'

Staines grimaced. 'I disliked him intensely. He reciprocated. In fact Cramb was the main reason I left the college.'

'How so?'

'His history lectures were full of militant rhetoric, like his published articles. Unconscionable, feeding such heady stuff to young ladies. But he garnered a lot of support. When I made my objections known in a forthright way, it became impossible for me to continue at Queen's.'

Staines was seized by a fit of coughing. He remembered all of it, the vilification, the white feathers, the rebukes from colleagues, the snubs from some of his own students.

Gregg pressed him for details, but Staines shook his head. 'That's enough,' he said. 'I've put it all behind me.'

Later, Gregg told Humph Latimer about this episode. 'Plucky of Staines,' said Gregg, 'to criticise Cramb publicly.'

'Mmm.' Latimer flicked ash from his cigarette. 'Just the same, it'd be interesting to know how others saw it. A cousin of mine studied at Queen's before the war, so she'd probably have been aware of a public altercation like that. I'll write and ask her.'

That evening the mood turned sour. For months there had been a variety concert every Friday, starting soon after dinner. A small committee solicited offerings and organised each program, the staple items being musical pieces, verse recitations and comic dialogues. No special talent was required, just a willingness to pitch in. This kind of concert had little appeal to Staines but he could see why others valued it. Devising their own entertainment kept the men's spirits up, and sooner or later most of them took part in something, even if only the chorus of a popular song. These occasions had always been good-humoured.

Things proceeded along the usual lines for about half an hour. One group, fond of contriving little skits in facetious music-hall style, regularly took the opening spot with a string of lame jokes, and this time their target was the food dished out at the Work Centre.

'Warder! The rice is disgusting. I've just found a beetle in it.'

'Don't tell the other men, or they'll all want one! Har har har.'

'How can you be so cruel about our gruel?'

'It takes a lot of practice.'

Someone from the audience called out, 'Talk about gruel! To sit through your act – *that's* gruelling!' And another, 'Our food's not as stale as these quips!'

After the warm-up jesters had been clapped and mock-hooted off the stage, it was Wally Bryce's turn. The satirical piece he recited was familiar, but because so many listeners had endured irrational arbitration at the hands of an appeal board they weren't tired of hearing about the Muckemdyke Tribunal's decision to send an appellant with a pegleg to the battlefront. '…It was our gallant hearts of oak that beat the foreign foe / And mahogany limbs can do the same – of course he's got to go!'

Next up was a thin youth who quietened them with a plaintive Chopin Étude, and then Humph Latimer's voice filled the big room with Hamlet's most famous soliloquy. Glancing around as Latimer gave his rendition of that vacillating speech, Staines could see it was causing some disquiet. These men had resolved to suffer slings and arrows rather than take up arms; but to many of them the sea of troubles must still seem endless. Some perhaps remained privately unsure whether their refusal to fight had come from courage or something less. 'Thus conscience does make cowards of us all' – uneasy, tense, they shifted in their seats when they heard those bitter words.

Politely applauded, Latimer returned to his seat. As three men took his place on the makeshift stage, their presence prompted murmurs among the audience. Staines recognised the trio: an unpopular group of self-styled anarchists known to others as 'the smirking shirkers.' He could put a name to one of them, a thick-lipped round-shouldered ruffian called Dicky Hoggett. From what Staines had heard, the way Hoggett and his associates behaved in public did much to explain the townsfolk's hostile attitude towards all conchies. Foul-mouthed and cocky, these three troublemakers liked to saunter around the streets of Princetown during their free time and give the impression of having a lazy life. Clods and curses were flung at them, someone told Staines, when they began to leer at local women whose fathers, brothers, sweethearts or husbands were under

fire in the trenches. And now, linking arms and grinning fatu-
ously at each other, they sang these words to the tune of Onward
Christian Soldiers:

> Off you go, brave soldiers,
> Leave your girls behind;
> Let us entertain them –
> Surely you won't mind!
> We'll teach them a trick or two,
> Show just how it's done:
> Keep their little bottoms warm
> And fornicate for fun!
> Off you go, brave soldiers,
> Leave your girls behind;
> Let us entertain them –
> Surely you won't mind!

Before they finished their reprise, angry booing broke out, with
cries of 'Shame!' Some men left the room in disgust; others
converged on the provocative trio and began to berate them.

'It's the likes of you that give genuine COs a bad name!'

'Got a lot to answer for, you coarse bastards!'

Doug Lindsay, usually as mild as milk, yelled at Hoggett,
'That vile smut is just disgraceful! Women deserve respect. Your
lewdness harms the cause of peacemaking!'

'Oh, hark at Namby Pamby!' Hoggett sneered at him. 'Only
a Quaker would be naïve enough to think women are all pure
as driven snow. It's a crude world out there, Lindsay, but your
soppy religion stops you thinking about that.'

The uproar had put an end to the concert, and the men
slowly dispersed, muttering. Back in his cell, Staines sucked
on a Woodbine as he mulled over this eruption of conflict.
Obnoxious though they were, the shirkers had struck a nerve.

There were mixed motives and illicit yearnings among the conchies, no doubt about that. Their views on politics and religion had always been visible, but beneath those public attitudes lay cloudier emotions. Being deprived of female company – and of women's respect, too, in many cases – was just one of the factors complicating the principles they espoused. Anyway, it seemed to him that the principles themselves were not only varied but sometimes questionable too, even opaque.

Coughing up phlegm, crouching over his slop pail, he thought about his own complicated feelings and the difficulty of hiding them behind a mask of imperturbability. Having scrupulously rejected any bargain with military authorities and accepted the harsh consequences without complaint, he'd gained a certain reputation: most conchies, and some soldiers too, admired his absolutist stance even if they didn't like him. But he knew that if the full story had come to light he'd have cut a very different figure. It ached like a hidden wound, his conviction that he deserved nobody's respect. To be punished for repudiating warfare was utterly unjust; but to suffer retribution – though of a displaced kind – was still no more than his due.

FOUR

‘*My dear Maud,*’ wrote Humph Latimer,

It’s several weeks since I received your letter, with its encouraging words of support. I do appreciate the effort to cheer me up, and the assurance that you don’t think ill of me for maintaining my stand against conscription. I’ve no excuse for being slow to reply, except that this miserable place can make a fellow quite downhearted and lethargic at times.

I yearn to be back with actors and audiences and footlights and green rooms. Remember coming to see me at the Savoy, in Granville Barker’s production of *A Midsummer Night’s Dream?* Just three years ago but it seems a century! GB went off with a Red Cross unit to the Somme, you know, and has written a little book about it. The longer this ghastly war continues the harder it is for me to imagine ever being able to enter a stage door again and find the same marvellous world of dramatic performance that we once knew. Journalists talk these days about the ‘theatre of war’ – a tasteless oxymoron, demeaning the noble profession of those who tread the boards.

Now I have a request that will probably seem a bit odd, but I take the liberty of sending it because you've generously indulged some of my whimsical enquiries in the past. Perhaps you may be able to give me a morsel of information about an incident that occurred, I believe, at Queen's College during your student days: some sort of altercation between Cramb the warmongering historian and a lecturer called Gavin Staines, who left the place after they fell out. Anything more to it? I'd like to know what happened.

It's a matter of merely idle curiosity to me, but because my time here is such an unpleasant mixture of tedium and hard labour almost any little distraction can seem worth pursuing – and, as you know, I've always been an inquisitive sort of chap. (I apologise for the inkblots. This coarse paper is the only sort they provide for our use.)

I trust all is well with you, Maud. You must tell me more about your studies at the Institute of Education. School teaching is a fine vocation, and I'm confident the training course you have undertaken will equip you well to thrive as a classroom mistress.

Please convey my respects to your parents, whose kindnesses I remember gratefully.

Your affectionate cousin
Humphrey

Glancing through what he'd written, Latimer paused over the phrase 'a matter of merely idle curiosity.' A bit disingenuous. Why, really, did he want to know more about Staines's past? Was it just that the man's enigmatic demeanour posed a challenge? No, there was also something about his physical appearance. Despite the pallor, he cut a fine figure. Latimer could imagine him on stage, commanding attention. His lean face. The strong jaw. Those dark grey eyes that glinted like chips of wet moor-stone.

While awaiting Maud's reply, Latimer looked for opportunities to probe beneath Staines's stubborn reserve. Each morning he walked beside him on their work gang's march to the high wall they were building, and again as they returned to the prison at the end of the afternoon. It was about a mile each way along the track that took them over Blackabrook bridge, affording plenty of time to try squeezing bits of information out of him.

'It's not the prison itself that wears a man down, is it?' Latimer began on one such occasion. 'It's being cut off from hearth and home. I don't have much in the way of close family ties myself, but most of the chaps here do, and they tend to take the separation hard, especially if their folk don't share their own view of the war. What about you, Staines? Parents support your stand, do they? Brothers, sisters? Or a wife or sweetheart perhaps?'

'I'm on my own, actually,' said Staines tersely. Interpret that as you like, he thought. Damned if I'll let you winkle out any details. But the question brought back to mind his father's livid face and spurning words, 'Since you refuse to do your patriotic duty, I can no longer regard you as my son.'

'Gavin!' his mother had cried out as her only child strode to the door, but he knew that she would have been compelled to swallow her distress. His name, he was sure, would never have been mentioned in the family home since that day.

Now Latimer was taking a different tack. 'When that big bruiser nettled you in the Plume of Feathers Inn, you told him you knew a lot about suffering in France. So what exactly happened to you over there? You were in that group of conchies the army took to the front last year, weren't you?'

With a curt nod and a grunt, Staines turned his head away to look across the river at the sloping fields.

'Rough treatment?' The phrase, ugly, hung in the air. Staines said nothing. 'Rumours, that's all we heard about it,' Latimer persisted. 'Talk of torture, and being left out in the open within range of shellfire. True, is it?'

Again Staines made no response – not until a few minutes later, as they were approaching the stone wall. Then in a tight strained voice, as if the words had forced their way out of his throat, he said simply, 'Field Punishment, they called it. Crucifixion, that's what it was.'

'Strung up, you mean?'

For the time being, struggling to maintain his equanimity, Staines would say no more about it. But the memories pressed insistently.

It had been so wretched in the dark cells of Harwich Redoubt – rotten floors, bitter cold, and moisture trickling down the walls – that he'd felt a sense of relief at the news they were going to be sent to France, all sixteen of them.

'Shipped there in irons,' a shrill young warder yelped, 'and then they'll put you under active service conditions! Anyone who resists will be shot! Don't expect to return. Make your wills before you go.'

Disembarking at Le Havre, they stood on the dockside for an hour in steady rain, unsheltered, roped together, watching stores being loaded on drays. Then a long trudge took them to Cinder City Camp, where tents and huts perched on a crust of slag and thick ash spread over the swampy ground.

Staines lasted only a day at Cinder City. The morning after their arrival, hustled and dragged out on parade alongside hundreds of soldiers, every conchy refused to obey when ordered to march off the ground with the rest. Deemed one of the most insolent resisters, Staines was shoved into a lorry with a couple of others and taken along muddy tracks to a Field Punishment Unit at Harfleur. He'd come to know well these two men who shared his attitude of quiet defiance. Cec Bilson, short and thin, had a habit of working his mouth soundlessly as if in silent rehearsal of an utterance that never emerged. Whatever that unspoken thought, he seemed certain of its validity because as his lips moved he would often nod in agreement with himself, turning his head slightly to one side like a cunning bird in an old fable. Although Staines felt sure Bilson's miming was a nervous tic, it infuriated military authorities as much as any deliberate provocation. The other man, Percy Gill, said little but his self-righteous air made him, too, a regular target for official hostility. Staines didn't have much time for him.

As their truck approached the Harfleur barracks it turned towards three wooden frameworks standing like artists' easels in a space behind the service buildings. The truck stopped next to these structures, each one a set of vertical posts with a crossbeam about five feet from the ground. 'Get out, you three!' someone bellowed. 'Now stand over there with a post hard against your back!' Ankles were strapped, and outstretched arms bound to the horizontal struts. For two hours they stood in the open. Rain burst overhead and the wind came whipping into them. Bilson, being so short, had to relieve the weight of his body on his arms by raising himself on tiptoe. They hardly spoke to each other. Staines could think of nothing but his own thirst, the tightly knotted rope around his ankles and the cramping aches in shoulders and innards.

The next day brought the same punishment, again the day after that, and so on for a week: two hours or more out there every morning, exposed to whatever the weather might bring and weakened by scant daily rations – just tea and stale bread while even the German prisoners, they heard, were given porridge. To take his mind off the pain and make time pass, Staines resorted to a device of distraction that had become habitual: eyes closed, shutting out the surroundings, he focused his thoughts on a linked series of haphazardly chosen words, pondering their shape and origin, tracing byways of association. *Endure*: to last, to persist for the *duration* – no, not just to persist but to toughen youself, derived from Latin *durus*, hard or harsh. Then there's that archaic phrase *durance vile*: long imprisonment, patiently borne. *Patient*: longsuffering – connected oddly to both *passion* and *passive*. *Conscience*: supposedly an inner knowledge of right and wrong, but perhaps just a figment that makes cowards of us all? *Coward…* No no, stop. Swerving away from that pang of memory, he forced himself instead to concentrate on his other well-practised method of self-containment: calling to mind one of the many sonnets he'd learnt by heart in earlier years. Line by line, he began to recite it under his breath.

> They that have power to hurt, and will do none
> That do not do the thing they most do show,
> Who, moving others, are themselves as stone,
> Unmovèd, cold, and to temptation slow…

And on to the poem's strange transition into a final image of sweetness turning rank:

> Lilies that fester smell far worse than weeds.

He repeated Shakespeare's puzzling poem in a slow murmur, and then again and again. Tomorrow morning, pinioned at the stake once more, he would try to distract himself by summoning up a different sonnet.

Each day after being taken back indoors they were ordered to carry out menial tasks. Time and again they refused. The sergeant in charge of them, nonplussed at first, became irate as the deadlock continued.

'Listen, Staines, you stubborn bastard,' he shouted, 'you're goin to take this bleedin shovel and dig a latrine trench. No arguments!'

'I won't do it. I don't recognise military authority, I oppose the war, and won't do anything that assists the army in any way.'

'We'll soon change your tune. Beat you until you're broken.'

'What use will I be to you then?'

'You'll always be bleedin useless, you lump of shit. It's your submission we want, Staines – not your bleedin services.'

'I'll never submit.'

'Ah – so if I decide to give Mr Cocky a thrashin, he's goin to fight me off, is he?'

'No, I won't use physical force to resist. The choice to refuse submission is in my mind.'

Tying the shovel roughly around Staines's neck with a piece of cord, the choleric sergeant punched him in the belly and walked out. Encumbered by handcuffs, Staines had to take the weight of the shovel with one cramped fist to lessen the strain on his neck.

Hours later, a black-skinned soldier who brought him the ration of tea and bread slipped a couple of biscuits surreptitiously into Staines's pocket and untied the shovel. They held each other's steady gaze. Dark eyes stared at their grey reflection, which looked back evenly. Then, at the same moment, both men gave a faint mirthless smile.

'I can't quite agree with your views,' said the soldier, 'but the treatment you're getting isn't right.'

Staines shrugged. 'I don't expect to be handled gently. From an army point of view we're just a big damned nuisance, I know that. We don't accept their rules, so they don't know what to do with us.'

The two men looked at each other again, silently, in an exchange of glimpsed understandings, before the soldier turned and left. Staines had heard that a few black men enlisted but it was startling to see one of them in uniform. What snubs and slurs would such a person have to endure in the army?

A few days later, with Bilson and Gill, Staines was manacled and bundled into the canvas-covered back of a truck.

'Where to this time? We seem to be heading north-east.'

'Who knows? Another of Normandy's picturesque nooks.'

'Pillar to post, anyway.'

After hours of lumbering and lurching, the truck deposited Staines and the other two on the cobbled quayside in Boulogne, where the barracks occupied an imposing stone building that still bore signs of its pre-war existence as a fish market. Hustled to a large dark room at the back, the three prisoners found themselves facing steps that led down to a wooden cage below floor level, set in a pit about twelve feet square, with more than a dozen men in it, all handcuffed like themselves. Prodded forward by an escorting soldier, the trio stumbled down into the crowded cage, greeted by a stench of excrement and vomit, murmurs of recognition, and familiar faces – their own group of conchies from Cinder City, who had arrived the previous day.

There they were all kept for a week. No light reached them except through slits between the thick planks of the cage. In the mornings a guard brought them water and individual portions of food: four hard biscuits and half a pound of bully beef each. Eating was an ordeal because of the handcuffs. To lie down, or even to lean against the dank walls, they had to take turns. Mostly they stood or crouched, day or night, sixteen men pressing close to each other, dreaming of elbow room, fresh air, beds. For as much of the time as possible they shrank away from the corner dominated by the single lidless latrine bucket. No paper to wipe themselves.

When at last an officer ordered them out of the dungeon, their trembling legs could hardly carry them up the steps. Putting an arm around Bilson, who seemed locked in a kneeling position, Staines managed to haul him to his feet and help him to climb; but when he staggered they both fell heavily. Guards dragged them to the top of the steps.

He felt disgustingly bedraggled and couldn't escape the smell of their filth. Flies were a crawling plague. After washing themselves and some of their clothes as best they could with the help of a grim-faced Red Cross nurse from the nearby base hospital, the conchies spent a mostly sleepless night on the floor, with only a scattering of mouldy straw to ease the chill. The next morning they were led to the Henriville camp. Soon after arriving, to their great surprise, they were introduced to a youthful Quaker journalist. Arnold Morecroft asked a string of questions about their attitude to the war and how the authorities were treating them. Taking detailed notes, he told them he would have a report sent immediately to his organisation in London.

'Thank God for wireless,' he said. 'Our people will make prompt use of my report. They have the ear of someone well placed in government circles.'

'So that explains how you got permission to see us?' Staines asked, and Morecroft winked, smiling.

Two days later the conchies were arraigned. Unsteady on his feet, almost overcome by giddiness, Staines felt too ill to pay much attention to the court martial procedure with its pretence of questions and its drone of accusations – *insubordinate, insolent, ringleader, refusal…* When the whole group had been propelled through the same stern routine, they were detained under guard in a small tent for half an hour.

Then a uniformed pair entered. 'Which one of you is Staines?'

They took him outside the tent. With his wrists still manacled in front, a wooden pole was passed behind him through the crook of each elbow, forcing his shoulders back and his spine forward. The two soldiers held the ends of the pole and marched him out to the centre of the parade ground, which was lined with hundreds of men standing to attention. Alone in the middle of the square except for the escorts who held him fettered, Staines heard an officer with a foghorn voice bark out the now familiar series of charges, all of which amounted to wilfully disobeying commands. Then the judgment:

'You have been found guilty. The sentence of the court is that you will suffer death by being shot!' Pause. 'Sentence confirmed by the Commander in Chief.' Pause. 'But subsequently commuted to penal servitude for ten years.'

Each of the other conchies was brought forth in turn and subjected to the same ordeal of protracted suspense, the same verdict, the same commuted sentence.

'You know what this means!' Bilson said jubilantly to Staines when they were back in the tent. 'We're all be sent back to England and put under the jurisdiction of civil authorities.'

Staines nodded. 'But I can't share your enthusiasm about that,' he said.

London and Perth

2015

FIVE

NOT FOR THE FIRST TIME SINCE COMING HALFWAY AROUND the world a week ago on this research trip, Tim Holmes was feeling more alone than he'd anticipated. London had shown him its most cheerless profile. He was weary of scowling skies, of puddled footpaths, of stale smells in the underground stations and in this cramped, ugly hotel room. The exchange rate meant that even basic expenses – accommodation, food, tube tickets – seemed exorbitant.

Again he caught himself in that absent-minded habit of his, the fingertips slowly rubbing his forehead as if to check whether the big birthmark was still there. Or to erase it. After twenty-four years he still hadn't quite got used to the stain on his skin, a raised brown blotch that spread above the eyebrow. So when something was troubling him he would often repeat this old unconscious gesture, like compulsively touching a scab. As he re-read now the email on the screen of his phone, thumb resting on his cheekbone, his fingers moved across the frown lines to feel an edge of the nevus.

Although the sheer distance from Perth left him thirsty for contact with friends, the eight-hour difference in time zones often made it awkward to exchange text messages promptly or connect through Skype or FaceTime. That meant relying mostly on email, but wifi links weren't always available and he needed to curtail the cost of data downloads while overseas, so he'd disabled automatic updates and resolved not to open non-urgent emails, especially anything with attachments. But he did have a quick peek at his inbox occasionally; and now, seeing there was a message from Valerie with the subject line Shocking News, he opened it at once.

Hi Tim

A hideous thing happened in our Uni grounds last night. Kemal Kaleli was found dead in the carpark outside the gym. Bashed. I can't imagine he provoked an attack in any way – didn't have an aggressive bone in his body. And the report said robbery wasn't a motive, because he still had his wallet on him, with cards and money untouched.

It's a horrible mystery, horrible.

The police will probably contact me sooner or later – they'll want to interview students who knew him. I guess they'll contact consular authorities so that Kemal's family back in Turkey can be notified. From what he told me, I know he was his parents' pride and shining hope. Eldest child, only son – they'll be distraught.

Can't remember when you're due to give your conference paper – perhaps the big occasion has come and gone? If not, best wishes for that. Too upset to write more now.

Valerie

Tim stared at the screen in disbelief. Kemal, of all people, bashed to death? Why would anyone want to hurt a guy like him? Must have been a random attack, maybe some madman off his head with drugs. Either that or an act of racial hatred, though to be brutally assaulted just for being Turkish seemed unlikely. Mistaken for someone from a less moderate Muslim country, perhaps?

There was something that made this grisly incident more troubling for Tim. A previous complication. He felt…what was it? Well, remorseful. Remorseful about having let Kemal become a source of tension between Valerie and himself. It was awkward now to know exactly how to reply to her message. Should he allude to their falling-out? In retrospect the thing that caused them to quarrel a couple of weeks before his departure from Perth seemed much less important than he'd thought it was at the time.

'It's a matter of principle, Valerie,' he'd said. 'Surely you can see that?' But when she dismissed his criticism as 'presumptuous and self-righteous,' the disagreement had escalated quickly.

It all came about because someone at Valerie's residential college, Lauren Holt, who was getting advice from her about assignments, mentioned that a fellow student, a Turkish friend in the first-year Politics class, was struggling to write essays. 'Kemal's quite bright but his formal English just isn't up to the task, Valerie,' Lauren had said. 'I've tried encouraging him to get assistance from the uni's learning advisers but he stubbornly refuses – thinks it will somehow count against him if he gets classified as having an academic literacy problem. I've assured him this wouldn't happen, but not passing the unit would certainly be a blot on his record. He won't take the point. What's unfortunate is that he's a really pleasant, hardworking guy, good in tutorial discussion, who's going to fail because he won't engage with the support system provided for people with written language difficulties. Seems perverse but I suppose it's a cultural thing, his aversion to official arrangements for students who aren't native English speakers. I don't think he'd reject informal help, one to one. Anyway I'd like to introduce you to him over coffee, Valerie – you've been so generous to me with pointers about assignments, and I'm sure Kemal will take advice from you if you're willing to give him a hand unofficially with written expression.'

So Valerie became Kemal's writing coach.

'Lucky fellow,' said Tim when she first mentioned this casual arrangement.

'Well, it's good for me too,' she said. 'A bit of mentoring makes me feel useful.'

But it turned out that 'mentoring' soon extended to major revisions of Kemal's draft material, even line-by-line editing. Tim discovered this when he spotted her sitting at a library carrel with her laptop and asked what she was working on.

'Oh it's this Politics essay of Kemal's – I'm really having to rewrite big slabs of it.'

Tim narrowed his eyes. 'Don't you think that's going too far?'

'I'm just getting him onto a level playing field, Tim. Imagine if you were studying in Turkey and had to produce assignments in a language that wasn't your own.'

'I'd never put myself in his situation in the first place.'

'What – so you disapprove of someone coming to Western Australia from Istanbul to improve his educational prospects?'

'Of course not. But…but I do disapprove…thoroughly disapprove of someone colluding with another person, whatever the circumstances, to get academic credit for work that isn't his own. You're letting Kemal exploit your generosity.'

'Not at all. There's something tangible in it for me, too – more than the satisfaction of giving a migrant a bit of practical assistance. As a quid pro quo, Kemal is giving me access to his circle of friends here for interview purposes.'

'Interview?'

'So that I can gather first-hand opinions from members of the Turkish community about Gallipoli commemorations – really useful for my research project.'

'The fact that you're both…both gaining something from the deal doesn't make it right. You're exploiting each other.'

'Oh, come off it, Tim! That's ridiculous. There's nothing unethical about exchanging benefits. It's the basis of human interaction.'

But he'd shaken his head, still feeling huffy. They argued until he stalked off. Although he'd sent a text message the next day and received her 'Apology accepted' reply, the cloud remained. They hadn't resumed their routine of coffee sessions and within a fortnight he was on his way to London for the long-planned research trip.

A silly squabble, he thought, looking back on it now from his London perspective. Having told her – and convinced himself – that it was all about 'the principle,' he now recognised a personal sting in it too. For a few months before Kemal popped up, Tim had been the focus of Valerie's attention, in fact almost her only friend in Perth, and her new friendship with this guy he labelled 'the Young Turk' made him feel supplanted. He hadn't examined closely his own attitude to Valerie until she'd introduced him to Kemal and sudden jealousy buzzed through him. Kemal had good looks, a warm deep voice and one of those shining smiles that would make some women melt.

Tim couldn't reasonably object to Valerie's idea of asking local Turkish people how they felt in this Anzac centennial year when their adopted country was so busy reviving memories of its ghastly old conflict with their former homeland. It might shed an interesting sidelight on her thesis topic, and meanwhile she could perhaps write a newspaper or magazine piece for general consumption, based on a few of the interviews. All of that made sense.

The real problem, Tim knew, was that he'd begun to suspect Valerie and Kemal might be in a sexual relationship or on the brink of it – yet he had no right to ask her what was going on. None of his business; he himself had no special status in Valerie's personal life, and her attitude hadn't suggested it was on the cards. So when he left on the marathon flight to London for his conference and some archival fossicking, nothing had been said to clear the air.

And now, after staring for several minutes at her email on the screen while these regrets bubbled in his mind and he nibbled the quick around his thumbnail, he composed a brief reply expressing 'dismay and sympathy' at the news she'd sent. The wording felt wooden but it was the best he could manage, so he pressed the send button.

For Valerie, Kemal's violent death brought to a jarring halt a six-month period of slow adjustment to her new habitat. It was as if a huge wall had suddenly collapsed on the way of life she'd begun to settle into. The developing friendship with Tim had been an important part of that settling process until their recent row over her dealings with Kemal.

She'd arrived during one of those extravagantly bright summers that people had told her to expect in Perth, a season replete with sun-dazzled sensuality. Day after day the river went on smiling broadly at her, and westerlies whistled across timeless afternoons. A great arc of azure overhead, long lazy beaches, limestone walls brimful with soaked-up sunlight, big sails bellying out on the wide water – it was like inhabiting a postcard. Each day the heat seeped through her body, almost alcoholic in its insistent pressure, loosening shoulders and suffusing everything with a hypnotic kind of languor. Calmly, soothingly, January stretched into April.

She'd had to keep reminding herself that she wasn't here for a holiday. Too easy to find idle distractions – reading a few novels, listening to podcasts, going to lunchtime concerts put on by the School of Music, becoming aimlessly familiar with the campus, and just pottering around. Too easy to put off her main task. Getting into a rhythm of work took time and self-discipline, she told herself, not only because the weather seemed to license a mood of sybaritic inertia but also because she'd been feeling her way so gradually towards a viable research project. Part of the difficulty was just in trying to gauge whether her tentatively sketched topic could eventually yield an original thesis. Perhaps she'd be unable to come up with something new to say about it. What's more, an inner voice kept asking whether, in any case, intensive scholarly activity was congenial. How sure was she of being cut out for dedicated academic enquiry at this advanced level? But then she'd hear a contrary voice, a no-nonsense superego: of course you can meet the challenge, it would tell her sternly. Of course you're cut out for this kind of thing. Your first-class honours result made that pretty clear, didn't it? So Valerie did her best to ignore the undercurrent of doubt. With Easter fast approaching, she'd soon need to buckle down and start formulating a more precise hypothesis.

The fact that Tim, as a fellow researcher, had shown appreciative interest in her line of enquiry made her feel less diffident about it. Their comfortable attachment to each other had crept up on her. When they'd first met, early in the semester, it was a pleasant encounter but didn't seem to hold a lot of promise. She could recall the occasion in detail.

SIX

———

THOUGH HIS VOICE SOUNDED WARM AND RELAXED, THIS young man with the strange birthmark right across his brow wasn't perfectly self-confident, she'd seen that straight away. An occasional faint hesitation showed it – almost the hint of a stammer; and he tended to avoid anything more than glancing eye contact. Yet Valerie, to her surprise, found herself enjoying Tim Holmes's presentation, and the questions it posed were giving her pause.

He'd caught everyone's attention at the outset by playing a jaunty old Beatles song from the sixties. The heyday of those Liverpool lads had been long before her time, but she remembered hearing this piece during childhood holidays, when her grandparents used to sing together as they washed the dishes. 'For the benefit of Mr Kite…' Though the tune was catchy, the lyrics were puzzling: they seemed to evoke some kind of circus fair, apparently belonging to someone with the odd name of Pablo Fanque.

Years had passed since she'd heard the whimsical words bouncing around the old Hornsby kitchen, and back then it hadn't occurred to her to wonder what particular situation lay behind this showground song. Now, unexpectedly, it began to make more sense. A history seminar at the University of Western Australia wasn't an obvious vehicle for information about it, but Tim's talk conveyed the significance of the curious world of Mr Kite, Pablo Fanque and their associates.

She'd come along not because the announced topic had any magnetic appeal ('Black Lives in Victorian Britain after the Abolition of Slavery') but because the seminar coordinator's email message made it clear that all the department's post-graduate research students and their supervisors were 'strongly encouraged' to attend. And as a newcomer to this university she knew she really should be there. The life of a doctoral student was mainly solitary, and if she hoped for collegial support when her own turn came to give a work-in-progress report there was a simple duty in the meantime to pay some attention to what her fellow research apprentices were doing. She might pick up a few handy hints, too, about methods of enquiry or tricks of presentation. Anyway she'd hardly met anyone on the campus yet apart from her uncharismatic supervisor, Dr Barry Plunket, so this series of monthly seminars was a useful opportunity to gauge whether there were any like-minded people around the corridors. So far it had seemed a much quieter place than the Melbourne department in which she'd completed her first degree. Perhaps Perth was more decorous than she'd anticipated – not that this would bother her. Probably she wasn't the kind of person who'd be likely to discover any liveliness that might exist here.

Tim's research paper turned out to be far from dull. It opened up for her a whole segment of Victorian culture about which she'd been entirely ignorant. The lyrics of that Beatles song, Tim explained, were taken directly from an old circus poster John Lennon found in an antique shop. Pablo Fanque was the name of one of the most famous entertainers in nineteenth-century

England, a brilliant rope-dancer and equestrian who became proprietor of a circus that remained enormously popular throughout the country for three decades, touring widely and drawing huge crowds. And he was black!

As Tim recounted the career of this remarkable performer and impresario, he deftly held the interest of the small seminar group. Engaging, Valerie thought, despite the trace of diffidence. She could see at a glance that everyone was listening closely. Tim's paper had sketched the historical background: blacks came to England in the late eighteenth century from several places – mostly the West Indies, Africa and America – and in many roles. Some arrived as servants; planters returning home from Jamaica and elsewhere would bring their black retinue with them. Some came as flotsam of the trade in bodies; commanders of slaving vessels berthing in Bristol or Liverpool could transport a few members of their cargo for personal profit. Some came as refugees; stowaways escaping plantation life occasionally managed to find their way to English ports. Some were former soldiers who had fought for the British in the American war and were then dumped back in England. And some were sailors who jumped ship. For all of them, England's abolition of the slave trade in the early nineteenth century was at best a mixed blessing. Blacks could no longer be treated as mere chattels, forced to wear a metal collar like a dog, but on the other hand 'liberty' simply released most of them into a limbo of poverty – thieves, unemployed beggars, or fringe workers finding only despised menial jobs, languishing as domestic drudges, crossing-sweepers, sock-knitters and the like.

Now Tim came to his summing up:

Only a few managed to lift themselves above that morass of misery, usually in the world of fairground entertainment as boxers, tumblers and animal keepers. Pablo Fanque, as I've explained, was the most celebrated emblem of this kind of success.

But an important question remains, and I put it to you in conclusion: how should we interpret this apparent exception to the common fate of a black underclass? A generously liberal inference might be that the British public respected exceptional achievement regardless of skin colour and cultural background. Some years after Pablo Fanque's death, a spokesman for the Showmen's Guild said his career demonstrated that 'in the great brotherhood of the equestrian world there is no colour-line.' Taking a more sceptical view, one might argue it was only because Fanque and a few other blacks of the same ilk were mere circus entertainers that they could achieve their popularity. They remained closely associated with animals, their fellow-performers: the caged lions and acrobatic monkeys, the dancing bears and prancing horses. Like those enslaved creatures, circus blacks were virtually captive to an alienating perception, admired for their freakishness rather than for their humanity. After all, Pablo Fanque himself rose to fame as part of a duo: he was the agile rider of a clever black mare called Beda, which (according to the *Illustrated London News*) was 'trained to do the most extraordinary feats of the manège'. This black man who seemed almost joined to his black horse must have been in the Victorian imagination like a kind of centaur, something not quite human.

Thanks for your attention.

The paper was applauded, questions were politely put and neatly answered. With a further flutter of clapping the seminar came to a close. As the group began to disperse and Tim was putting his notes away into a folder, Valerie approached him with a tentative smile.

'Thank you,' she said. 'Your topic's very different from mine, but there were surprising connections.'

'Good, good. Such as?'

'Oh, little conceptual things. Images. For instance what you said at the end about seeming to fuse man and beast together – it brought to mind a remark from a book on war memorials: that in some statues, Australian military horsemen look almost like centaurs.'

'Interesting. Why've you been reading about war memorials?'

'That's my research project – how soldiers from the Great War were commemorated in Australia and England respectively. At least, that's what I think it's going to be. Hardly more than a proposal at this stage. I'm just starting, but your thesis seems to be well on its way.'

'I don't…don't recall seeing you around here before now?' An enquiring eyebrow accentuated his birthmark.

'I'm new to Perth. Valerie Morton. Did an honours degree at Melbourne Uni, but I wanted a different environment for postgrad research, and UWA offered me a scholarship. What about you?'

'Always lived in Perth. Did my undergrad studies here.'

There was a fractional pause as he glanced quickly at her eyes and then looked down before adding, 'Like to continue this conversation over coffee?'

'OK. Where?

'What about the Uni Club?'

'Isn't that just for staff?'

'No no, postgrads can be Club members too. I belong. You'll be my guest.'

They sat on the shaded terrace. A light breeze had come up, softening the day's heat. Across the lawn opposite, outside the Arts Faculty building, the resident peacocks stepped noncha-lantly. Like an airy thought, an errant frisbee went spinning past nearby.

Tim wiped a fleck of coffee froth from the corner of his mouth. 'Well, you've spent a fair bit of the afternoon listening to me rattle on about my research. So tell me more about your own. Why war memorials?'

'Can't say much yet, because I'm still standing on the threshold. It's only a few weeks since I arrived in Perth, and I've been trying to find my feet. The PhD proposal grew out of my honours thesis, where I had a look at the Australian public's attitude to Vietnam veterans. So I'm going back now to an earlier war, the bigger one that was supposed to put an end to all warfare.'

'A comparative approach, you said – Australia and Britain. What do you hope to show by putting them side by side?' Before she could respond he added apologetically, 'Sorry if I'm sounding like the Grand Inquisitor...'

'No problem – I need to practise an explanation. Well, there seem to be differences between memorials here and in England. That's what my preliminary reading indicates. So I want to look into those differences more closely. Perhaps they point to underlying cultural patterns.'

'Such as?'

'Such as the fact that Australia, unlike England, has no established national church. One scholar suggests the absence of a state religion made secular war memorials more popular in our country than elsewhere. Obelisks, for example – they have no specifically Christian associations – and practical amenities rather than just sacred monuments.'

'Amenities? Like what?'

'Oh, district meeting halls, community hospitals, bus shelters, drinking fountains, public gardens, things like that.'

'So war memorials in Britain are different?

'More likely to be chapels, shrines, crosses. Plus special features in churches – stained glass windows, bell towers and so on.'

'But I've seen a few religious memorials around Australia too.'

'Oh yes, it's not a stark contrast. But the predominant kinds of memorial do seem to differ from one country to the other.'

Tim gave a nod of encouragement. 'Worth looking into, certainly.'

'And there's more to it than the religious angle,' Valerie added, warming to her theme. 'According to another book about World War 1 commemoration, Australian military leaders tend not to be glorified the way they usually are in Britain. We put a distinctive emphasis on the common soldier. More celebration here of the act of volunteering, too, because none of our servicemen were conscripted.'

'All volunteers – I hadn't thought about the significance of that.'

There was a pause. He picked up the sachet of sugar from his saucer and fiddled with it. As she was glancing around the café, he took the opportunity to scan her profile quickly. An assertive nose. Lower lip pushed slightly forward, almost in a pout. A firm neat jawline. Her dark hair pulled back in an unfashionable ponytail. Nothing glamorous, but he liked the look of her.

SEVEN

———

IN THE FOLLOWING DAYS AND WEEKS THEY OFTEN MET AGAIN for coffee. Their conversations moved along harmoniously, and they soon exchanged the circumstantial details people usually talk about as a friendship begins to form. Valerie was staying at one of the University's colleges, St Catherine's; Tim was also living close to the campus, sharing a rented flat in Claremont with someone who'd been a mate of his since their high school days. The contours of their families appeared to be almost symmetrical. Valerie's mother was a schoolteacher, and Tim's a school librarian; both fathers worked in the public service. She was an only child; he said he'd often felt like one, because his brother was much older and had left home while Tim was still a kid.

Becoming more relaxed in each other's company, they tolerated not only questions but unspoken curiosity as well. He didn't mind that she sometimes stole a glance at that tea-coloured stain on his forehead. She didn't mind that he sometimes took a sly squiz at her cleavage. They weren't uncomfortable with their differences, either. He adjusted to her complete lack of interest in parties, popular music, sport or even drinking at the campus tavern. She no longer felt defensive about being at a more tentative stage of her research project than he was with his. He readily accepted the fact that her approach to history had a leaning towards literary and cultural studies rather than being tightly bound up with politics as it was for him.

'The thing that's always interested me most,' she explained one afternoon, 'is how our sense of the past gets shaped by images and texts. The monuments I want to write about, what they're generally doing is combining sculpture with inscriptions to make a statement about basic human experiences. Death. Sacrifice. Gratitude...' Her voice trailed away. She frowned.

'Been to see the big Cenotaph up in Kings Park yet?' Tim asked.

'The State War Memorial? Not yet. I've looked at images of it online, of course. Going there should be high on my list, but actually I've been putting it off because I'm a bit of an agrophobe. The idea of finding my way around a big open space like Kings Park is a bit scary, to be frank.'

'I could walk there with you, if you like.'

'Would you? That's a sweet offer. I'd be grateful.'

'What about...what about tomorrow morning, then, before the day heats up too much? Your college is close to the edge of the Park, so I could meet you at the front entrance of St Cat's – let's say nine o'clock? – and we'd be into the Park in a couple of minutes. Then it's a bit of a walk along one of the main avenues, but with some protection from the sun. On this western side the climb is fairly gradual, really. Probably half an hour up to the Cenotaph, and plenty to look at on the way there.'

'Sounds great! Thanks, Tim. Tomorrow at nine. See you then.'

❖

It began pleasantly enough. As they walked together up into Kings Park, a honey-eater circled them, undulant, scalloping the morning's edges. Already soaked with warmth, the air was dispersing a pungent smell of lemon-scented gum-leaves.

'I remember that aroma from years ago,' said Tim. 'Often used to come to Kings Park on family picnics. Always loved it. Plenty of space to romp around. The views are exhilarating, especially from the slopes near the Cenotaph. Until recently I hadn't been here for quite a while, but a couple of months back I found myself standing in an old familiar spot when I was part of a protest rally.'

'Wouldn't have picked you as a protester.'

'I don't make a habit of joining demonstrations. But my housemate Pete Fleming does, and he persuaded me to go along to this one – a show of support for refugees, detainees, asylum-seekers.'

'That's your friend's particular political cause?'

'Not really. Pete's an all-round libertarian. It's only in the last month or two that he's targeted the government's border protection policy. For much longer, gay rights has been the thing he's most passionate about.'

Valerie paused to digest this information before asking, 'And you're very close to Pete?'

'Known each other for years. Same high school class… Oh – I see what you're getting at. No no, not close like that. I'm straight myself. Totally. We're different in other ways, too, Pete and me. He's very much the political activist, in the same mould as lots of law students with an arts background. Pete majored in politics before enrolling in his JD course. He can be a bit wild, and experiments occasionally with drugs, which I don't touch. Passionate about social justice, so he's into legal aid work, petitions, protest marches. He sometimes gets quite hot-headed. I'm inclined to tease him a bit – like to tell him he acts as if only those who share his opinions have a genuine conscience. For his part he reckons I'm just an armchair philosopher - "over-fond of calm conservative rationality" is how he describes me. He reckons I "don't live fully and feelingly in the present world." Some truth in that, probably!'

'If he's so different from you, sharing the flat with him must be a strain?'

'Not really. He makes me laugh. Pete has an amazing fund of memorised lines of poetry, and draws on it at the drop of a hat to recite something appropriate. Sure, he can be pretty intense at times, but then there's a jokey-blokey side to him too. Tells some hilarious stories – always claims they're true, but you never know.'

'Such as?'

'Well, there was his mock epic tale about seeing an uncon-scious-looking body way out beyond the surf at Swanbourne and swimming as fast as he could through the big waves, intent on rescue, completely exhausting himself, only to find that it was an inflated sex doll, ridiculously curvacious. "I wouldn't have minded," he said, "if its gender had been more to my liking." He's a funny guy, Pete is. A bit crazy. Lives on the edge.'

Valerie laughed but didn't comment. The footpath was continuing to rise and she wanted to save her breath for a while. She became conscious of the heavy thud of her sneakers as she strode along the firm bitumen surface. ('You're such a clomper, Val,' her mother had once remarked in a tone of mild reproof. 'Far from elegant. Do try to cultivate a cat-like tread.' But refining her gait would have been too much bother.) Tim was moving along more softly, more smoothly – almost gliding over the ground.

A pair of large black birds waddled near them.

'The clumsy way those crows walk!' Valerie pointed. 'Or ravens, are they?'

He shrugged. 'Never been sure which is which. Whatever they're called, they always sound discontented. Snarky carpers.' She laughed, and he felt gratified.

They came to a T-junction. Long avenues of eucalypts stretched out on both sides, and under every tree there was a metal plaque bearing the name of a dead soldier. Turning right into Lovekin Drive, they walked more slowly now, reading inscriptions, waving the persistent flies away.

It was another sweaty quarter of an hour before they passed the statue of Lord Forrest, portly and berobed, and reached the summit of Mount Eliza with its various buildings – kiosk, gift shop, café and the rest.

'Ice-cream?' Valerie offered.

'Thanks – the perfect reward.'

Licking busily, they strolled down to the grassed area near the memorial forecourt. With a sweep of his hand Tim gestured to the vista. 'Your new territory as you've never seen it before,' he announced.

'What an astonishing vantage point!' Valerie stood there in a trance until melted ice-cream trickled over her fingers. Though trees and monuments interrupted what would otherwise have been a grand panorama, she took in Perth's central buildings to her left; then, down in front of her, part of the Swan separating the southside peninsula from the city; and in the far eastern distance a flat line of low hills.

Tim followed the direction of her gaze. 'That's the Darling Scarp stretched out there,' he said, 'like a long sleepy lizard. Round to the right you've got a glimpse of the river's widest reaches, extending all the way over to Applecross, where the Canning joins the Swan.'

He had an impulse to describe for her the view further westward, not visible from their position, as the river curled sinuously this way and that in the final stages of its glistening passage to Fremantle. He wanted to tell her, too, about the well-hidden osprey nest he knew about, not far down from where they stood, its arrangement of sticks looking like a pile of kindling for a phoenix. But he stopped himself. It wasn't for the scenery, primarily, that he'd brought her all the way up here.

'Want to have a look now at the State Memorial?'

She nodded.

'The precinct has a few component bits,' he explained. 'Just over here beside us, that's the ceremonial flame. Burns continuously in the middle of the forecourt. Surrounding it on that semi-circular wall are the names of the biggest world war battle-fields, with plaques at ground level for each of the VC winners from Western Australia. Perhaps you'd like to have a look at that area on our way back up from the main monument, the Cenotaph. There are other things you'll want to see too, scattered around nearby – a Light Horse memorial for instance, and a Jewish memorial. But let's walk straight down to the Cenotaph first. It makes quite an impact.'

She nodded again, wiping the last of the ice-cream from her fingers, and they crossed the grassy slope to the formal pathway.

'So many long lists of names,' he went on, as they approached the monument, 'that's what hits you. Panel after panel. All from this state, and all prematurely dead. Thousands of names down there in the undercroft. To get into the space we have to walk down those steps at the side of the obelisk, where that big group is milling around.'

'What's going on there, do you think? Seems to be some commotion.'

Only when they began to descend the steps did they see what the people gathered there were looking at. The whole external wall facing them had been defaced by graffiti. Red spray paint proclaimed WAR IS AN EVIL SCOURGE and TOTALLY WASTED LIVES and THEIR BLOOD IS ON THIS

NATION'S HANDS and RITUALS OF REMEMBRANCE =
INAUTHENTIC CONSCIENCE.

'No, no!' Valerie moaned, covering her mouth with her hands
as if to stop herself from vomiting. 'How could anyone do this?'
Turning away, she ran back up the steps and began to stride
along the path towards the forecourt with its flickering flame.

Hurrying to catch up, Tim fell into step beside her.

'Tasteless, isn't it?' he said.

'More than that!' she cried, coming to a sudden stop. 'It's
mindless! A self-righteous expression of facile pacifism by
people who've never grown up – young morons who get a kick
out of irreverent anti-social protest gestures and know nothing
about warfare.'

The hiss of her anger startled Tim. 'What makes you think
they're ignorant young morons?' he asked, looking at her askance.
'Could be middle-aged morons who do know something about
warfare.'

Cheeks flushed, she glared at him, but he went on in carefully
measured tones. 'I mean there's nothing to indicate who made
those statements. Or what their motivation and personal experience might be. Couldn't the perpetrator be a returned soldier?
Maybe someone who'd seen action in Iraq or Afghanistan and
felt bitterly disillusioned?'

'Anyway,' she said, refusing to engage with that possibility, 'I
think it's despicable, whoever did it. Something built to honour
so many lost lives ought to be treated as a sacred place. Political
protests don't belong here.'

She walked on. Tim called after her: 'Don't you want to look
around the Cenotaph?'

'Not today. The visit's been spoilt. I'll come back another
time.'

Frowning, he caught up with her again. 'This has really
distressed you, hasn't it?'

'Look,' she said, 'it's personal. My grandfather fought in Vietnam. I'm proud of his service there, but like other Vietnam vets he had to put up with a heap of shit when he returned to Australia. Public hostility towards the war and towards people who'd done their duty. Bloody hell, they were the first men in Australian history to be *conscripted* for service on foreign soil – they didn't ask to fight! They were told to go, and they went, and then look what happened after they came back. At best they were ignored; at worst they were reviled. I totally detest that attitude.'

'Fair enough. There's a special Vietnam memorial here in the park, along one of the other avenues. If you'd like to see it we could go there on the way back – not much of a detour.'

'Some other time. I'm too upset now.'

EIGHT

'TELL ME,' said his housemate, 'about this chick you're seeing a lot of.'

'Chick? You mean Valerie Morton? She's no chick, Pete. Far from it!'

'What – acts the formal young lady, does she?'

'Not exactly. Valerie's sort of upright, I s'pose. Upright and sometimes forthright. As if she'd been transplanted into the present from a few decades ago.'

'A throwback!'

'Well, I'd say just an old-fashioned girl, with strong convictions. She's her own person. Independent. Doesn't hesitate to speak her mind when something provokes her. Tends to be fairly reticent most of the time, though. Valerie's got the proverbial old head on young shoulders. In some ways she probably feels more affinity with her parents' generation than with her own, I'd say. Like, f'rinstance, she regards social media as a total blight – disdains Facebook, detests Twitter. She's very bookish. Really into historical novels. And her taste in music seems to be confined to classical stuff – you know, chamber groups and all that.'

'What the hell d'you find to talk about, then?'

'Oh, we have some good conversations. When she speaks she's unhurried, deliberative. Quite a serious manner. That's totally OK by me.'

'And so?'

'Well, she takes an intelligent interest in my research.'

'Oh yeah. Pumps up your tyres, does she?'

'Cynical bugger, aren't you! No, Valerie's not into flattery.'

'What's she look like?'

'No especially attractive feature that I can call to mind. Overall she looks good. Different. Doesn't try to match the style of most women around the campus. Reminds me of a school prefect.'

'Not exactly a fashion leader?'

Smiling, Tim shook his head. 'No way. Her hair, clothes, things like that – they make a conservative statement. Like she's aligning herself with the decorum of many years ago.'

'Strait-laced, eh? Sounds as if Miss Prim might need to be vigorously aroused…' Smirking, Pete rolled his eyes in a lasciv-ious pantomime.

'You're a coarse animal, Fleming. I doubt that she needs anything, actually. Seems quite self-sufficient, far as I can tell.'

The next day Tim had been crossing the footbridge from the Arts precinct to the library entrance when he saw Valerie coming straight towards him. Her folded arms gave the impression that she was embracing herself, or perhaps just protecting the curve of her breasts from lewd attention. He slowed to a stop and smiled at her – but to his astonishment she turned abruptly away, right in front of him, and walked down the stairway to the ground level. This snub was so jolting that he stood still for a few moments, mouth open, unable to follow her or call out. What had he done to offend her? Yesterday, when they'd parted after returning from King's Park, she'd been subdued but he hadn't detected any tension between them.

He couldn't let her ignore him like this without explanation. Pulling out his phone, he texted her: 'What's up – why the big brush off?' A curt reply came at once: '????' He retorted: 'Just now, near the library, u walked right past me.' She explained: 'Didn't see u! Prosopagnosia.'

Pro *what*? He googled it on his phone. *A disorder of perception where the ability to recognise faces is impaired while other aspects of visual processing remain intact.* He sent a quick text.

'Just looked it up. Wow! I was totally unaware.'

'Not v observant yourself, then!'

Her terse response brought an odd little incident to mind. When they'd been having coffee in the Club a few days before, someone went past their table, lifting a hand in greeting – at which Valerie had asked, 'Who was that guy?'

'Huh?' Tim had thought at first she was kidding, but she looked genuinely puzzled. 'You didn't recognise your very own supervisor?'

'That was Barry Plunket?'

'None other. Those puffy eyes are unmistakable. And the way his head droops to one side.'

She'd made a moue. 'I'm not much good at faces.'

So now he sent another message. 'What about a reconciliation coffee this arvo at 4, usual place? You'll recognise me OK this time – I'll be doing a headstand on the table to attract your attention.'

Before long they were laughing at each other and themselves. She felt more relaxed with Tim than with anyone else. So on a later occasion, when misrecognition nearly made her bang into her mirror image in a department store, she wasn't too embarrassed to tell him about it.

But more than a month had passed since then, and they were no longer close. The distance that had lately come between them exceeded the 15,000 kilometres separating Perth from London. She'd kept herself remote from him by withholding warmth, and it was no more than he deserved – he could acknowledge this to himself as he checked his inbox in the hope of another message from her, even just an update on the Kemal incident.

He tried to stop himself from dwelling on the breach with Valerie but the possibility that he might never regain her friendly trust made him feel forlorn. She meant more to him than he'd let himself acknowledge until now. Not just pleasant to be with. Not just a person whose conversation he enjoyed because of like-minded interests. Beyond their everyday congeniality, something more had begun to develop. Though he shied away from giving it a romantic name, the painful fact was that he missed her company, missed it in a way that had little to do with general homesickness. Part of it was visceral; but in trying to subdue the stirring of lust, not wanting to seem like an opportunist who was coming on to her in a rush, he hadn't been fully conscious of the ways in which their friendship became broader and deeper. While he was intent on stopping his hands from reaching for her body, their minds had been edging closer together.

Then he'd bloody well spoilt it, hadn't he, with his jealous criticism of her involvement with Kemal. All he could do now, here in the wrong hemisphere, was to keep in amiable contact, hoping Valerie would soon put their tiff behind her.

A couple of days passed without further news. Meanwhile, conference over, he decided to send her an email about the new research lead he was going to pursue. Wanted to get an apology off his chest, too.

Hi again Valerie

Anything more come to light about Kemal's murder? I keep

thinking about the poor bugger, wishing we hadn't argued about him. The fault was mine. I got things out of proportion. My harsh words must seem really stupid now that this appalling thing has happened. Very sorry.

You asked about my conference paper. Got a good reception – lively Q&A. One tantalising bit of information, it could be important for my thesis, came up in a comment right at the close. A guy from Manchester called Frodsham, an expert in circus history, has put me on the trail of a black man, Joshua Dunn, who may turn out to be suitable for a case study. All Frodsham could tell me is that Dunn worked for Fanque's circus as a boxer in the 1860s but then somehow fell into crime and ended up imprisoned in the Dartmoor gaol at Princetown. A few quick searches online indicate it will probably be hard to get any further info about him. The National Archives at Kew don't seem to hold information on prisoners except for census lists – which weren't compiled in the relevant years. Nothing in the Devon Record Office either, according to its website. I'd hoped records held at the prison itself might reveal a few things about him, but they were largely destroyed when an administration block there was burnt out during a riot in the 1930s. So disappointing!

Call me impulsive but I'm about to head off down to Dartmoor anyway, to see whether I can find out more about this guy Dunn from any of the material kept in the prison museum. Unlikely, I know, but if I draw a blank there'll still be time to do some further delving into files in London and Sheffield – e.g. circus history – before I return. Still got some of my research leave left, and I've now arranged to add a couple of vacation weeks to that, so there's latitude in my schedule.

Hope your own project is going well. I really miss our conversations about what you're doing.

Best wishes

Tim

The next morning he found she had replied while he slept.

Good luck, Tim, for your sleuthing expedition to Dartmoor. Watch out for the dreaded Baskerville hound!

There's been nothing in the media since that first news item about Kemal, but I've remembered a little incident that could have some bearing on what happened to him. Now I may be quite mistaken, but I think it involved Omar – that Somali student who's friendly with your flatmate Pete. I just can't be sure, though. Anyhow, a day or two before his death I saw Kemal (I'm definite it was him, despite my usual uncertainty with faces – we'd spent enough time together over the previous few weeks for me to recognise him), talking with Omar (if it was actually Omar) and a third person, standing in that arched passageway at the back of Winthrop Hall. Nearby there were other groups of Muslim-looking students too, so I guess they'd just finished one of those prayer meetings they hold in the undercroft area.

Well, I walked past quite close to them, and although I only heard a few loud phrases exchanged I could tell there was a heated argument going on. Seemed to be something about Islamic attitudes to sex. Perhaps it was a Sunni versus Alevi thing – I told you, didn't I, that Kemal belongs to the Alevi faith, a Shi'a offshoot, which is the largest religious minority in Turkey. I didn't hear the third guy say anything and I don't know what he looked like. Had his back to me.

I've been fretting about whether to get in contact with the police and mention this, but it's so vague I'd probably make a fool of myself. May be wrong anyway in thinking it was Omar arguing with Kemal. I met the guy just the once, when you introduced us outside the library – and I didn't warm to him. Smooth on the surface but uptight, that was my impression. The way he said 'Kemal told me about you' sounded disapproving. I imagine he's one of those severe religious moralists who'd take a dim view of friendship between a Muslim man and a self-reliant western woman.

Best

Valerie

Tim remembered clearly that brief uncomfortable conversation with Omar and Valerie near the library entrance. Earlier in the year he'd heard Omar speak at a rally in Kings Park, and then encountered him a few times around the campus in Pete's company. Valerie's intuition might well have been accurate; probably Omar wouldn't approve of her close friendship with Kemal, guessing it might have a physical element. For a different reason Tim felt much the same about it, and was beginning now to see its implications in the light of this reported quarrel between Omar and Kemal over different attitudes to sex. Valerie herself may even have been the particular focus of their quarrel and therefore part of the reason for Kemal's death.

But surely Omar, whatever argument he might have had with Kemal, wasn't capable of *killing* him?

NINE

———

A PHONE CALL FROM HOME IN MELBOURNE PUSHED ALL thoughts of Kemal and Omar out of Valerie's mind. It was her father's voice, quivering. 'Something nasty has happened, Val. The police called me about your Grandpa. He's in hospital. Bashed by a bunch of hooligans. They broke into his home.'

Nausea plucked at her. 'Oh no! Why would...' The words felt misshapen as they slid from her trembling mouth. 'Why would anyone...?' Tears welled up.

'Random robbery, I suppose. But they weren't content with taking cash and his medal. They beat him up, the bastards. Police won't tell me a lot and the hospital won't let me speak to him on the phone yet. All I know is he's badly hurt – face smashed up, busted ribs. Seems there's nothing life-threatening, though complications could develop at his age. Anyway I've got a seat on the plane to Sydney first thing tomorrow and I'll stay there as long as I need to. Sorry to give you such upsetting news, Val. Soon as I've seen him I'll be in touch.'

Before his next call she read online the *Herald*'s brief report of the incident.

A 75-year-old Vietnam veteran with a distinguished service record, Mr Sam Morton, was assaulted in the early hours of this morning when he confronted three youths who broke into his home in Hornsby. He sustained multiple injuries and a hospital spokesman has described his condition as serious but stable.

When her father phoned again he still couldn't say much. 'I've just been with him. His face is all swollen and bruised,' he told her. 'Cheekbone and nose broken. Deep gash in his scalp. His eyes are so puffy they've nearly closed up. He can hardly speak, but doesn't seem to want to talk about it anyway. The police were back for a second interview while I was there, and when they asked him to describe his attackers he gave a shake of his head and just repeated, "Three young fellers." I reckon he's holding something back.'

Pushing aside the sickening thought of his wounds, she tried to recall her grandfather as he'd been in the past – a genial patriarch. Over the next few days her memory kept returning to cheerful times spent with her grandparents in years gone by, those regular summer holiday visits when she used to go with mum and dad to stay in the little bungalow in Hornsby. If she closed her eyes now, an album of miscellaneous memories opened. There she was as a toddler, earnestly tending the vegie patch with her miniature plastic watering can. Wriggling to get comfortable at bedtime on an over-inflated rubber mattress on the floor. Hearing whip-birds in the darkness, and the spooky barking owls. Watching that wondrous albino echidna amble across the back lawn one morning. Grandma was still alive in those days, and it had been a treat to hover in her kitchen while the elaborate Christmas meal was being theatrically prepared – 'the Grand Production,' Grandma used to call it; but Valerie cherished just as much the scraps of conversation with Grandpa in his big shed where he plied his hobby of restoring old army vehicles, often humming quietly to himself.

As a child, she assumed the 'veteran cars' he talked about must belong to veteran soldiers – some sort of vehicle fleet owned by the RSL. He had a particular enthusiasm for Jeep engines, dating back to his time in Vietnam. When she'd first asked why he liked taking a motor apart, he just waggled his ears at her and replied facetiously, 'So I can put it back together again – and perhaps there'll be enough parts left over to make a wigwam for a goose's bridle.' In her early teens she enquired again, persisting when he shrugged the question off. 'Be serious, Grandpa. Why do you keep tinkering with these bits of machinery?'

He pointed with his spanner at the framed photo of a Jeep on the shed wall. 'That, young lady, is the acme of functional design! It's a MUTT, an M151. Not glamorous, just plain simple lines – a great performer.'

'But an engine isn't as interesting as a person.'

'Interesting? I'll tell you this: no engine ever tried to harm anyone. A person can be vicious.'

His harsh tone startled her, but the moment passed and she gave it no further thought.

As she grew towards adulthood and saw him less often, he gradually became in her mind a kind of silhouette epitomising the laconic modesty she associated with an older generation of Australians. The courageous things he'd done in Vietnam were all the more admirable, she thought, because he never wanted to talk about his award for valour. Once, at her insistence, he rummaged in a desk drawer and bashfully produced the medal with its striped ribbon. 'Aarh, nothing special, really,' he said with a shrug, putting it away again. 'A gong doesn't mean much.'

Grandpa had been a Tunnel Rat in Phuoc Tuy, her dad told her: a sapper who often faced extreme danger. Booby traps to detect and remove, caves and bunkers to clear. And because the Yanks couldn't aim straight, bombs overhead were as hazardous as mines underfoot. His Military Medal citation said he'd shown great gallantry in organising the safe evacuation of several wounded men despite his own injuries after a mine explosion in their midst had killed the commanding officer.

Knowing these things gave her a blurry sense of pride, in which family merged with nation. Surely the values embodied in people like Grandpa expressed something distinctive about the Australian character. A stereotype, yes – she could recognise that; but wasn't there a factual basis for it in qualities like simple decency, quiet bravery, pride in one's country?

His patriotism wasn't narrow, not by any means. According to her dad, Grandpa had spoken up in loud support of the Vietnamese boat people when big numbers began arriving in the years after his return to Australia. Helped them in practical ways, too, through local charities. Still talked about them compassionately.

'They were *real* refugees back then,' he'd said a few months ago, when she was in Sydney with her parents for his 75th and they'd slid into an edgy debate about asylum-seeker policy. 'Not like a lot of opportunists nowadays who get themselves smuggled here because they just want a more prosperous life – middleclass Iranians and such. Those boat people from Nam, poor buggers, were escaping from a desperate mess we'd left them in after the fall of Saigon. Fact is, we'd failed to protect them from Charlie – the Viet Cong – and so I reckon we owed them a safe place here…'

Safe place! The remembered phrase had a bitter ring now that he'd been attacked in his own home. Valerie found it hard to settle to anything while he was being kept in ICU for tests and surgery. Her impulse had been to fly at once to Sydney, but her father dissuaded her.

'There wouldn't be much point at this stage, Val. They've got him heavily dosed up, so he sleeps most of the time. They'll need to operate to fix the cheekbone and nose. Surgeon says it's complicated because they've given him blood-thinning medication to reduce the risk of clotting.'

'I wish I could sit beside him and hold his hand and talk to him.'

'Just keep those text messages coming. I read them out and they cheer him up.'

Valerie couldn't settle to anything. She sent Tim an email about the attack on her grandfather, told Lauren what had happened, and let her supervisor know that she wanted to fly to Sydney for a few days to see her grandfather as soon as the hospital let him go home. Meanwhile she had no appetite for her research project. Lauren tried to coax her back into it. 'Work is therapeutic,' she told her. 'Truly. Moping won't do your grandfather any good.'

'I know. But I can't stop thinking of the damage to his face – cuts and swellings.'

'He'll soon be on the mend,' Lauren assured her. 'In your mind's eye, instead of visualising injuries, you could call up an image of him looking hale and hearty.'

'I've been doing that.'

'When you picture him in his prime, what do you remember?'

'Oh, he was still a handsome man when I was little. Dark eyes, deep set. And I liked the uneven line of his mouth, turning down in one corner. But it's hard to separate his looks from his whole manner. Grandpa's quite gentle. The sound of him, too: his voice is really rich and sweet – used to make me think of a cocoa drink.'

'And while you're recalling what he's like, you've been smiling again.'

Later, in response to news that he had improved and was expected to be home within a fortnight, Valerie's agitation began to subside. Once he was discharged she took a weekend break to visit him in Hornsby.

He opened the door with a crooked smile of welcome. She tried not to look at the weals on his face. Moving slowly, he ushered her towards a chair as she murmured a question about how he felt.

'Aarh, the ribs are still giving me a bit of gyp, that's all.'

After he made coffee, they chatted on casually about this and that until she put him on the spot.

'Dad reckons you know something about your attackers that you haven't divulged.'

He turned his head away and gave an unconvincing cough.

'Grandpa? Who were they?'

'Nobody I knew, Val.'

'But you must have got a good look. What were they like?'

He sniffed, cleared some mucus and stared vacantly into his coffee cup.

'Grandpa?'

Meeting her gaze, he sighed. 'Between ourselves, then?'

'OK.'

'Vietnamese.'

'You sure? Not some other Asians?'

'I know the difference, Val, believe me. Can recognise their language too.'

'But here? I didn't think any Vietnamese were living around Hornsby.'

'They probably weren't North Shore types. The *Herald* says some young Viet crooks are becoming much more mobile these days.'

'Why didn't you tell the police anything about them?'

There was a long pause before he replied.

'No point, really. Anyhow – keep this to yourself, Val – when I remember things our soldiers did to civilians over there in

Nam, it wouldn't be right to complain now. There's an odd sort of ugly justice in what's happened. Specially the fact they took my medal. I'm glad to be rid of it.'

Shaking his head, he sucked in a noisy breath. 'See, I've never forgotten something shameful that happened during the war there. I didn't do it myself but I stood by. Should have spoken up...' His voice trailed off, like a small motor running quietly down.

'Grandpa?'

'Ah, may as well get it off my chest. Our men went into this village, see – miserable ramshackle place it was, nearly empty. We had the jitters, knowing Charlie wasn't far off. Orders were to push them back and we'd been moving forward for days but they just kept melting away invisibly in front of our advance. Must have had a lot of sympathisers in the villages, passing on information. Very frustrating for us, and our sarge got really worked up. Nasty piece of work he was. Brutal bugger. Anyhow at this particular place, in one of the huts, there was a little old stooped fellow, looked ancient though he was probably about the age I am now, and when the sarge shouted questions at him he just grinned back. The sarge went livid, yelled louder, but all he got out of this old grandfather was more grinning. Defiant? Uncomprehending? Who knows? Well, the sarge hit him hard with his fist, and then used the rifle butt on his face, no mercy, until there was blood everywhere. Horrible bashing. The little fellow said nothing.

'So I won't be saying anything either – outside this private conversation – about what happened here to me a few weeks ago. And I trust you not to repeat what you've just heard.'

Looking back from the gate as she left, Valerie saw him making his unhurried way towards the shed to commune with his Jeep engine.

Dartmoor

1917

&

London

1913-16

TEN

———

'TEACHING YOUNG LADIES AN APPRECIATION OF LITERATURE: now that would have been very pleasant, I imagine.' Leaning against the big stone wall, Humph Latimer wiped sweat from his forehead.

Staines gave him a wary glance. 'Meaning what?'

'Just that it seems an enviable role for a young man, lecturing at Queen's College with all those damsels hanging on your words.'

'Not on *my* words, Latimer.' Staines carefully stretched his back and shoulders. 'The aim was to have them hanging on the words of great poets.'

'Of course, of course. So what reading did you prescribe?'

'Most of my classes were about the English lyrical tradition, especially the sonnet form. The students responded well to that kind of poem, with its tight structure. Shakespeare's sonnets most of all.'

'Ah,' said Latimer with a snicker. 'Just the thing to put the lovelorn into a swoon. "Let me not to the marriage of true minds admit impediments" – and so forth. Very sweet.'

Staines frowned, scratching at a callus on his hand. 'You undervalue the poetry, I think. That sonnet sequence covers a

93

range of moods beyond sweetness. And you underestimate some of the young ladies, too: the best students at Queen's are quite capable of reading with their heads as well as their hearts, I assure you.'

'All right, all right,' Latimer laughed, raising his hands in an exaggerated gesture of surrender. 'I shouldn't disparage fine poems or anyone who appreciates them. All the same, Shakespeare's plays are so much richer than the sonnets, wouldn't you say? Not just their wonderful *language* as grand dramatic poems but all that subtle interplay of characters as well, and the suspenseful way the action unfolds…'

'But the plays need to be staged for their fullest impact, don't they? Some of the young ladies at Queen's probably hadn't ever seen a first-rate theatrical performance. The sonnets could speak to them directly from the page.'

'Enough chitchat, you two laggards! Back to work!' The supervisor strode towards them.

'Just taking a short breather, Mr Higgins,' said Latimer, as they turned back reluctantly to the pile of rocks. 'You can't begrudge us that. We're not machines, you know.'

That evening, as the men sat around the common room sipping from tin mugs of over-steeped tea, Latimer found a quiet corner where he could resume his conversation with Staines, moving the subject around to an angle that might, he thought, provide entry through the other man's defences.

'That sonnet sequence: some excellent poems in it, I grant you. But to my mind they're just warm-up exercises for the plays. When Shakespeare brings poetry to the stage it carries more power, don't you agree?'

Staines didn't respond. Lighting a cigarette, Latimer shook the match and watched its flame go out before he continued.

'The sweep of events, the array of characters, they enrich his language. And the dramatic form gives him scope for larger themes. The whole gamut of goodness and nastiness.' He blew smoke rings, watched them drift and dissolve as he went on in his orotund manner. 'The subject-matter of the sonnets, love's yearnings and pains and so forth, it's all there in the plays too, but much else along with it. Vaulting ambition. Comedy that can be genial or mordant…The poems give us nothing to match a creature like Falstaff, whose actions ludicrously belie his words. "The better part of valour is discretion" and so forth – buffoonery with a sting in it…'

'True enough.'

'And the villainous characters too – the dark intrigue, the devious passions. Not least, all the excruciating agonies of conscience – now there's a theme that ought to resonate deeply for everyone cooped up with us in this place, if they weren't preoccupied with trivial games of cards and dominoes.' He gestured sweepingly to the many tables around their large common room.

'At the concert,' said Staines, 'when you declaimed Hamlet's soliloquy about conscience and cowardice, it seemed to bother some people.'

'Good, good! That was my aim. Too many of the men here speak glibly about their "conscientious" principles. If they knew Shakespeare better they might deepen their thinking on the subject. Conscience means different things to different people.'

Staines nodded. 'I'm sure many soldiers on the western front would say conscience led them to enlist.'

'Exactly. It's an uneasy word. In Shakespeare's tragedies and histories it keeps recurring, mostly with a little mist of shifty meanings around it. Do you know *Richard the Third*?'

'Not well. Haven't read it since school days. Never seen it on the stage.'

'In performance it can be gripping. Villainy on a grand scale! I once played a minor part in a spirited production, so I know the play well. I'd quite like to organise an acted reading of a couple of scenes from it for one of our concerts here. King Richard's role would suit you down to the ground, Staines: it needs a saturnine demeanour and you've got that. Can I persuade you to speak his lines?'

'No chance. Not the kind of thing I'd ever want to do.'

'Ah. Pity. You know, *Richard the Third* has plenty to say about conscientious scruples. I remember especially a couple of lines near the end, when the king admits confusion: "My conscience hath a thousand several tongues," he says, "and every tongue brings in a several tale." Now that's what conscience is really like, if you ask me. Not some simple black-and-white certainty about right and wrong but a clamour of internal voices, each one shouting or whispering a different story about what ought to be done. A thousand several tongues! – I kept hearing them in my head when I was trying to decide whether I should oppose this stupid war. What about you, Staines? What does conscience mean to you?'

Gavin Staines was silent for a minute or more, scratching at a scab on his elbow. 'I understand your point,' he said at last. 'I've heard it too, the babble of contradictions telling me how to act. To go this way – no, that way. To do something or not to do it. To be or not to be, et cetera. Sooner or later it all resolves itself into a definite sense of what's the right decision. But sometimes that comes too late, when you've already made the wrong choice.'

'Sounds as if you're thinking of a specific case.'

'Perhaps.' Staines shrugged and turned his head away to cough. Someone started singing raucously at the next table, and the confessional moment evaporated. Latimer knew he wouldn't get anything more out of him. Not now. Not yet.

But the letter from his cousin Maud was in his pocket. While confirming that Staines had left the college – an abrupt dismissal, reportedly – because of his public spat with Cramb,

Maud also remembered a vague rumour of something else too, some whiff of suspected impropriety on his part. No specific allegation, as far as she knew.

Lately Gavin Staines had been finding it harder than ever to quieten the tumultuous feelings stirred by self-reproach. Harder to forget things said and done to her. Harder to dismiss the obsessively repeated sequence of pictures flickering silently behind his eyes, as if a newsreel film continued to show the same few images over and over again. Rooms where their minds had met and mingled. The long narrow lecture hall at Queen's with its green walls, its frieze of chained white flowers, and its marble mantelpiece framed by plaster cherubs holding platters of fruit; the library with its large armchairs, carved table, florid carpet, and portrait of its august founder; that room upstairs with its view over the lead roofs of the mews into cobbled yards where horses snorted at coachmen. And other remembered spaces beyond the confines of the College, along those parks and streets where they had walked. Hyde Park. Harley Street. Wimpole Street. Piccadilly Circus. Regent's Park.

Day and night for nearly five years the commotion in his heart had never subsided for long. As he lay shivering in prison cells, stood fastened to the punishment stake, toiled at the tall stone wall or sat disconsolate among the other conchies, there was little respite. Often sleep eluded him for hours, his blood pulsing with the rhythm of those lines that had first brought them together:

> Love is too young to know what conscience is;
> Yet who knows not conscience is born of love?

It had all begun when she approached him as he was gathering up books and papers after one of his Friday lectures to the senior pupils.

'I must tell you, Mr Staines,' she said, 'I'm learning such a lot from the way you've talked about poetry this term. Truly illuminating. Especially whenever you read any of Shakespeare's sonnets aloud to the class.'

'Very kind of you to say so. It's Miss Remington, isn't it?' He glanced sidelong; beneath dark brows her eyes were wide open. She was probably 18. Three-quarters of his own age.

'Lavinia Remington. After your lecture last week I looked along the library shelves here and found Malone's edition of Shakespeare's poems. I've been absorbed in them.'

'I'm glad to hear it, glad to hear it.' The silly echo in his phrasing annoyed him. He added, more firmly, 'I have a personal copy of that edition myself.'

'Well, I want to become completely familiar with all of them. And take the whole sequence of sonnets as my subject for the extended essay you've asked us to hand in at the end of term.'

'Ambitious undertaking!' Difficult to bring himself to look at her directly.

'Oh, I'm nearly halfway through already. I can make sense of most of the poems so far, but a few things seem obscure. I'd be grateful if you could discuss some passages. Explain the difficult lines.'

'I'm impressed by your diligence, Miss Remington, but your fellow pupils probably wouldn't want me to squeeze comments on more sonnets into the lectures, even if I could manage it. There's only limited time available in class.'

She glanced back over her shoulder. The last of the other girls were disappearing through the doorway at the back of the room.

'We can talk after one of the sessions, can't we? Just the two of us?' Her manner seemed somehow both bold and shy at once.

He hesitated. 'Perhaps a brief conversation when you've read carefully through the rest of the sonnet sequence. Along the way, just jot down questions when they occur to you.'

Questions were taking shape in his mind as well. The intensity of her interest – not just just in the poetry but also in him, apparently – made him wonder about the appropriate way to respond to her. He hadn't encountered this kind of thing before.

A week later she waylaid him again after his lecture, eyes sparkling.

'I've finished them. All one hundred and fifty-four! Marvellous poetry, isn't it?'

'I'm delighted it's made such an impression on you. And surprised you've been able to spend so much discretionary time on literature, because I believe there's a great deal of required reading for other subjects. Especially for modern history: I've heard that Professor Cramb expects you all to immerse yourselves in his warlike writings about what he insists on calling the destiny of imperial Britain.'

'Do I detect, Mr Staines, some distaste for Professor Cramb's kind of patriotism? Yes? Well, a few of us disapprove of the emphatic way he advocates aggression towards Germany, though I must say we're in the minority. He has plenty of enthusiastic supporters. Some of my fellow-pupils like nothing better than being harangued as he strides around the classroom.'

Staines drew in a deep breath. 'I won't disguise the fact that I do strongly object to Cramb's use of lectures to promote a battle-hungry mood among impressionable young people. Warmongering sickens me, Miss Remington, and I make no secret of my pacifist position. You've probably seen ILP pamphlets recently on the library tables here, and in the foyer, arguing that England must do all it can to keep the peace? Well,

I'm the one who distributes the pamphlets. But let's not get distracted now by all of that. You were telling me about being absorbed in Shakespeare's sonnets. Have some of the difficult passages become less puzzling?'

A pause before she replied. One of those disturbingly direct looks, with a hint of…irony, was it?

'They have, yes. Most of the obscure bits have dissolved. I just kept going back over them with dictionaries until things became clearer. But there are still a few details that perplex me, so I've done what you said. Made a note of them.' Her smile was a friendly bridge and she took a step towards him, holding out a folded piece of paper. 'Actually most of my queries are about one particular sonnet. It seems rather different from the rest.'

Taking the proffered note, Staines put it straight into his pocket. 'I'll look at this later,' he said, trying to re-establish a formal distance. 'Can't linger now, Miss Remington – need to get to an appointment. We may be able to discuss your questions after next week's lecture.'

Back in his lodgings, Staines took out the piece of paper Lavinia Remington had given him and glanced at her neatly inscribed questions. Almost all of them concerned one of the last poems in the sequence; he recognised at once its opening lines. Pulling his copy of Malone's edition from the bookcase, he turned to number 151 and stood there, elbow resting on a shelf, while he read it slowly. With a shake of his head he put the volume aside.

During the next couple of days, perusing the lines again several times did nothing to quell his misgivings. When the time came for another lecture at Queen's he was still unsure what he would say to her afterwards. Her presence in the front row, just a couple of yards beyond his lectern, disconcerted him: she would write rapidly in a notebook, look up at him with her tongue moistening her lower lip, and then busy herself again with her pencil.

When the lecture was over she stood in front of him, arms folded, dark eyes unblinking, as they waited for the room to empty. The postponed conversation started awkwardly as he tried to find a delicate way of conveying that this particular poem probably wasn't suitable for the eyes of young women and he wouldn't feel comfortable going into its details with her. Anyway some of its lines were a bit…odd. Oblique. Best, he suggested with a husky cough, to set it aside.

'I'm not a child, Mr Staines,' she'd said. 'I can't grasp it all, but I think it's a poem about lust.' Her gaze was no less direct than her declaration. Looking away, he muttered a faltering reply.

'Well…yes, that may be. One could summarise it in those terms, I suppose. It does seem to be unusually…unconventionally physical in its implications.'

She was waiting for more. He cleared his throat. 'Well,' he said. 'I can't…actually…discuss it now. Something rather urgent has come up. Need to leave.'

Hurriedly he tucked his lecture notes into a folder, gave her a little nod and turned away.

As he went out into the street, head down, he almost collided with the College's Principal, Sir Henry Craik.

'Poetry lectures going smoothly, are they?' Craik asked with his customary briskness.

'I believe so, sir,' said Staines, conscious that Craik, whose own literary enthusiasms didn't include verse forms, would probably prefer the pupils to be reading the *English Prose Selections* that he himself had edited. 'There are some rather clever young women in the senior group here. Eager to go beyond the set reading.'

'Good, good. Who stands out, then?'

'Oh, there's Miss Remington, for example. Has a keen appetite for…for Shakespeare.'

'Ah yes, Lavinia Remington. The lawyer's daughter. Notoriously precocious, that one. Can be high-spirited, though she keeps to herself much of the time. The family's very wealthy, you know. And influential. Large country estate. Hmm. Well, I mustn't dawdle. Good afternoon.'

❖

She buttonholed Staines again after the next lecture, startling him with her frankness.

'Is this poem saying that, from a masculine point of view, love can't be separated from the pleasures of the body?'

He prevaricated, trying not to meet her gaze. 'Hmm. Not sure it's quite so straightforward. The lines follow the structure of an argument, apparently, and yet the logical steps aren't altogether clear.'

'Parts of it might be easier to comprehend if you would read the whole thing aloud to me.'

'Not appropriate in this case, I think.'

'Please do.'

From the corner of his eye he could see that she had clasped her hands imploringly. Frowning, he said, 'A poem of this kind doesn't really lend itself to an elocution exercise, Miss Remington. If anyone were to come into this room and hear me voicing certain phrases…'

'Then can't we go somewhere else to read it and talk about it?'

'Away from the College? No no, I don't believe that would be permissible.'

'Oh yes, it would! It would! Queen's is quite liberal, you must know this, about letting us leave the premises, as long as nobody is alone. Apart from class times, we're mostly free to come and go. I've often walked around the city for hours with one or two of the other girls.'

'That's entirely different from going off somewhere in the company of a man! Think what the lady visitors would say!'

She shrugged. 'Hah! We refer to them privately as the titled interlopers.'

Staines smiled. The so-called lady visitors were persons of rank and fashion whose informal duties included monitoring informally the social life of the college, radiating a spirit of gracious condescension, sitting occasionally at classes with the pupils in a quasi-chaperon capacity, discouraging undue enthusiasm for the suffragette movement, and acting as intermediaries between professors and parents. He'd encountered two or three of these visitors.

'Nobody takes them seriously,' she said. 'Anyhow you're not a male companion in any ordinary sense, Mr Staines. You're a visiting lecturer, so adjourning elsewhere to discuss literary matters would just be an informal extension of your teaching role. Professor Rippmann, until he left the College last year, used to issue extramural invitations to some of us regularly.'

From a glance at her face he couldn't decide whether she was being naïve or wily.

'Nobody can object,' she went on. 'It's a lovely sunny afternoon. Perfect spring weather. Don't be such a sobersides! Let's stroll into Regent's Park and talk about poetry. Please.'

Nonplussed, he yielded to her insistence. And to that disarming smile of hers.

When they crossed the York Bridge and walked on into the Park, he was seized by the heady notion that they had suddenly entered a state of nature unconstrained by social propriety, where there were no limiting rules, only liberties. He knew it was foolishly fanciful to think so, yet everything around them – the expanse of greensward with its bushy fringes, the beaming flowerbeds, light flickering on shiny leaves, a perky-tailed squirrel practising a pirouette, a bevy of waterbirds frolicking in the lake – glowed with the pristine freshness of an earlier world, edenic, in which both of them seemed for the moment entirely free.

They found a secluded bench. She handed him the little volume of sonnets and raised her brows expectantly. He cleared his throat, found the page and began:

Love is too young to know what conscience is;
Yet who knows not, conscience is born of love?
Then, gentle cheater, urge not my amiss…

She broke in. 'I don't quite understand that bit – "urge not my amiss": what does it mean, exactly?'

'It's an old use of "amiss" as a noun, in the sense of failure or fault. So the speaker asks his mistress not to castigate him – presumably for moral or physical shortcomings – because, as he goes on to say, she may be just as blameworthy herself:

Lest guilty of my faults thy sweet self prove.
For thou betraying me, I do betray
My nobler part to my gross body's treason;
My soul doth tell my body that he may
Triumph in love; flesh stays no farther reason,
But rising at thy name, doth point out thee
As his triumphant prize…

Brusquely she interrupted his reading. 'There seems,' she said, 'to be a bawdy play on words.'

He gave an embarrassed laugh. 'I've never heard any woman speak in such an uninhibited way as you do, Miss Remington.'

'I believe in being forthright. The ribaldry in this poem doesn't bother me.'

Staines blinked, took a deep breath and read on slowly:

Proud of this pride,
He is contented thy poor drudge to be,
To stand in thy affairs, fall by thy side.
No want of conscience hold it that I call
Her 'love,' for whose dear love I rise and fall.

She took the book from his hand and stared at the page. 'It verges on the obscene, doesn't it?' she said. 'His rising flesh points at the lover! And then words like "proud" and "stand" continue this carnal meaning, don't they?'

'I – well, I suppose so.' He hoped he wasn't blushing. 'Apparently there isn't much in this poem that you haven't already managed to explicate for yourself. This knowledge of yours…'

'Where does it come from? Well, I haven't been up to any wickedness myself, if that's what you're wondering.' She gave a tinkling laugh. 'Our College library has some remarkably informative books, Mr Staines. Illustrated histories of classical art, for instance, showing Greek vase paintings with satyr figures in a state of high arousal. Besides, on my family's property I've watched farm animals mating. We have three fine stallions standing at stud – fascinating to see them in action.'

'You're extraordinarily outspoken. You want to shock me with your candour, I think. Anyway it's evident you don't need any help from me in interpreting this poem.'

'But I wanted to hear you reading it to me. It's as if your voice makes the words vibrate inside my body.'

He didn't know what to say next. Her thoughts always seemed to move more quickly than his, and so audaciously that whenever she spoke she caught him by surprise. They looked at each other in silence for a lingering moment. Then at last, breaking the trance, he took out his pocket watch and showed her the time. She nodded and sighed, strangely subdued now. Without further conversation he escorted her back to the College entrance in Harley Street, gave a slight bow, and walked slowly away.

'Love is too young to know what conscience is…' – the words kept rolling around in his head, at times attaching themselves her youthfulness and at times to his own. He was conscious of his complete inexperience in dealing with women on anything but a formal basis. No sisters. No female friends while growing up. Very few young ladies alongside him in the classroom when he was a university student. To date, his life had been a sheltered one. What little he knew, or thought he knew, about sexual activity was filtered through the euphemisms of his reading. And conscience? It was an abstraction that couldn't easily be connected to the bodily hunger he had begun to feel in Lavinia's company.

The following week, after his lecture, they went again into Regent's Park, making their way right across it to the zoo on the northern side. As they paused in front of the tigers' cage, a pair of the sinewy creatures shook off their sun-sodden inertia and began nonchalantly to copulate. Lavinia drew her arm through the crook of his elbow and squeezed it. He held his breath, unable to disengage himself from her or from the spectacle.

'Someone from the College will see us together before long,' he said as they strolled back later through the park, 'and busy-bodies will gossip. We can't continue with these walks.'

'Pah!' Lavinia waved her hand dismissively. 'Let the prattlers prattle. Surely, after all the freedoms gained in recent years, it's possible to have friendly, open conversations between a man and a woman without their becoming social outcasts!'

But when he persisted in voicing his qualms, she proposed a discreet compromise arrangement: from now on, instead of setting out together from the College in Harley Street, they would go separately to the park and meet inside it, on York Bridge. He would make his way there straight after his lecture finished and she would join him a few minutes later. 'There! You can't find fault with that plan!' she said triumphantly. No, he couldn't, or wouldn't. She seemed to have taken charge of him.

'Until next Friday, then,' she said. He inclined his head, raised his hat, and was beginning to turn away when she spoke again. 'Where are you walking to now, Mr Staines?'

'To my lodgings.'

'Where do you live?'

'Oh, not far from here. A few hundred yards.'

Catching his eye, she held his gaze for a moment, but said no more.

When the time for their next excursion came around, low cloud had darkened the sky. As Gavin Staines emerged from the College buildings there was a smell of imminent rain in the air, and before he reached York Bridge a shower came at him suddenly, flung by a sudden gusty wind that made his umbrella ineffectual. He walked back towards the gate. She would probably have the good sense, he told himself, to stay indoors while the weather was so unpleasant – but there she was now, hurrying along the puddly path towards him, grinning as the rain thickened.

'You'll get soaked,' he said.

'You sound like my mother!'

'Really, you ought to return to the College straight away!'

'No, not to the College!' She spoke vehemently. 'Let's go to your lodgings. We can dry out while you read to me.'

'That would invite scandal.'

'Fiddlesticks! You worry too much, Mr Staines. Besides, we aren't likely to encounter anyone in the building at this time of day, surely?'

He gave a helpless shrug. Getting wetter by the minute, they walked up to his rooms in a tingling silence. He lit a fire and they stood with their backs to it, side by side, saying little, waiting for the warmth to do its gradual work.

'This place must look shabby to you. I took it furnished. Not quite my taste, but it's conveniently located.'

'Nothing to apologise for. The fireplace is a boon at a time like this. My skirt must be beginning to dry, I think.' Staines watched her lift the hem above her slender ankles and bend down to feel the damp leather of her boots.

Picking up the scuttle, he tipped some coal on the flames.

She stepped closer and rested her hand on his forearm. They stood face to face. No words came to him. The blood was thudding in his temple, in his chest, in his groin. The sudden dumbfounding thing that had gripped them seemed to have a clumsy volition of its own. By now he felt powerless to resist any longer.

TWELVE

OVER AND OVER, DURING SWEATY NIGHTS OF BROKEN SLEEP, Gavin Staines continued to wrestle with himself, unable to still an agitated inner voice insisting that what they had done was wrong, indefensible, and the fault was plainly his. Although Lavinia's impulsiveness had been startling, that didn't excuse him in any way. He bore the responsibility. She was hardly more than a girl, and he should have foreseen what might happen. Should have known to keep his distance. He'd been weak.

But he also heard something else, the whisper of concupiscence subverting conscience. You'll never, said this voice, resist the lure of her dark eyes, her milky flesh, the way she draws your hands to her breasts, the way her mouth opens wide in mirth or ecstasy.

Weeks went by. Autumn rains had settled in. She contrived to visit him again in his rooms, and again and again. During their conversations he tried repeatedly to tell her that they could not go on in this foolish headstrong way, that it was full of risks and bound to end badly, but she brushed his compunction aside each time with that throaty laugh of hers.

❖

Finding the College library empty, Staines pulled a sheaf of pamphlets from his coat pocket and was in the act of placing them on the tables when he heard the door open. With a swish of silk, a short plump woman entered, mouth pursed and small eyes as dark as currants in the shiny surface of a pale bun. Recognising her as one of the supercilious 'lady visitors,' Lady Sarah Corkindale, he greeted her with formulaic politeness, which she acknowledged minimally with a slight nod of her head.

She picked up a pamphlet and read its title aloud. 'A Labour Case Against Conscription.' Slowly she turned its pages. 'This seems,' she said with cold disapproval, 'a most unsuitable publication for you to be distributing here, Mr Staines. Does it have even a tenuous connection with the subject matter of your lectures?'

'None, Lady Corkindale.'

'Do you have the Principal's permission?'

'No. My own beliefs authorise me to provide an antidote to the militaristic views being propounded so aggressively by Professor Cramb in his classrooms.'

'That,' she said as she swept from the room with a pamphlet in her hand, 'is a very rash presumption on your part.'

A few days later Staines came face to face with Cramb himself in the gloom of the main corridor. They had never previously exchanged more than a few words, but this time it was clear as they approached one another that Cramb intended to accost him. Refraining from any salutation, the older man spoke curtly. 'I believe you've bin making critical remarks about my lectures. Surely y' wouldnae claim any expert knowledge of military history?'

Like a heavy curtain lowered over his mouth, Cramb's thick moustache muffled his words, already being squeezed through the grainy filter of a Scottish burr. Listening to his antagonist,

Staines remembered that Cramb was reportedly a close friend of Craik the Principal; the two were countrymen, after all.

'How you interpret past events, sir,' said Staines, 'is not my concern. I do take exception to your use of lectures here to impose on young minds a particular notion about present-day patriotic duty.' Cramb blew an exasperated puff through his moustache as Staines went on. 'To me it seems quite wrong that you urge pupils of Queen's College to join the chorus of those who advocate war against Germany. Instilling such a belligerent attitude goes beyond the role of a teacher, in my view.'

There was an angry flush in Cramb's cheeks. 'On the contrary,' he shouted, 'influencing the attitudes of one's pupils is precisely what a teacher should aim to do. Surely that's bin part of your own purpose when you've stood at the lectern.'

Before Staines could shape a reply, Cramb had stalked off. By the following week their dispute had become the talk of the College, and Staines could see plainly that his own opinion attracted scant support. When he came into the common room muttered conversations would stop; some pupils began to look askance at him in class; and on one occasion as he came up to the lectern he found a white feather waiting for him there.

Only one of his fellow lecturers, instead of shunning Staines silently, made any direct reference to the matter. Eric Crupper, the music teacher, a friendly soul, spoke to him one day as they were both leaving the College building. 'I imagine you must be feeling somewhat isolated, Staines. This dispute with Cramb.'

A shrug. 'I didn't expect my position to be popular.'

'Whereas Cramb certainly knows how to whip up enthusiasm! He's quite the orator, I'm told. Besides, there's a lot of sympathy for him at the personal level, you know. Invalid wife, crippled son. Not in good health himself.'

'I didn't know any of that. But it doesn't alter the fact that he flagrantly abuses the privilege of his academic status to persuade

young women that war between England and Germany is desir-
able. The last thing our country needs is more of the mad
nationalistic fervor that killed thousands of soldiers and civilians in the Boer War. Terrible suffering and waste, disguised by
romantic rhetoric.'

Then something drove all thoughts of the Cramb controversy
from his mind. Late one afternoon, opening the door to Lavinia,
he saw at once that she was pale and unhappy.

'What is it? Are you unwell?'

No response. Slowly she drew off her gloves and sat down
near the fireplace, staring at the embers in silence. When at last
she spoke it was with a deep sigh. 'My monthly courses have
always been regular, but I'm now more than a fortnight overdue
and I've been feeling light-headed. I must be carrying a child.'

His hand went to his chest, as if to steady the lurch of pertur-
bation. 'Have you spoken to anyone about this? Friends? Family?'

She shook her head. 'My parents will be enraged if they find
out. Mother is very pious and strict. Father is likely to disown me.'

He squared his shoulders. 'Not if you're wedded, surely.' The
imploring words tumbled out hastily. 'And I do want you to be
my bride, Lavinia. Just tell me you agree, and I'll ask your father
to consent to our marriage.'

'No no, he'd never permit that. You mean well, I know, and
it's a gallant offer, and I'm grateful, but I'm afraid he'd regard
your financial prospects as much too limited.' Her rueful tone
became bitter as she added, 'Father has always made it quite
clear he intends me to be a device for linking our family's
property with the assets of some suitable landed gentry.'

Staines protested. She needn't subject herself to her father's
ambitions; she had a mind of her own... Lavinia's retort was

blunt. She had no money of her own, no real independence. And tiresome though her parents were, she was their only child and she simply couldn't bear a family rupture.

'So you won't marry me?' The question hung there, drooping, as hope drained out of it. He drew in a long breath. 'Then what do you plan to do?'

Pressing her clasped hands to her lips, she looked into the dying fire. 'I need to think carefully about that. Privately.'

'But we must consider it together.'

Resisting his entreaty, she rose and moved towards the door.

'It's something for me to deal with alone. I'll let you know later what I decide, but in the meantime please don't make contact with me.'

He began to remonstrate, but she raised a restraining hand and left the room abruptly.

Bitter apples: according to a medical book in the College library, that was the common name for it. Colocynth extract. Procuring the powder from a street-seller proved surprisingly easy. Lavinia took the small packet up to her bedroom.

Just a teaspoon of it, she had read, should produce a sufficient purgation to dislodge the thing growing inside her. With trembling fingers she measured out twice that amount to be sure of its efficacy, mixed it with water, and swilled down the acrid potion. Within a few minutes it had a drastic cramping effect. Clutching her belly, she hobbled along the corridor to the lavatory. There she vomited violently, uncontrollably, and then the diarrhoea began and would not stop. Pangs became fiercer.

Nothing like this had happened there before, and the College authorities did all they could to keep the matter quiet. It would be 'needlessly distressing,' the Principal told the assembled students, to let parents know that a young lady had died suddenly, by her own hand, on these premises. On no account should the sad circumstances be publicly mentioned. Even among themselves, speculation about the cause of Miss Remington's plight would be entirely inappropriate, showing a deplorable lack of respect for her family's privacy in its time of profound bereavement. All classes would be suspended for a week, and during this time every girl would devote herself to individual study and reflection.

Only when he walked into the College common room two days later did Staines learn about the catastrophe. 'Lectures cancelled?' he exclaimed after glancing at the noticeboard. 'Why?'

'A shocking death,' murmured a colleague. 'One of the young ladies. Miss Remington. Appears to be suicide.'

Speechless, numb with his private grief and self-recrimination, he returned at once to his rooms and stayed there for several days. Tormenting questions jostled in his mind. Had she indeed killed herself deliberately? Or did an intended abortion procedure go terribly awry? Either way, he was certainly culpable. Did anyone suspect his involvement? Had he been observed walking with Lavinia? Had she, despite her avowed discretion, perhaps told a confidante about the liaison with him? Should he himself confess it? But to whom, and to what end? Declaring himself to have been Lavinia's lover and the unwitting cause of her dreadful death could serve no purpose, give nobody any comfort. His role, it seemed, would have to remain forever on his conscience, an unabsolved secret.

Then a short letter came from Sir Henry Craik, summoning him to the Principal's study at the College the next morning 'to discuss a grave matter.'

In the dark-panelled office Staines sat rigidly, hands clasped, eyes lowered.

Craik came straight to the point. 'I regret to say, Mr Staines, that I have received serious complaints about your conduct.'

Staines nodded, suffused with guilt and shame, resolving to deny nothing and to surrender himself to whatever judicial process and punishment would be forthcoming. He waited to hear this stern square-jawed Scot utter Lavinia's name.

Astonishingly, that didn't happen. The complaints were about something else altogether: his pacifist activities. By distributing disreputable political pamphlets, Craik informed him, and by publicly criticising Professor Cramb's patriotic sentiments, Staines had not only upset many pupils but also provoked strenuous protests from staff and parents. The matter was serious, extremely serious.

'This College,' intoned Craik, 'proclaims in its title a profound homage to royalty. With the distinct possibility of war on the horizon, we cannot tolerate here your advocacy of what is tantamount to sedition. Your part-time appointment as a lecturer will be discontinued forthwith.'

'But sir…' Staines began.

Craik interrupted, gesturing impatiently. 'No, no. Nothing more to be said. Please leave these premises without delay.'

THOUGH NEVER OSTRACISED UNTIL NOW, GAVIN STAINES had long been familiar with isolation. An only child, shy and earnest from an early age, he felt drawn to solitary pastimes and private reveries. It could hardly have been otherwise; his father, an irascible banker, seemed preoccupied with business matters, generally kept his thoughts to himself, and seldom – except when erupting in a fit of drunken anger – spoke more than a few words at a time to his son or even to his wife, who herself had shrivelled into defensive taciturnity. In a home that offered little conversation and no companionship, young Gavin immersed himself in the solace of reading. Characters in books became a substitute for friends, with stories of stoical self-reliance exerting a particular appeal: Defoe's Crusoe and Dickens' Copperfield seemed kindred spirits. The storehouse of poetry opened wide its doors when an aunt gave him for his 15th birthday Palgrave's *Golden Treasury of the Best Songs and Lyrical Poems in the English Language*. He went over and over his favourite pieces until he could recite them aloud to himself. Repeating long passages from memory became a cherished comfort, a shield against loneliness.

Bookishly reclusive throughout his undergraduate studies at University College London, he attracted the attention of the Quain Professor of English there, W.P. Ker, because of the excellence of his final-year assignment work. An essay on variant forms of the English sonnet won him the prestigious Brassington Prize. Not long after his graduation, Ker encouraged him to attend meetings of the newly formed English Association, introducing him there to Sir Henry Craik and later writing a glowing testimonial to recommend his appointment as a lecturer at Queen's College. 'Mr Staines is well on the path to becoming a fine scholar,' said Ker's letter, 'and although temperamentally inclining towards a quiet, reserved demeanour, he can speak with uncommon clarity on literary topics. He would be, I have no doubt, a highly competent lecturer, capable of inspiring the best of your pupils.'

His role as a visiting teacher at Queen's had required little in the way of sociable interaction. He came and went, came and went, arriving unobtrusively for his scheduled lectures and usually leaving soon afterwards. His ingrained tendency to turn inwards, somewhat disengaged from those around him, had gone unchecked until Lavinia insisted on seizing his attention.

Yet now, with her horrifyingly abrupt departure from his life, Staines found that his previous habit of seclusion had not prepared him to cope with the sudden spurning that followed his dismissal from the College. He was doubly outcast, cut off both from the world of work and from his family. He knew his father's rejection of him, already implacable, would be even more furious if he were to learn that Gavin had not only become a pacifist and forfeited his occupation but had also debauched one of the students placed in his charge, causing – albeit indirectly and unwittingly – her violent death.

Repudiated by his parents, and with no gainful employment to which he could turn, he faced penury as well as social exclusion. These things might have been easier to bear if not for the appalling circumstances of Lavinia's death. His feelings of utter loss, compounded by guilt, could not be shared with anyone. It was as if they lay locked under his tongue or lodged in his throat.

Days dragged. When the sun shone he stayed indoors, often lying on his bed fully clothed for hours on end, idly turning the pages of this or that book. When rain fell he walked for miles around the streets, aimless, cold to the bone, loitering here and there under a dripping umbrella, his trousers and boots wet through. On one of these meanders he was traipsing along Marylebone High Street, coat wrapped tightly around him, when he stopped outside a shop he greatly admired: a long-established antiquarian bookseller proudly bearing the name of its mid-Victorian founder Francis Edwards. The business, he knew, had moved from the West End a couple of years ago to occupy these new premises, claiming to be the world's first bookshop specifically designed and built for the purpose. What caught his eye now was a small handwritten notice in the window:

WANTED:
SHOP ASSISTANT
WITH WIDE KNOWLEDGE OF BOOKS.
APPLY WITHIN.

A week later he began work there. Although the wages were meagre they covered his frugal living expenses, and the duties proved to be generally congenial enough. When customers sought books to suit their interests, he was glad to help with a suggestion or two; when there were routine tasks such as shelving newly acquired items, he seldom found them tedious; and when the shop was quiet he could browse some of its stock. Occasionally he would come across old books that had a particular allure for him. He pored over Samuel Johnson's *Lives of the Most Eminent*

English Poets, relishing the rhythms of Johnson's vigorous style. With reverent care he turned the pages of an early edition of the *Songes and Sonettes* anthology popularly known as Tottel's Miscellany, which assembled poems by the Tudor courtiers Thomas Wyatt and Henry Howard; Staines lingered over their rendering of Petrarchan sonnets into English, their experiments with rhyme and metre. He browsed through several publications of the Early English Text Society, particularly some of their erudite editions of previously inaccessible medieval writings.

If he had supposed that this immersion in an antiquarian frame of mind would distract or even liberate him from his recent preoccupations, he soon found he was mistaken. Barbed words would suddenly reach up from the page and accuse him. In one of Wyatt's poems he was abashed by the phrase 'lust's negligence,' and in another by the paradoxical image of being held tight in an unlocked prison. Even the mere title of a book could disconcert him: he came across a Philological Society edition of a 14th-century Northumbrian poem by Richard Rollo called *The Pricke of Conscience*, and from the same period a Kentish treatise retrieved by the Early English Text Society, Dan Michel's *Ayenbite of Inwyt, or Remorse of Conscience*. In modern books, as well, there were passages that spoke to him with unnerving directness; Bradley's *Oxford Lectures on Poetry* suggested that Shakespeare understood well 'the pain of self-reproach and self-condemnation, and of the torment to which this pain might rise.'

Apart from these saltings of his wound, the simple repetitive bookshop tasks brought him a kind of sedative relief, helping the time to pass. One month drifted into the next, and the next. Seasons shifted placidly and Staines began to think that nothing would come of the persistent talk about imminent conflict with Germany. But then, somewhere in the Balkans, some crazed assassin lit a pile of kindling and soon the bursting flames ignited Europe. By early August, Britain's soldiers were on the march – straight towards carnage. Before the end of that same month a *Times* correspondent was reporting from the battlefront on 'terrible losses': the British Expeditionary Force, so recently mobilised, had already been reduced to 'a retreating and a broken army.' To Staines's dismay, recruiters turned this humiliating news into an opportunity to exert moral pressure, reinforced by jingoistic press articles, with the result that many thousands of new volunteers were sworn in within a week and the government quietly persuaded several leading authors, among them the creators of Peter Pan and Sherlock Holmes, to sign an open letter – and urge many literary colleagues to do so too – appealing to 'all the English-speaking race' to support the fight against the 'Blood and Iron of Germany's assault on the highest European ideals.' He was pleased to see that the bold freethinker Bertrand Russell, a shining light for pacifists, refused to sign it.

With tighter control over military censorship and government propaganda, information about what was going on in France soon became so sanitised, so thoroughly disinfected, that Staines could ascertain very little through official press channels. Instead he relied on meetings and publications of the Independent Labour Party to glean some insights into the real situation. Reports collated by ILF writers on the basis of several informal sources, including clandestine interviews with maimed and repatriated soldiers, drew a horrific picture: there had been no significant troop advances, only stagnation; no heroic exploits, only dreadful slaughter; no clear strategies, only confusion. But for the British public at large it was all happening far enough away to be suffused with a haze of patriotic fervour, and to pose no immediate threat – until May of 1915, when an inaugural shower of incendiaries from Zeppelin balloons fell on the East End, killing a mere handful of civilians but striking fear into the hearts of all Londoners. A few months after that, a much heavier freight of Zeppelin bombs hit the city centre near St Paul's, destroying prominent buildings, starting many fierce blazes and sending more than 20 people to their deaths including half a dozen children. Warfare had come to England – and a week later so would three large convoys of wounded men, the largest influx of them yet, arriving by boat train at Waterloo Station to be lugged to the King George Military Hospital, where well over 1000 half-living bodies were already crammed into wards and corridors. This latest trio of shipments comprised Australians and New Zealanders from the Dardanelles, most of them mangled or deranged. Such things could not be kept quiet.

Yet still, to Staines's frustration, a large majority of his fellow citizens seemed to be wilfully ignoring the insane pointlessness of the conflict being so savagely waged on foreign soil. How could they cling with such stubborn tenacity to the illusion that some innate attribute of Englishness would guarantee before long a glorious victory over their country's barbaric foe? How could so many of then go about their ordinary business while thousands upon thousands on both sides of the conflict continued to be killed – and many more of them degraded, cruelly crippled, tormented into madness?

At his employer's request he attended in September a meeting of the International Association of Antiquarian Booksellers, where most of the members looked twice his age. He was appalled to find how pettily commercial their concerns were. They fretted at length over the wartime restrictions on paper and printing that made it difficult to produce catalogues promoting their sale items. They lamented the decline in sales of second-hand books. 'Everyone wants to read the latest drivel about this damned war!' expostulated one man, so tremulous with indignation that his tea slopped into the saucer. 'Can't interest them in *belles lettres* these days!'

When he did encounter someone who wanted to talk about the conduct of the war his interlocutor turned out to be a former military man, a proud veteran of the Boer campaigns, who specialised in selling publications on army history, gave his Kipling-thick moustache a brisk twitch at the end of each sentence, and emphatically championed the cause of international bellicosity as 'England's destiny and duty.'

Readying himself for an argument, Staines told the mustachioed militant that for his own part he had no interest in books about warfare.

'No interest? What do you read, then, young man?'

'Mainly poetry. Sonnets in particular.'

'Ah, sonnets – then you'll know that rousing one by Wordsworth about British freedom?'

'I'm not sure that I…'

'Magnificent climax. Ends like this:

> In our halls is hung
> Armoury of the invincible knights of old.
> We must be free or die who speak the tongue
> That Shakespeare spoke, the faith and morals hold
> That Milton held. In everything we are sprung
> Of Earth's first blood, have titles manifold.

Fine sentiments, eh? Marvellous turn of phrase.'

Staines wanted to say that a patriot's century-old rhetoric, perhaps forgivable in the era of Trafalgar and Waterloo, had no relevance to the loathsome butchery of present-day warfare. But there were some people one could never convince. He turned away from the twitching bristles.

Early in 1916 the long-anticipated legislation came into force. The Military Service Act required nearly all men aged from 18 to 41 – exceptions were few – in England, Scotland and Wales to be subject to army enlistment. Any man objecting to his call-up could apply to a local tribunal, which was empowered to grant conditional exemption from service under certain narrowly defined circumstances.

Staines put his case firmly and responded with patience to unsympathetic questioning. No, his conscientious objection to military service did not stem from religious beliefs. No, he was not eligible for exemption on the grounds of being married or widowed with dependents. No, he was not willing to undertake work as an unarmed medical orderly, or support his country's military action in any other way. No, he did not consider himself a traitor. No, if his objection were to be dismissed he would not recognise any military authority – let alone obey it. Yes, he was certainly able to explain his intransigent position: for him it was a fundamental principle that no civilisation worth the name should compel any person to act with violence towards any other. Yes, he did understand that such obstinacy on his part would lead to imprisonment.

Later, being taken to his cell in the Harwich Redoubt, he asked himself whether he would have given a fully candid answer to a further question, if the tribunal interrogators had thought to ask it: whether his complete renunciation of violence had any more personal underlying cause.

Hard to explain, except to his mother. She alone shared what he had suffered at his father's hands. Like her son, she had known how unpredictably moody that bull-necked man could be, how suddenly his rages could erupt. She too had felt the force of his fist and the thump of his walking stick.

Perth

&

Dartmoor

2015

ELBOWS ON DESK, EYES CLOSED, FINGERTIPS PRESSING against her forehead, Valerie sat in her college room and tried to steady her mind.

More than a fortnight ago, after her return from Sydney, Barry Plunket had asked her to produce a tentative outline of likely subtopics for her thesis, and she still couldn't get started. 'A page will do,' he'd said. 'You'll find it useful as a basis for the structure. A history thesis is just a series of chapters, after all. Thematically linked essays arranged in the shape of an argument.'

It was hard to concentrate on scholarly pursuits after the double eruption of violence. Her grandfather's case still upset her whenever she thought about it, though it no longer seemed to be a cause for serious worry; he was on the way to recovery. The hideous attack on Kemal would always stay in her mind, and meanwhile it had a direct impact on her research project because he had been on the point of setting up meetings for her with various Turkish friends so that she could ask, with his help as translator, how they viewed the Gallipoli commemorations. There would have been a chapter in that, but none of it could proceed now. Anyway, a setback to her research work was trivial beside the terrible fact of Kemal's death, which left her mind floundering. Why did he die?

To sort out the jumble of her thoughts, Valerie took a sheet of paper and jotted these notes:

POSSIBILITIES

1   Random attack. Not specifically targeted, K just happened to be a victim of brutish violence. 'Motiveless malignity' – somebody's comment on one of Shakespeare's villains.

2   K was targeted as a Muslim by someone ferociously hostile to that brand of religion.

3   K was targeted as a Turk by someone irate at how Anzac commemorations this year are representing Turkish soldiers not as mortal foes of the diggers but as their honourable peers.

4   K was targeted as a Turk by someone taking revenge for the slaughter of well over a million Armenians in the same year as the Gallipoli conflict.

5   K was targeted as an Alevi Muslim, a 'heretic,' by a Sunni fanatic.

6   K was targeted by someone with a personal grievance against him.

Then, sipping her coffee, she reflected on each conjecture in turn.

Assaulted for no reason by some nutter in a murderous rage? Doesn't seem likely, she thought. I've never heard of vicious gangs or individuals roaming around this uni precinct. Occasional opportunistic assaults on women, maybe, but not on men. Drug-fuelled thugs itching for a fight gravitate towards bars and nightclubs, don't they? Not campuses, though I suppose a mundane situation anywhere can quickly turn nasty. Perhaps some nasty drunk asked him for cigarettes or money, and became furious when K wouldn't hand anything over. Not very different, in that case, from what happened to Grandpa: started as robbery, escalated into brutality.

Or it could have been a wild attack in revenge for lethal aggression by Islamic fundamentalists against Australians – the stabbings in Melbourne a few months ago and the Lindt Café siege in Sydney? Lots of Western Australians died in the Bali bombings, though that was years ago and most of their friends and families seem to keep their grief quietly to themselves. There have been a few anti-Muslim incidents around Perth, such as graffiti on mosque walls, but not violent crimes. Even if racist hotheads came onto the campus in search of a sacrificial human victim, they wouldn't be aware K was a Muslim, because there was nothing about him, not the way he dressed or anything else, to proclaim his religion.

But did someone, knowing K was a proud Turk, get so agitated over the positive tone of current media commentary about Turkish soldiers in WW1 that beating him to death seemed a suitable protest? Seems hard to imagine, she thought. There's been a lot of chauvinistic flag-wagging this year, and the Gallipoli centenary could have made a few people rabidly resentful towards the country that killed thousands of Anzacs there – and maltreated POWs, with nearly one in four of them dying in captivity. But making a Turkish student the scape-goat for retribution so long afterwards? That's too a big stretch, surely.

If K's death had anything to do with events of a century ago, isn't it more likely to have been an act of revenge for the slaughter of over a million Armenians? Pointing in that direction is recent publicity about the Turkish government's refusal (and also Australia's) to acknowledge this as genocide. But there's only a handful of Armenians in Perth, and as far as I know they haven't been agitating about that distant atrocity.

K told me that he and his family belong to the Alevi community, which Turkey's Sunni majority regards as heretics. According to Dr Google, Alevis don't worship in mosques and don't share many of the dominant Muslim beliefs and practices. They encourage women to be educated, to choose whatever occupations they like, to dress in modern clothes, and to mix freely with men. Alevis don't pray at fixed times, they don't observe Ramadan fasting or Hajj pilgrimages, and generally they support the concept of a secular state established by Attaturk, which Erdogan's government is steadily dismantling. There were mass killings of Alevis by Sunnis in the 1970s and 1990s, and just last year Alevis staged big public protests at the oppression they still suffer. So although I'm not aware of any open Sunni animosity towards Alevis in Perth, it wouldn't be surprising if conflict had somehow developed between K and Sunni students.

Pushing back her chair, Valerie made herself a cup of coffee and slowly chewed on a couple of ginger biscuits, the first thing she'd eaten since lunch. The time for an evening meal had come and gone without any hunger pangs. She looked over what she'd written and tossed it aside with a sigh. Music: calming music was what she needed, and she turned to her stack of CDs. Tim had been amused at her preference for this 'outmoded format,' but she liked it – liked the little ritual of taking a disk from its plastic case, inserting it into her old machine, and reading the booklet of album notes as the music played. On top of the pile was something she'd bought recently from the Zenith store in Claremont: a Vaughan Williams selection containing his Pastoral Symphony. Listening in a kind of trance, she tried to picture Williams working as a medical orderly in the mud of France, lifting maimed men onto waggons and then, after the war, distilling all that sorrow into these elegiac sounds. 'A monument of loss,' the descriptive notes called it.

Monuments of loss. Could be a title for her thesis? If she ever got around to writing it. Regaining enough purposeful energy to feel properly committed to the project seemed beyond her for the time being. Listless, she was finding it hard to give any serious thought to a program of research. The nearest she could get to her topic was to bathe her mind in listening to music written around the time of the Great War and in reading fiction that evoked aspects of it. She'd just finished Pat Barker's novel Regeneration, moving in its use of episodes from the real-life wartime experiences of Siegfried Sassoon and Wilfred Owen, and their attempts to devise a new poetic idiom that would express without lyrical evasion the horror of this piteous conflict and its lingering aftermath. In the book's title she heard a commemorative tonality: the story itself, in a lest-we-forget spirit, was enacting regeneration, bearing witness to all that suffering.

Her lateral exploration into music and literature could be justified as soaking up the aesthetic climate of the period, getting a sense of context for the more solidly monumental forms of remembrance and testimony that constituted her chosen subject matter. But she knew that in fact it was an evasion, an indefinite postponement of the task of developing and testing a research hypothesis. Adrift: she felt adrift.

Her iPhone interrupted this pensive haze, vibrating with a Reminder Alert: Lauren Holt was due to knock on her door in five minutes for another informal tutoring session. This was one of the 'value-added' services provided to resident under-graduates at St Cat's. Postgraduates like Valerie were available, in return for discounted college fees, to offer occasional study advice to first-year students. Valerie found most of these casual sessions pleasant enough, especially with Lauren, a clever and personable girl. Between them now there was also a particular bond, a bond of grief at Kemal's senseless death. Lauren, his classmate in a Politics unit, had been the person who approached her on his behalf when he was struggling to write his assignments.

Kemal. The timbre of his voice. Valerie found herself replaying fragments of conversation, just ordinary things they'd talked about. His earnest words. His laughter, too. Hard to accept that he'd been silenced forever.

A familiar rat-tat. She wiped her eyes, blew her nose, opened the door to Lauren and welcomed her in. That beguiling smile of Lauren's, with its hint of wantonness. The lift of her pert breasts under the tight blouse.

'Coffee?'

'No thanks. I've brought something else.' Lauren pulled a bottle of red from her bag. 'Let's have a glass or two while we talk.'

'I'm not much of a drinker.'

Lauren grinned. 'Do you good to relax a bit.'

So as they discussed assignment topics, they sipped and then quaffed and refilled. And became drowsily sentimental.

'Without you, Lauren, I'd never have met poor Kemal. A lovely man, wasn't he?'

'I can't stop imagining his last moments. Lying there on the concrete, his skull cracked open, life slipping away. Alone.'

'Terrible. I've been picturing that scene too. Try to push it away but it keeps coming back. Not able to get on with my work or do anything much. Don't even feel like spending time in the Postgraduate Common Room here. Having to be sociable – it's just not my mood these days. Rather stay here in my room and think my own thoughts. Pathetic, eh?'

'Well, it sounds, like, a bit lonesome. But I know how you feel.' Lauren refilled Valerie's glass. 'What about that friend of yours, the cute one with a birthmark? Doesn't it help if you talk about it all with him?

'I can't really. Kemal's death happened soon after Tim went off to England on a research trip.'

'What's he researching?'

'Tim's thesis is on blacks in Victorian Britain.'

'Phew! Isn't that, like, a totally risky topic?'

'Risky? Why?'

'Well, a white guy presuming to write about the experience of black guys! I mean, he can't possibly know what they felt, being part of a minority group. How they saw things. Can he?'

Valerie gave a sour smile. 'That's the orthodox line in Humanities tutorials these days, is it, Lauren? The notion that we're disqualified from writing about anything outside our own race or gender? What – so my own research project on war memorials ought to be left entirely to the RSL blokes? Kate Grenville shouldn't have written *A Secret River*, because it's impertinent for a female novelist to put herself compassionately in the shoes of one of her flawed fore-fathers? Shakespeare's temerity in writing *The Merchant of Venice* offends female lawyers and Jewish financiers because he could never know how it actually feels to be Portia or Shylock and so his empathy is illegitimate? I think this possessive, censorious kind of identity politics is a totally stupid ideology!'

Lauren's jaw had dropped. 'Wow! I really pushed a button there, didn't I?'

'Sorry, not rebuking you personally – just sounding off. It gets my goat, the way some self-righteous academic custodians of identity try to shut down independent inquiry.'

'I guess I haven't thought a lot about all that, so it's fair enough for you to challenge what I said. Anyhow, I admire your loyalty to Tim and his project.'

'Loyalty? I don't know. The ironical thing is, just before he left here we had a big row. Over Kemal.'

'Over Kemal? Why?'

'He thought I was giving Kemal too much help with his writing. Got on his high horse about it. There was a personal edge to it, too. I could see Tim thought Kemal and I had a physical thing going, and he was a bit jealous.'

'Was he wrong?'

'Quite wrong. I wasn't intimate with either of them, actually. Not in that way.'

Lauren gave her a hug.

Valerie stood up, and then put her hand on the back of a chair for support. 'Whoo,' she said. 'I feel a bit giddy. Not used to this much wine, especially on an empty stomach.'

'Do you good,' Lauren repeated.

'Before you arrived I was listening to some music from nearly a century ago,' she said. 'Vaughan Williams. Like to hear it?'

Lauren nodded. 'Sure. But I should have worn something warmer. D'you have a rug I can wrap myself in while we listen?'

They snuggled together on the couch, a blanket around them both, and the Pastoral Symphony took them to other places. Bugles were echoing forlornly across distant fields. *Poco tranquillo*. Valerie's breathing deepened. She closed her eyes.

When she opened them in a groggy haze she looked blearily at her watch. Three in the morning! Lauren, snoring gently, lay with her her head on Valerie's shoulder, and her hand on Valerie's thigh.

FIFTEEN

Hi THERE, VALERIE

Any further news of the police inquiry into Kemal's death? And what progress with your work on war memorials?

I miss Perth but must admit August weather in England can be quite pleasant, even in this famously wet and windy region where I've spent the last couple of days. People joke that Dartmoor is all 'fogs, bogs and dogs,' but since my arrival it's been almost cloud-free here, with enough cheery warmth to make me think I may start turning into a little sunbeam myself.

I'm staying in the Plume of Feathers Inn, Princetown's oldest building (late 18th c). Perfect atmospherics for a visiting historian: thick granite walls, wooden beams etc. You get a sense that old stories probably lurk in every nook. Not luxurious here but the food is hearty and my room is snug. In the evening, groups of hikers crowd into the bar, brimming with rowdy chatter about their rambles on the high moorland. I may explore one of the walking trails myself if this weather holds.

You can guess from my upbeat tone that I've already had a bit of luck on the research front – though there's been some frustration, too. Coming down to Dartmoor on spec could have been a complete waste of time, but the excellent prison museum was well worth a visit and a little library in the Community Centre has also proved useful up to a point. That ex-circus black man I've been seeking information on, Joshua Dunn, does get mentioned in a newspaper of the time, and the report is about a really strange episode. The background, it seems, is that Dunn had left Princetown in early 1889 after several years incarcerated here. When released he was put on a train to London. But then a few months later – this is the bizarre thing – he's caught trying to break back INTO the prison! The news item I've seen is about his arrest. Why did he do it, and what happened next? Don't know yet – the files here are patchy. So far I haven't located any account of the subsequent trial, which would probably indicate his motivation, and maybe what kind of person he was. Frustrating not to be able to get more info at this stage.

Suspense isn't something a line of research usually produces. I've been trying to fathom what could explain this peculiar reversal – not a Great Escape but the opposite, a breaking-and-entering exploit that brings a discharged crim voluntarily back inside. Might it be simply that, after so long shut away, he'd found no place for himself anywhere out there as a 'free' black man? Nowhere to go, no employment, no friends. Perhaps not even much food or shelter. Living rough, I'd bet. In contrast, although Dartmoor prison wouldn't have been a pleasant place, I guess returning to the routines of a familiar little world where he probably had still some mates doing time may have seemed more attractive than struggling alone in London.

Or was there some other reason?

There's got to be a record somewhere of what was said in court, perhaps including a statement by Dunn himself. I'll keep looking.

Tell me how you are, Valerie.

Best, Tim.

Her brief reply came within half an hour.

> Good luck, Tim, with your hunt for more info about the unfortunate (and perhaps unhinged?) Mr Dunn.
>
> No, nothing more has emerged publicly about Kemal's murder. As for what I told you about overhearing part of his squabble with Omar just before his death, I can't believe that's likely to be relevant to the crime. It was something about the kinds of sexual activity that the Koran permits – Sunnis and Alevis presumably have quite different views on that topic. Anyway, whatever tensions there may have been between those two guys, it seems totally improbable that Omar would assault Kemal lethally. He certainly hasn't been taken into custody, because I saw him in the distance a couple of days ago. At least I think I saw him – you know how unreliable I am when it comes to recognising people!
> Best
> Valerie

A moment before receiving that, he'd pressed the send button on a quick follow-up to his previous email.

> Hi again, Valerie
> Here's a P.S. to the long message I sent a few minutes ago. I meant to tell you I came across a little display in a corner of the museum here that would have really interested you. It commemorates an odd but important period in the prison's history, nearly a century ago. Until I saw this particular set of exhibits – just a few photos with captions and commentary – I had no idea that during part of WW1 all the Dartmoor criminals were transferred to other gaols around England so that more than a thousand conscientious objectors could be held in what the government relabelled the Princetown Work

Centre. Some were given menial tasks indoors but most were sent out each day in work gangs on the moors – hard labour, harsh conditions. There were other Work Centres in different regions, too, to cope with the large numbers who refused to enlist, about 16,000 in all. There's a memorial to conscientious objectors erected in Tavistock Square, London – you can find it easily online. Perhaps you already knew about all of this, but it was a revelation to me. Might your research project extend to a pacifist memorial like that one? Or to another more recent monument that I've just been reading about on Wikipedia – the 'Shot at Dawn' memorial in Staffordshire, dedicated to more than 300 British and Commonwealth soldiers executed in WW1 for 'cowardice.' No Australians among them, because all our countrymen found guilty of offences punishable by death had their sentences commuted. Some Kiwis, Canadians and West Indians weren't so lucky.

I'll make time to see the Tavistock Square conchy memorial when I get back to London, but there's something else I need to do here first, which may take a few days. I'll tell you about it later, if I find what I'm looking for. Anyway, let me know how your work is going.

Best

Tim

The next day's weather looked fairly settled, and the moorland was so close to the western edge of Princetown that on impulse he went on an exploratory hike up towards the radio mast on the high dome of North Hessary Tor, about a mile from the town. Though the slope was steep and he had to watch his footing on wet and mossy patches, he pressed on further, exhilarated by the cool air, as far as Hollow Tor with its disused quarry and pair of granite stacks. From the vantage point of Hollow Tor he had a clear northward view across to what he assumed, because of its imposing height, to be Great Mis Tor. This harsh ancient landscape presented him with a puzzling blend of the strange and the familiar. Its time-smoothed rocky outcrops reminded him of granite crags in the Darling Scarp east of Perth, and down south near Albany and in the Porongorup Range. Yet while Dartmoor's mighty boulders mirrored what he remembered from those parts of his distant homeland, it was a reflection bleared by differences. Here the granite peaks and clitter stood out starkly because most of the surrounding expanses of hummocky moorland looked so bleak, almost empty: tors dominated the scenery for miles in every direction, vegetation being scant, low-lying and inconspicuous. In contrast the great grey stones of Australia's southwest were generally set within bushland. Besides, although native inhabitants of his home region had known it intimately for thousands of years, they left few conspicuous traces of the way they had lived there – no cleaving of the granite, as far as he was aware, and no manipulated stone structures. But the prehistoric denizens of Dartmoor had left their mark on the solid material around them, hewing it into serviceable shapes, lining cavities with it, hauling it into rows and circles for long-forgotten ritual purposes. Clouds were now blotting out the sun and the sky had begun to look leaden. He hurried back down into the town.

Over his evening meal Tim jotted down a memo list of research tasks he would need to pursue when he returned to London. But he wasn't yet ready to leave Dartmoor. He had something else to undertake first, an investigation of a different kind.

While absent from Perth he'd been in touch with his parents by email or text a couple of times a week, as promised. Although it was over a year now since he'd moved out of the old family home and into his flat, he knew how important to them it still was to maintain frequent contact with him, especially because his brother lived so far away down south and kept to himself. Usually Tim would spend part of each Sunday evening back at his parents' place – a hearty meal, an exchange of news and political opinions, a pleasant reinforcement of the values that bound them together affectionately. Now that he was overseas for a while, regular messages were serving the same purpose.

When his mother knew that Tim was going to add some vacation time to his research leave and spend a few free days in Devon, she asked him for help with a line of genealogical enquiry she was trying to follow. She'd become an enthusiastic family tree cultivator, addicted to ancestry.com and TV re-runs of *Who Do You Think You Are?*

> While you're in the Dartmoor area, Tim, could you make time to check parish records for me in a little town called Chagford, not far from where you'll be? If it's not a nuisance? Mum used to say part of the family came from there – that's on her maternal side, back through my great-grandmother. Nothing comes up from my usual ancestry.com sources, and there's no census data available online after 1911, which is before Great-Grandma was born, so tracing that family line back doesn't seem possible from here. I don't want to put you to any trouble, but if you can have a bit of a look at the parish registers on the spot – births, deaths, marriages – perhaps you'll find something relevant. I'll send a follow-up message with a few details, the little I know about names and dates, and you'll see where the gaps are…

The minibus to Chagford ran only once a week, a Saturday service. From Princetown it took him up the B-road through

Postbridge and on towards Moretonhampstead before winding slowly around narrow leafy lanes to his destination. This small northeastern corner of Dartmoor was surprisingly different from the bleak moorland he'd seen the previous day. As the bus turned this way and that, Tim glimpsed thickly wooded hillsides, splashing streams, dark waterlogged ditches, a deep river gorge. He was conscious of his Australian ignorance, lacking the local knowledge to find appropriate descriptive terms for some of the landscape features he could see. Was this clump of bushes what people here might call a copse? Was that tenebrous gully down there a dingle? Or perhaps a dell?

After checking into the Globe Inn, where he'd booked a room for a few nights, he ate a light lunch at the bar and then went for a stroll around the placid town. Chagford was a smaller place than he'd expected, hardly more than a village now, with few traces of its proud past as one of the stannary towns that monopolised Devon's tin-mining trade for centuries.

Its dominant structure was a tall rectangular tower, and he made his way towards it. The Church of St Michael the Archangel, a brochure in its vestibule proudly stated, had a history that went back to late medieval times. There had been a place of worship on this site for at least seven and a half centuries. Religious belief had no hold on Tim's mind, but as a historian he found pleasure in imagining a continuous pattern of churchgoing here over such a long period. Inside the building there were many things to admire: the granite columns and arches, the colourful neo-gothic windows, the carved oak pews and ornate pulpit. Most of the memorial inscriptions on wall-mounted brass plaques were conventionally pious, but among them, oddly, he found a quatrain recognisable from its sentiments and distinctive asymmetrical rhyme as coming from a translation of Omar Khayyam's *Rubaiyat*:

If in this Shadowland of life thou hast
Found one true heart to love thee, hold it fast,
Love it again, give all to keep it thine.
For love, like nothing in the world, can last.

As the name of that medieval Persian poet crossed Tim's mind, it triggered thoughts of the latter-day Omar he knew back in Perth, possibly implicated in the case of Kemal's murder. What a contrast! Omar Khayyam, if the translators could be trusted, was a wry sceptic with a hedonistic bent who thought of paradise as 'a book of verses underneath the bough, / a jug of wine, a loaf of bread—and thou…' That genial philosophical version of Islam, contemplating fate with a shrug and a smile, seemed utterly different from the stern moralism expressed by Omar the Somali student.

Re-emerging into the daylight, he walked down through the sloping church grounds to where the town's war memorial stood, surmounted by a tall stone cross. Beneath it was a large wooden bench, and from that spot he could see across part of the Teign River Valley. Was this a vista that any of his relatives had enjoyed in the past? Did the surrounding graveyard contain bones with a DNA matching his own? The parish records that might hold answers to such questions wouldn't be accessible until Monday afternoon. In the meantime the town seemed to offer little for him to see or do. That evening an immoderately cheerful waiter, presenting Tim's dinner of beef pie with mashed potatoes as if it were a royal feast, confirmed that hiking trails were the most popular attraction for visitors to the town. 'Wonderful walks around here! Oh yes! Wonderful!' Back in his room, Tim studied the leaflets he'd picked up from the reception counter and an ordnance survey map bought from the tourist information centre.

He had to fill in the next day somehow, and a long trek seemed the best option. If nothing else, it would give him a more directly physical impression of Dartmoor than he'd got from reading documents or glimpsing scenes through bus windows. Before going to bed he put plenty of snack food in his backpack. Not such a cheerful repast, he thought ruefully, as the *Rubaiyat*'s jug of wine and loaf of bread would have been – but anyway there was no 'thou' to share a picnic with him. The lack of Valerie's company preoccupied him until at last sleep arrived.

SIXTEEN

WHAT BECAME KNOWN AS THE PIG'S HEAD INCIDENT hit the campus like a galvanic jolt and left it abuzz for days. Social media sizzled with vapid commentary and perfervid condemnation. Various student and staff groups issued formal statements, vying to outdo each other with protestations of outraged offendedness.

This furore, this pervasive clamorous agitation, came at a time when Valerie, or part of her, was already turning inwards, and it deepened her need to sequester herself. Never gregarious, she'd become increasingly withdrawn from ordinary interaction with other students. Friendship had receded. Tim was overseas and somewhat estranged, Kemal was dead, and she'd kept away from Lauren since that episode of sleepy semi-conscious intimacy, unsure what to make of it. She postponed a couple of scheduled meetings with Barry Plunket, her supervisor. Most of her time was spent in the quiet seclusion of a library carrel or her room at the college. Tending to avoid more public spaces, she began to recognise that a heightened agoraphobia was afflicting her. It had always been there, latent, and the attack on her grandfather, coming so soon after the death of Kemal, seemed to have triggered its resurgence.

Now this latest provocative act, appalling in its grisly symbolic violence, made her want to retreat further from everyone and everything around her. The confronting report was there on the front page of *The West*, accompanied by a gory photo: somebody had found a severed pig's head shoved into one of the Turkish-style squat toilets next to the Muslim prayer room under Winthrop Hall. Police were said to be focusing their attention on right-wing groups antagonistic to Islamic students. The journalist quoted an incautiously speculative comment from 'a university spokesperson' to the effect that such a deplorable occurrence lent some credibility to the idea that the recent campus killing of Kemal Kaleli may have been a hate crime.

The next day Valerie's mother phoned from Melbourne. 'Darling, we've just been listening to a radio news item about the awful thing that's happened over there. The disgusting business with a pig's head. It must be really upsetting for you, coming so soon after the killing of your Muslim friend. Are you OK, love? We haven't heard from you for a while.'

'Yeah, sure, I'm OK. Not bright and cheery, but coping.'

'You do sound a bit down. Not letting yourself get too isolated, are you?'

'Nothing to worry about, Mum. Most of the time I feel quite self-sufficient.'

'You've always been like that. Comes from being an only child, I suppose. But Val, everybody needs a few mates, you know.' Meaningful pause. 'No boyfriend in the picture, then?'

'Come on! I don't need a boyfriend. Coupledom isn't my thing.'

'What about that nice-sounding fellow you mentioned a while back – Tim, isn't it?'

'Oh, Mum, cut it out! Intense relationships are not – repeat, *not* – a high priority for me right now.'

'Well, if you say so. All the same, when I was your age I was already engaged to your Dad. I know this postgraduate study is something you want to concentrate on, but don't wait forever to think about…you know – finding someone to set up a home with. Just saying…'

'Oh, pur-lease! You sound so twentieth-century. Nineteenth, more like. Look, Mum, let's get this clear. Family is important to me in retrospect, not in prospect. I'm glad of my lineage, the way it connects me with our past generations, but I don't want to look forward to more of it. Not at this stage, anyway. Happy to be a daughter and granddaughter et cetera. Can't see myself as a progenitor.'

'All right, I hear you.' Change of gear, audible in the tone. 'How's your research project going?'

'Ah. Not brilliantly, to tell the truth. No momentum – I'm a bit in the doldrums. I've yet to convince myself there's much to say about my topic that others haven't said already. But people tell me this is a pretty common feeling in the early phase of thesis work.'

'So keep calm and carry on, eh?'

'Something like that.'

They chatted briefly about her grandpa's convalescence, about the family dog's laziness, and about things that were making her mother's schoolteaching work less satisfying than it used to be; but Valerie found it hard to focus on the conversation. After it ended, she stared vacantly at the wall of her room. *If I'm not destined to be either a baby-incubator or a scholarly apprentice,* she mused, *who exactly am I turning into? Might I end up as a woebegone hermit? Would that be so very bad? The conventional wisdom is that humans are social and sexual creatures above all else, but why can't some of us be singlemindedly reclusive?*

❖

More than a month had gone by since Kemal's death, and still she couldn't stop mulling over the mystery of it. Couldn't curb the habit of reviewing again and again the possible explanations she had summarised on paper. Couldn't bring herself to go near the part of the campus where his body had been found, in the carpark behind the gym. There had been no mention of the matter for more than a week now, no press update from police on their lines of enquiry. Public attention was shifting to other stories. She felt a pang of anticipatory sadness at the thought that before long, even here among those who had been his fellow students, everyone would have forgotten about Kemal. It seemed disloyal to his memory that she'd done nothing except wait passively for the crime to be solved. Wasn't there anything at all she might contribute to that investigative process? An examiner's report on her honours thesis had praised her 'sleuthing skills' as a historian. Couldn't she somehow deploy those skills now, in the present, beyond the rituals of academic analysis?

Again her mind went back to the ding-dong altercation she'd half-overheard between Kemal and Omar – if it was actually Omar! Mightn't the cause have been connected to Kemal's Alevi allegiance, as she'd thought before? Being a Somali, Omar would almost certainly have strict Sunni convictions, so no doubt he'd fiercely disapprove of the liberties taken by the Alevis of Turkey. Perhaps, in that scene near the back of Winthrop Hall just a couple of days before Kemal died, Omar was admonishing him for Kemal's supposedly immoral ways. Or were they arguing about something quite different, perhaps a purely personal disagreement unrelated to religion? Anyhow it might well have escalated later into a full-on angry conflict.

It was her duty, she saw this clearly now, a duty of friendship and remembrance, to seek out Omar and try to get him talking about what happened to Kemal. Draw him out. Probe his feelings. It wouldn't be easy: not only did she have to overcome her growing reluctance to interact with other people, especially with a Muslim man at a time like this when he was likely to be tense and touchy because of the swinish insult to his religion, but there was also the practical problem that she didn't know how to make contact with Omar – didn't know what subjects he was studying, or where he lived, or even his full name. But then it occurred to her that there was in fact a fairly simple way of getting in touch: she could wait near that prayer room entrance, in the area where she'd overheard the argument. As an apparently devout Muslim he would be sure to go there at the usual daily worship times. She knew from conversation with Kemal that one of the obligatory prayers, *dhuhr*, began just after midday.

So the next day as the sun approached its zenith she took up her position in a shaded doorway opposite the eastern end of the Winthrop Hall undercroft, a scarf demurely covering her head, and observed the young men converging for their *wudhu* ablutions and *salat* ritual. Although North African students stood out distinctively from the larger groups of swarthy Middle Easterners and light-brown light-framed Indonesians and the small sprinkle of pink Caucasians, she didn't feel confident of recognising Omar. Was that him now, very slim and tall, with much darker skin than most, striding briskly to the entrance? Irresolute, she stayed where she was and he disappeared from view. About a quarter of an hour later as she continued to watch, that same person – it was the same, wasn't it? – emerged and stood still for a moment, checking something on his phone. Uncertainly she walked towards him.

'Omar?'

He looked up.

'Excuse me. It is Omar, isn't it?'

A small nod, wary. Maybe every second Somali male is called Omar, she thought.

'I'm Valerie Morton. We were introduced a few weeks ago by Tim Holmes. Peter Fleming's friend.'

'I remember, yes.' A husky quality in his voice, a sidelong flicker of his eyes. Was he on his guard, or just avoiding her gaze for polite cultural reasons?

'I knew Kemal Kaleli quite well, and I think you knew him too. I'd like to ask you about him, if you have a few minutes to spare.'

Omar frowned, looked at his watch, glanced to left and right. 'Very busy time for me now,' he said.

'Only a few minutes. Please.'

He hesitated. Looking up at him, she gestured towards the cloister alongside Hackett Hall. 'Can we just stand over there, out of the sun and wind? For a moment or two?'

With a barely perceptible shrug he followed her into a sheltered spot, but slowly, keeping his distance. Self-contained. Eyes lowered, hands clasped in front of him. Big strong hands. A powerful physique despite his slender build. She remembered Tim saying Omar had spoken eloquently at a political meeting, a rally for refugees, and she could well imagine that he'd hold a crowd's attention. Something compelling about him, even charismatic, yet potentially intimidating. You wouldn't want to be on the wrong side of him.

'Omar...,' she began, and then wasn't sure what to say next. She cleared her throat. 'Omar...It's very hard for me, not knowing how or why my friend Kemal...well, what happened to him. Perhaps there have been some discussions among Muslim students about his death? I thought you might have heard rumours?'

Omar shook his head, eyes averted. 'No rumour. Nobody is knowing anything.'

Valerie took a deep breath. 'Omar, I saw you arguing with Kemal just over there,' pointing, 'a couple of days before his death. Can you tell me what that was about?'

'No arguing. Not me and Kemal.'

'Well, it certainly sounded like an argument. Something about the teachings of the Koran, wasn't it?'

Omar turned his head away. 'I don't think so. Nothing important.'

'About the kinds of relationship that a Muslim man is permitted to have with a non-Muslim person?'

Seeming startled, he responded sharply, his voice rising. 'You make a mistake. No argument of such a kind.'

She persisted. 'And there was a third man standing with you, listening to what you and Kemal were saying. Who was that?'

Omar shook his head again, looked at his watch again. 'Very late,' he said in a tone that conveyed unceremonious finality. 'I must go now.' Turning on his heel, he stalked quickly away, long legs slicing the air like scissors.

She watched him go. How to make sense of his stonewall refusal to engage? Hiding something? Or just in a huff at being accosted and cross-examined, especially by a kafir woman? Either way, whether he was withholding relevant information or had nothing to divulge, she was none the wiser. Zero result. You're not cut out to be a detective, Val, she told herself. And what do you think about Omar? Not sure. Behind that handsome ebony exterior, what he thinks and feels is unreachable, at least for someone like me. He may be a person of great personal dignity and calm, or capable of intense aggression – how would I know? Difficult, in any case, to believe that a person as pleasant as Kemal could arouse such anger, in Omar or in anyone else, whatever the reason, that it would lead to his brutal death.

SEVENTEEN

O N Sunday morning, as the wisps of valley mist evaporated, Tim set out on a southwesterly route that would lead him through part of Chagford Common and around the eastern and southern sides of Fernworthy Forest towards the randomly chosen destination of his walk, a pair of ancient stone circles known as Grey Wethers. By then he'd be nearer to Postbridge than to Chagford. With the rise and fall of the land, an excursion that far and back again would take several hours and be strenuous enough to tire him out. Fair weather had been forecast.

From Chagford he followed at first the road to Fernworthy Reservoir until he came in sight of the thick conifer plantation. Then he went along the Two Moors pathway in search of a double stone row shown on his map. After climbing steadily up to a ridge, he saw the two lines of jagged granite, roughly parallel. Perhaps they were the tips of half-buried walls running beside a pathway? But what function might they once have served? Practical? Ceremonial? He couldn't guess. What they signified now, like so many other archeological remains around here, was something more general: the unimaginably protracted expanse of human habitation in this forlorn part of Dartmoor. The ordnance map was thickly dotted with markers of prehistoric stone structures – cairns, hut circles, funerary cists and tumuli, pounds, stone rows...

By the time he had moved on around the southern side of the forest, his legs were tiring and he wished he hadn't attempted such an ambitious walk. But he knew he must now be close to the Grey Wethers and at last he reached them.

Set on grassy plateau, the two large circles were nearly contiguous, almost forming a flattened figure of eight, an hourglass shape aligned north/south. Some of the great dark stones were almost perfectly rectangular, and the one nearest to him had such evenly placed spots of white lichen on its surface that it was like a chunky half-buried domino tile. The fanciful thought struck him that if the pieces forming each ring had been placed a little closer to one another, and then one of them fell, they would have gone on toppling, each one against the next in a series of mighty concussions, until all lay flat.

Sitting with his back to one of the giant dominoes, he ate what was left of his snack food, massaged his calves and fell into a sombre reverie.

Among the countless generations of men and women inhabiting this region in the past, some of his own forebears might once have walked where he had walked today. Five thousand years ago, ten thousand, what kind of landscape was it here? Perhaps the moors were less dismal in ancient times, more wooded? The immeasurable vista of prehistory stretched far back beyond his ken. This Dartmoor, this almost ageless place, seemed to mock the tiny circles of routine enquiry he'd been trained to follow as a historian.

Drowsily he watched shadows from the tall stones inch across the grass as the sun began its gradual decline over the moors. Time sank with it, not just the time of day but also the very notion of calculable progression itself, drawn down into the ancient land by a slow absorbing suction. As his mood sagged, every past or present human thing felt momentarily miniscule and pointless. You could lose your bearings here, map or no map. Misplace yourself.

He jerked his head back, as if to dispel such doleful thoughts. Only a few days ago in an email to Valerie he'd told her how cheerful he felt. Was it just the absence of companionship that was now turning him into a gloomyguts? If his friends were here, they'd soon tease him out of the doldrums. He could almost hear Pete Fleming's sardonic voice: 'Perk up, mopey goth!' And Valerie would be forthright in her own way: 'Melancholy doesn't suit you, Tim. Snap out of it.'

Getting to his feet, shouldering his backpack, he found as he began to make his way back towards Chagford that his thoughts were returning, little by little, almost reluctantly, from prehistory's shadowland into the enclosed world of recorded human lives in this part of the country. It was as if, having lost his footing and been submerged beneath time, he had now come up again to the surface.

Back at last in the Chagford hotel, Tim eased his aching body into a hot bath, glad he would spend much of the next day sitting quietly, even if his search of genealogical records turned out to be unproductive. The information his mother had sent didn't give him much to go on. No dates, and some uncertainty about names. Parish documents were unlikely to yield much information anyway – at most, the barest facts of lineage, which would hold little interest without some knowledge of personal stories behind them.

After almost nodding off in the bath, and again over a meal of roast lamb and Yorkshire pudding with a bottle of local ale, Tim fell into bed and slept heavily.

Over breakfast he re-read his mother's hazy email about her grandparents.

…In our hearing, mum (that's Joan) always referred to her mum as 'your Grandma Phyl': short for Phyllis, probably. Born during the Great War, I think. Oddly enough, and frustrating for me, there's no family record of her maiden name. All we know (or think we know) is that she came from the Chagford area. I have no information about her husband – my maternal great-grandfather – except that he was evidently a Hardy. Grandma used to joke about her married name, Phyl Hardy: she said her husband thought she had a reckless streak, so he liked to call her Foolhardy. Mum believed he died during the Spanish Civil War, late 1930s, when she was just a tot. Quite a few English volunteers fought there on the republican side. But the casualty lists I've checked online don't contain anyone of that name.

Well, perhaps you can find something in a local marriage register from the early 30s, though I can't be sure Grandma Phyl did get married in Chagford or even near there. There may be a birth notice for Joan in 1933 – her birthday was 8th June. And possibly a death report of someone called Hardy, time of the Spanish war?

For the relevant period, Chagford parish registers were not voluminous and Tim worked steadily through them in a few hours, only to draw a complete blank. Nothing at all for Hardy in the marriages, births or deaths. He also dipped into regional newspapers from those years but with fading hope.

In the late afternoon, eyes tired, he gave up and walked back dejectedly to the Globe Inn. Ordering a pint of Otter Bitter, he eavesdropped idly on a conversation between two other drinkers nearby. When he heard mention of the Local History Society he turned towards them. A pair of retirees, he guessed. They looked approachable, so he took the liberty of introducing himself and explaining his reason for coming to Chagford. They nodded receptively, made encouraging noises, and he went into more detail. 'Not often we meet a fellow historian from the other side of the world,' said one of them with a genial smile. As Tim talked, the other man – 'Wilf Robertson, round here they call me Robbie' – frowned thoughtfully and began to scratch the hoarfrost stubble on his chin and cheeks.

'You'll still be in town tomorrow?' he asked, after Tim bought them a round of drinks.

'I can be. Haven't worked out yet, anyway, how best to travel back to London from here.'

'Well, there's something I could show you tomorrow,' said Robbie, 'that may interest you. I've almost finished writing catalogue notes for a large batch of correspondence donated recently to our History Society. Letters written in the 1920s and 1930s by a notorious Chagford gossip to her sister in Tavistock. Hilda Moss, that's her name. Wrote every week for many years, and she was a real Nosy Parker, to be frank. Knew everybody's business, passed on tittle-tattle about half the folk in the district. It's a long shot, but who knows? – You might just happen to find some mention of those people you've been searching for. Worth a look.'

Before lunchtime the next day, Tim had uncovered what looked as if it could be the tip of an astonishing family secret. Making full sense of it would take him a while, he told himself as he boarded a bus for Princetown that afternoon. He'd need to sort carefully the relevant details strewn across the pages of scribbled notes he'd taken from Mrs Moss's tattling correspondence, and then sketch out their possible genealogical implications.

He'd check back into the Plume of Feathers Inn, have a quick meal and then make a start on sifting through those notes.

But by the time he reached Princetown something else, something seemingly unrelated, had pushed all such thoughts aside. As the bus rumbled towards his destination, he was browsing for the first time through a small book he'd bought a few days before in the Prison Museum, a compilation of 'stranger than fiction' Dartmoor tales by a local amateur historian – and in it, to his delight, he came across a lively account of what the courtroom proceedings had revealed following Joshua Dunn's arrest in 1889. Dunn was evidently a fascinating figure and his confessed motive for breaking into the prison was darker than Tim had imagined.

The impulse to share his news at once was irresistible. So that evening, before reviewing the notes he'd made from Hilda Moss's letters, he sat with his laptop and sent a message to Perth.

Hi Valerie

Well, it's been quite a day of discoveries! In the morning I stumbled across some startling info tucked away in a cache of old correspondence. It may hold the key to a little mystery in my family's past. Long story, and I'll save it for another time, because this afternoon my attention was pulled away suddenly from that topic when I chanced on a report of the trial of Joshua Dunn, the black prisoner I've been searching for – and what I've found out is extraordinary!

According to the little book that summarises Dunn's case, there were two judicial hearings – the usual thing back then for offences of this kind. First, Dunn was taken to Tavistock and charged before a magistrate. There he spoke openly about his purpose in breaking into Dartmoor Prison: it was to take violent revenge on the Chief Warder, a man called Starkey, for all the cruelty he'd suffered – being treated, he said, 'worse than a wild animal' because of the colour of his skin. So, having confessed to a seriously unlawful act, Dunn was committed to the Devon Assizes in Exeter, where a few weeks later they tried him for burglary (but oddly enough, not for attempted murder), sentenced him to a year's hard labour, and also indicted him on a separate charge of stealing a sheep from the prison farm – he'd been so famished after walking all the way from London to Dartmoor that he'd killed the beast with his bare hands and eaten part of it raw.

The report I've read gives a few incidental scraps of information about Dunn, e.g. his age and the fact he'd previously been convicted of manslaughter, serving time in Liverpool. But his voice comes through in a couple of quoted comments on his maltreatment, and I've begun to form a picture of him. It's likely that by this stage of his life he was an unsavoury piece of work, but that's a sure result of so many years oppressed by demeaning conditions. I guess his attitude was partly shaped by slavery somewhere in the family background – enough to fill anyone with resentment. And then just imagine what those long periods of penal servitude would have done to him. Gaols were fiendishly cruel places back then, and a black man would get the roughest end of it all. Probably he'd been reviled and beaten, and that sort of brutalising experience would grind anyone down and produce ferocious reactions. So Joshua Dunn, treated 'worse than a wild animal,' had his humanity taken from him by a degrading and unconscionable system. What a sad case, eh?

Let me know how you're going, Valerie.

Best

Tim

Her reply came quickly.

Amazing story! I'm not convinced, though, by your idea that Dunn's intended act of vengeance shows his treatment made him subhuman. You could see him in a more positive light, couldn't you? From what you've summarised, my take on the episode would be that by breaking into the prison to confront his tormentor, this guy is refusing to be dehumanised. It's an assertion of manly courage and ethnic pride. He's standing up defiantly against injustice, wanting to make a big statement to other prisoners and shake his fist at a system of law and order that's so brutally administered. OK, he wasn't successful – but he's still a kind of hero, isn't he?

    Best
    Valerie

Tim responded straight away:

Perhaps you're right, Valerie. But are you tending to idealise some forms of violence? Whether perpetrated by a hapless criminal or by soldiers listed on your war memorials? To me, Dunn would be more of a hero if he'd found a non-violent way of resisting. Reminds me of a passage from Martin Luther King's book Why We Can't Wait – it's here in a file on my laptop. I've just looked it up and this is the quote: 'The negro was willing to risk martyrdom in order to move and stir the social conscience of his community and the nation… He would force his oppressor to commit his brutality openly, with the rest of the world looking on.' That's the principle of civil disobedience, a lot different from lethal vengeance.

    Anyway I can't hope to understand Dunn's character and motivation without knowing more about the circumstances of his life, especially the gap between his circus days and the prison. Census data wouldn't help because it's a fairly common name – scores of Josh Dunns in England in the Victorian period – and I have no idea where he was living at particular times. He probably moved around a lot. I'm hoping my investigation hasn't reached a dead end. After leaving Dartmoor I may still have time to get up to Sheffield and search the National Fairground Archive there.

Best

Tim

Within a few minutes her reply hit his in-tray.

What you say, Tim, about heroism and non-violence gives me pause. I probably need to rethink my notions about military courage etc. in the light of something my grandpa has told me – I'll try to sort it out on paper for myself, and talk it over with you when you're back here.

Meanwhile fingers crossed for your efforts to fill out Dunn's story. Of course even if you strike it lucky with archival material and sift through it meticulously you still can't expect to uncover more than some surface facts. Finding out what life actually felt like to someone like that – on the edge of society, leaving hardly a trace – well, it's beyond the scope of historical research, isn't it? For my own part, I'm starting to see how limited the work of any historian is. Sticking purely to verifiable evidence means our findings will often fall short of what we really want to discover. Makes me envy the novelist's freedom to imagine a person's innermost thoughts and feelings! Don't you wish you could tell the story of this Joshua Dunn in an unhampered, inventive way? Perhaps I've been reading too much fiction lately to be comfortable with the scholarly rituals of perusing documents and developing cautious hypotheses!

Best

Valerie

Tim lay awake for a long time, recalling his own recent ramble from Chagford to Grey Wethers and trying to picture what it might have been like for Joshua Dunn, perhaps walking wearily over the very same terrain on his way to Princetown, no doubt cold and hungry much of the time, filled with hostility, intent on revenge. What kind of person was he, this hapless black man? What had drawn him into a life of violent crime? So many questions – and perhaps unanswerable, as Valerie said, by any amount of historical research.

Liverpool
to
Dartmoor
1869–90

EIGHTEEN

HIS BLACK BUNCHED HANDS HAD BROUGHT HIM HERE. For years they'd been proclaiming what kind of man he was, demanding caution and even something close to respect from those who might otherwise have treated him contemptuously. Around the Liverpool docks and streets a fist had the power to ward off trouble, to turn an object of disdain into a feared persuader. In fairground booths all over Lancashire he'd boxed his way to money – enough to live on without begging or thieving. And now, in this grand circus ring, surrounded by a clamorous crowd, he stood facing the legendary Jem Mace, bareknuckle champion of all England.

It was nothing like the kind of contest he'd dreamed about. Instead of being in the role of genuine challenger, eagerly measuring his prowess against the yardstick of Mace's pre-eminence in the sport of fisticuffs, he was going through the charade of a fixed match.

'Now listen here, Josh,' he'd been told, 'you're a strong fighter, we know that, but it's Jem Mace who brings the crowd to us. They want to see him win, and we've given him a quiet assurance he won't be hurt. So put on a good show, eh lad? But pull your punches and let him look superior.'

Josh had to accept the arrangement with a shrug. Besides,

he didn't begrudge his opponent the crowd's adulation. Mace had done well for himself, coming from a gypsy background, and good luck to him. But Josh, holding back his own natural aggression, felt his heart was a boiler full of steam, near to bursting.

The fight took its predetermined course. Although Josh jabbed away at the older man's ribs, and once gave his ear a sharp clout just to let him know what he could do, he made sure none of the blows he landed was at full power. Mace, a clever boxer as famous for his dancing style as for his accurate hitting, kept moving around him quickly, smiling at him, confident and poised. When the exhibition had gone on long enough, Josh dropped his guard, let one of Mace's punches through, and fell back as if stunned. There was an eruption of yelling and whistling and clapping. He picked himself up slowly. Mace waved to the crowd, walked over to him and shook his hand. 'Well done, lad,' he said with a wink.

Josh had been with Pablo Fanque's travelling circus for six months now, and despite the occasional frustration of needing to restrain himself in the ring these had been the best months of his life. Having enough money for good food and shelter was part of it, but the most important thing was belonging to a group – a group that felt almost like a large family, and amazingly it had a black man at its head. Although Mr Fanque was getting quite elderly now, everyone knew what a brilliant horseman and rope jumper he'd once been. His popular success in recent years as showman of the Circus Royal was well deserved, many of the performers said so. He and Mrs Fanque were widely respected for the way they looked after the people who worked for them, making sure everyone was well fed and arranging benefit nights in cases of hardship.

In Mr Fanque's own life there had been much that was hard, much misfortune to surmount. Josh had heard the stories. Fanque's father was a former slave, and in his boyhood the family had suffered destitution. Then, in the early days of the Circus Royal, the spectre of financial disaster often hovered nearby. There were times when stormy weather damaged equipment, times when creditors forced him to sell his trained horses, times when the crowds stayed away because his competitors were offering more spectacular entertainment. And worst of all, the first Mrs Fanque had died in that terrible accident at a show in Leeds when a wooden gallery collapsed, crushing the ticket booth where she was stationed. But despite every adversity Mr Fanque had persevered, and his past troubles made him a considerate, compassionate man. Towards Josh as a fellow black man he showed particular kindness.

Josh's exhibition fights came early in an evening's program, and he liked this arrangement. It meant he had time to wash himself down and get dressed before the performance that always thrilled him. Tonight, as usual, he took up a position near the front of the ring where he could watch her every move. Perhaps, after the show, he would find the courage to speak to her for the first time.

Here she comes now, as the ringmaster shouts her name. Madame Caroline! The beautiful acrobat and aerialiste! The crowd greets her with enthusiastic applause, and Josh watches open-mouthed. Arms and legs thrillingly bare, torso clad in a close-fitting blue satin doublet with spangles at the tip of each breast, she climbs the long rope ladder, higher and higher, until she is standing on the small platform sixty feet above the ground like a tiny bird in a treetop. Josh has seen her perform many times but still feels the same mixture of admiration and apprehension. The sight of those pale naked limbs, flexing as she ascends; her slender but womanly shape in that bright costume; the sparkling circlet crowning her head; the spill of blond curls over the nape of her neck; the regal manner in which she waves to the multitude of upturned faces when she reaches the top of the swaying ladder – they make him breathe heavily, and saliva rises around his tongue. He never takes his eyes off her.

She is bending to pick up a pair of hoops from the platform, extending her lovely white arms, and stepping out onto the tightrope. The crowd has gone quiet. Slowly she makes her way forward, a steady progress all the way to the central point of the rope, where she begins to twirl the hoops around her forearms. This part of the display always worries Josh; it must be extremely difficult to keep her balance while the hoops are spinning. And now, just as he is thinking this, she stumbles, slips! Gasps and cries surge up from the people around him, and he hears himself groan her name as the hoops drop away and she grabs at the rope to save herself from falling. Far above the shocked crowd she hangs there by her hands, a dangling pendant. Her shoulders flex as she tries to haul her body up to the rope, but her arms aren't strong enough. She seems too frightened to be able to move her hands sideways and inch herself along the rope towards the ladder.

In all the commotion and consternation, one person is decisive: Pablo Fanque has appeared at the entrance to the ring and gives quick instructions to the men with him. Then he beckons urgently to Josh, who runs over to his side.

'I've sent someone to fetch the rigging man,' says Fanque. 'Tom should be able to lower the rope part of the way, but it won't come close to the ground. When it's as far down as Tom can get it, she's going to have to let herself fall. You're the biggest and strongest man here, so I want you to take up your position underneath and break her fall, catch her if you can. Won't be easy, mind you. Could injure both of you.'

Josh nods. 'I won't let her be hurt, Mr Fanque. You can trust me.' He can hear that his croaky voice reveals the anxiety he is trying to disguise.

Tom the rigger arrives and gets quickly to work on the winding mechanism at the back of the tent. It seems an age before the rope begins to sag, bringing her gradually lower and lower. Josh braces himself, worried that she may be unable to keep her grip on the rope. Her hands and arms must surely be tiring; but his own will hold her tight when the moment comes.

Then, abruptly, the slow descent of the rope stops. 'That's it,' Tom the rigger calls to Pablo Fanque. 'Can't get her no further down than that.'

She is still at least twenty feet above them. Cupping his hands around his mouth, Fanque shouts, 'Madame Caroline! You'll have to let go! There's a man waiting here to catch you safely!' Others yell encouragement. Josh steadies himself, head back, arms out in front of him, palms upturned, as if imploring the heavens to guide her into his protective embrace. He tries to imagine he is already holding her.

She is looking down at him. With a fearful cry she releases her grip and plummets. Almost instantly her body is upon him and as he clasps her they both crash heavily to the ground. But he is underneath: he has managed to cushion the impact for her. She is sobbing and her nose is bleeding but as others help her to her feet it seems that, miraculously, nothing is broken. The crowd is applauding, cheering. He has saved her. His twisted knee and ankle are painful, his ribs too, but he is happy.

Two days go by without sight of her, though Mr Fanque tells him that she has recovered well. She is probably resting, getting over the shock of it all. Josh has not been sleeping well; his leg throbs and when he tries to change position in bed his ribs hurt. The incident keeps repeating itself behind his eyes. He thinks carefully about what he will say when she comes to thank him, as surely she will soon. He'll make light of his bandaged leg and the ache in his side, though the injuries will hamper his boxing for a while. He'll brush aside modestly her words of gratitude, telling her how very glad he is to have helped with her rescue. He'll ask when she intends to resume her performance routine, and whether she is going to modify it. And then perhaps he will hold her again in his arms.

But still she doesn't come to see him. So on the third day, as all the circus equipment is being dismantled and packed in preparation for their move to the next town, he goes looking for her, limping around the tents and cages and carriages, leaning on a stick. And there she is now! She makes her way across a corner of the field near him, laughing with her head thrown back as she clasps the arm of Cummins the ringmaster. Josh hops and hobbles in her direction, calls her name: 'Madame Caroline!' She stops and looks towards him, frowning as if she doesn't recognise him. Josh lifts his cap. Clears his throat. Stammers something about being glad to see her in good health.

Turning to her companion, she asks in a tone of cold disdain, 'Who's this nigger cripple?'

NINETEEN

'**V**ERY SORRY TO SEE YOU GO, JOSH,' SAID FANQUE. 'AND I really don't understand why you want to leave the Circus Royal at a time like this, when you're so out of kilter. You won't find it easy to get other work until your ankle-bone mends. We can tide you over here, you know.'

'I'm grateful, Mr Fanque, truly. You've been good to me. I won't give my reasons for going. A private matter.' How could he begin to tell another black man about such a mortifying rejection from the woman he'd adored, sneering at the colour of his skin?

Fanque sighed. 'What will you do about money, Josh?'

'I don't know. I'll find something.'

Fanque drew a purse from his pocket, but Josh shook his head. 'No, no, sir. I won't accept any more payment, now that I can't work.'

'Nonsense. False pride. Take it, lad. It'll keep body and soul together for a little while. Go on, I insist.'

In the miserable weeks that followed, he could do little else but wait for his injuries to heal. No plan. Always able to rely on his strong body until now, he was suddenly at a loss. He couldn't yet go back to the fairground tents where he'd previously fought – not while he was so lame. Perhaps there'd be some light work he could pick up soon at the docks, near where he'd grown up. Perhaps he could find his sister, if she still lived in the Merseyside port district, and see whether she'd give him a roof over his head for the time being.

Making his way by train to Liverpool, he limped to the waterfront.

Beyond the sheds and warehouses he could see familiar thickets of masts and yards, but now with many tall steamer funnels among them. Steam vessels, he'd heard men say, would soon replace sail altogether for cargo shipping. Hard to imagine it.

The quays were even rowdier and smellier than when he was last here. Yelling, banging, clanging on all sides. Thunderous oaths from boss porters. The bass rumble of barrow wheels. An unmistakable stink of guano mingling with scents of tobacco and brandy. Slowly, painfully, he made his way past stacks of timber, wine barrels, cotton bales, boxes large and small. Liverpool had become a great greedy maw, gorging itself on commodities from around the world.

To find dockside work could be challenging even for ablebodied men, Josh was well aware of that. The supply of workers here always far exceeded demand, and for most of them it was never steady employment. Having a barrow, a cotton-bale hook and a strong back was insufficient to guarantee being hired. Anyone who wanted a labouring job on the docks needed to know how to handle every different kind of packaged produce, how to weigh, mark, stow and trim them all. To earn the higher pay of a stevedore he must also know how to load a ship, how to work the hatches and manoeuvre goods safely and economically into different parts of the hold. At dawn on the quays a large ring of men would be waiting, more than a hundred at every shed entrance.

Getting work was hard enough; getting somewhere to live in the meantime was an even more pressing need. If he had to rent a room and buy food before he started earning wages, the money Mr Fanque had given him wouldn't last long. So it was urgent to find his sister Beth. Last he'd heard she was living around these parts with a docker, Charlie something…Watkins or Watts. Josh spent the afternoon going slowly from one alehouse to another, asking if anyone knew their whereabouts. Shrugs, blank looks, head shakes – until one lumper, wrinkling his brow, said 'Charlie Watts? Fellow of that name used to work in the holds a while back, heaving coal and bushelling grain, but he got sick. His lungs, I think. Haven't seen him for nigh on a year. Heard he was renting a cellar down one of them alleys near Vauxhall Street…'

For another hour or more Josh hobbled up and down foul-smelling passages in that neighbourhood, eventually encountering someone who nodded at the mention of Charlie Watts's name and pointed to a doorway down narrow steps nearby. By this time, daylight was leaking away and pain had spread from Josh's swollen ankle into his knee and hip.

When his sister answered his knock she looked so pinched and careworn that for a hesitant moment, in the gloom of the doorway, he could hardly be sure it was Beth. And though she welcomed him warmly, Josh had to mask his dismay at the squalor of her home. A damp smell drifted up from the floor to accost him, mixed with the stink of stagnant drain-water. The entrance opened straight into a cramped room – their only room, was it? Through the single smeary window he could see that the ceiling was on the same level as the flagstones in the lane outside. Furnishings were scanty: a three-legged deal table, two rickety chairs and a stool, a battered dresser for a few plates, and a lumpy mattress on the floor.

'Charlie, look, it's my brother Josh, come to see us.'

Pushing back his chair, a thin stooping man rose slowly, hand extended.

'Well, you'll be wondering what brings me here,' said Josh

after an exchange of greetings. 'Truth is, I'm at a loss. There was an accident at the circus where I had a job. Broke my ankle. So I've made my way to these parts – couldn't think what else to do – in the hope you'll let me stay with you for a week or two. Just while the ankle mends. And then perhaps I can get myself hired for loading cargo.'

Frowning, Charlie shifted a quid of tobacco with his tongue to a different corner of his mouth. 'We can give you shelter,' he said. 'But to be frank, a man who gets himself hurt won't find much work. Look at me.' He coughed and hoicked. 'Used to do heavy labour, grain-bushelling mostly, till the dust started clogging my lungs. Been sick for months now. We'd starve if Beth didn't take in washing. Best I can expect when this phlegm lifts off my chest is a few scraps of work helping a freight clerk or tallyman. Good luck to you, but until you can put full weight on that leg I reckon nobody will hire you.'

There was a long silence. Josh looked down at the palms of his big hands as if they could tell him something useful.

'But stay with us for a while, of course you can,' said Beth, 'though there's not much food to go around, I'll be frank with you. It's just this for tonight' – she pointed to a half-eaten loaf of bread – 'and some cabbage soup I'll boil up.'

'I can buy us food for a week or two,' Josh told them. 'There's some money in my pocket.'

'We're not too proud to have your help,' said Charlie. 'We've had to pinch and scrape, that's the truth of it.'

'There's but the one mattress, mind,' Beth said, gesturing towards it. 'You'll be dossing there with us. Top and tail.'

With a shrug of acceptance, Josh looked around the room. There was a small cot in one corner. Empty. Beth followed the direction of his glance.

'Our baby girl died last year, poor mite,' she said. 'It was the croup took her. And now I think I'm in the family way again.'

He sensed her anxiety and guessed what was kindling it. Not just the prospect of trying to keep an infant's body and soul together as the family slipped further into poverty. Something underneath that: Beth would be troubled by the knowledge of what happened to her own mother – their mother. She had died of childbed fever a few days after Beth was born. Josh, barely two years old at the time, remembered nothing about her now. The children were consigned to a slovenly aunt on their father's side, who provided little more than a leaky roof over their heads. Her regime of slothful neglect soon taught Josh the need to be self-reliant and to keep a protective eye on his sister. He became adept at foraging, rummaging, skirmishing, pilfering, begging.

They'd seldom seen their father. When they did he was hopelessly drunk. Embittered, self-pitying, a dribbling sot, he used to rail obsessively against the government for discarding him along with other black soldiers, most of them Jamaican recruits, who'd fought against Napoleon under the Union Jack. 'Washed their hands of us! Dumped us on the docks here, soon as the Peninsular War was over! No pension money for the likes of us. Not a penny. It's wrong!'

Josh still pictured him slouching against a dockyard wall, slack-jawed, his lower lip protruding in such a pout that a seagull might almost perch on it.

But that was years ago. Their father and foster mother were long since dead. Josh had left Liverpool with a troupe of fairground boxers when Beth, at the age of 14, was taken into domestic service and didn't need to rely on his protection any more. For a good while after that, there had been no contact between them. Unable to read or write, Josh knew nothing of his sister's welfare until a circus worker relayed a message about her marrying Charlie. If it hadn't been for his broken ankle and his decision to return to Liverpool, he might never have seen her again. But here he was now, under the same roof as Beth, just a stone's throw from the neighbourhood where they'd grown up. Being back in this narrow joyless world made him feel that he couldn't take a deep breath. No wonder Beth had already lost her youthfulness: her face had the crushed look of a flower trodden underfoot.

The day after his return he spent luckless hours lingering around quayside sheds and then bought bread and sausages for their evening meal. He was approaching the dark alley that led to his cellar lodging when he heard a woman's muffled cries. As he rounded a corner, he saw Beth struggling to fend off an assailant, a brawny ruffian who was pushing her hard against a wall with his forearm across her throat while his other hand groped under her skirt. With angry shouts, Josh stumbled towards them, half-skipping. The attacker swung round to face him, snarling, releasing his hold on Beth and raising his fists, but a single hefty punch from Josh sent him staggering backwards. As the man toppled, his head struck the sharp edge of a brick wall with a loud crack. He twitched and then lay prone, motionless, blood pooling around his broken skull.

Beth was sobbing, hands pressed to her face. Josh put his arm around her and they began to move slowly away. Two men came around the corner, took in the situation, and yelled at him. 'Hey! Whatcha done to our mate Ned?' Ignoring them, Josh helped Beth down the steps to her cellar. As he closed the door behind them and glanced back up, he saw that one of the men had followed and now stood there threateningly, pointing at them as if his finger were a dagger.

The next day Josh was arrested. Soon afterwards a summary conviction of manslaughter condemned him to languish for ten years in a Liverpool gaol.

❖

On a wretchedly cold Ash Wednesday in 1880, emerging from a decade's imprisonment without money or hope, he turned at once to thieving. Stolen train tickets soon took him to London, where he made it his habit to loiter around Euston railway station, mingling with crowds and picking pockets.

Caught a month later 'in possession of stolen property, namely two pocket watches, a silver snuff box, a tortoiseshell comb and a silk handkerchief,' he was sent to Pentonville for the usual nine-month initial period of solitary and silent confinement, to be followed by further incarceration in Dartmoor's Princetown Prison for eight years of penal servitude: hard labour on public works. His mood when sentenced was one of dull resignation, tinged with a sense of relief. In prison he would at least be sheltered from foul weather, and would no longer have to scrabble desperately for food.

He had yet to encounter Dartmoor's Duke.

TWENTY

AT THE BEGINNING OF THE 1840S, ALTHOUGH THE triumph of Waterloo had receded a quarter of a century into the past, Field-Marshal His Grace Arthur Wellesley, first Duke of Wellington, was still an eminent public figure. As a rigidly conscionable elder statesman he had his detractors, and his glory days in warfare and politics were well behind him, but the septuagenarian Duke remained a minister in the Conservative Government, served as Leader of the House of Lords, and resumed his position (albeit mostly ceremonial now) as Commander-in-Chief of the British Army.

So when Edward Starkey, having served enthusiastically under Wellington as a junior officer in the Peninsular campaign and continued to venerate him, became a father on Midsummer Day 1841, he conferred on his newborn the national hero's personal names. Growing into boyhood, Arthur Wellesley Starkey received frequent parental reminders that his christening was auspicious; and as he often impressed this same information conceitedly on his young companions in the hope of commanding their esteem, they soon began saluting him with friendly mockery as 'Duke.' By the time he reached adulthood, big-boned and hard-hearted, that nickname had lost its teasing edge and become warily respectful. As a prison officer, Duke Starkey perfected the art of intimidation, insisting on deference from those around him and rising rapidly to the rank of Chief Warder at the grim Dartmoor establishment. He ruled the place. Even the Governor's ostensibly cardinal authority depended on the pivotal role of the Chief Warder.

Duke Starkey was waiting at Princetown's prison gates when Josh and two other miscreants arrived on a jolting waggon from Tavistock, each of them trussed like a bag of turnips. For most of their journey, the clopping rhythm of draught-horse hooves had been the only sound accompanying them. The scruffy pair travelling with Josh, huddled in the far corner, had exchanged a few grunted words with each other but cast only sidelong glances towards him. Did they despise him because of his colour? Fear him because of his muscular bulk? Either way, he didn't care.

They came to a sudden stop under the forbidding entrance archway. Looking up at this dark angular structure, Josh could see a pair of inscrutable words incised across its capstone. Not English, as far as he could tell. Not intended, anyway, for the likes of him, he was sure of that.

A tall thickset man came up to them with a sheet of paper in his hand. 'Get out!' he barked. Hands still tied, they clambered down awkwardly from the back of the waggon.

'I'm the Chief Warder. Mr Starkey to you.' He looked down at the paper. 'Which of you is William Hibbins?' The sallow-cheeked one coughed and nodded.

'And James Gorton?'

'That's me,' said the other, his face inflamed with carbuncles.

'That's me, *Mr Starkey!*'

'That's me, Mr Starkey.'

The Chief Warder swaggered towards Josh and stood straight in front of him, up close, exhaling loudly. 'So you're Joshua Dunn, then.' Starkey gave a derisive snort, poking him in the chest with a truncheon. 'Dunn, eh? Your skin's darker than dun. Another black bastard. I know your sort, so be warned, Dunn: don't expect an easy time of it here.' Turning to a pair of henchmen, he added with a peremptory nod, 'Bath-house and barber for these three, then to their cells.'

The warders took them first to a shed partitioned with small closets on either side. In a long trough extending beneath the half-walls of corrugated iron that separated each compartment, the scummy communal water lay like cold mutton broth.

'Clothes off, and into the water you go.'

As the men undressed, Josh saw boils and weeping sores all over Gorton's skin. After a cursory dip in the greasy water, they shared an old stained towel for rubbing themselves dry. The clothes they had removed were thrown into a bucket and they had to don coarse ill-fitting broad-arrow uniforms. On Josh's jacket the cuffs came halfway between wrist and elbow, and the shoulders were so narrow he could hardly flex his arms.

'This is who you are from now on,' one of the warders told him, affixing a small metal plate to the right breast of Josh's jacket and pointing to the registration number marked on it. 'For as long as you're here, you'll be F13. No names to be used. Forbidden in this place.'

The boots were roughshod: an arrow pattern nailed into their soles would leave the government's imprint wherever the prisoners walked. More like a crow's foot than an arrowhead, Josh thought, though either way the symbol mocked his situation: a bird and a pointed shaft could both move freely through the air.

'Bid your hair goodbye,' said the warder. A scraggy barber, his hands like little bundles of bent sticks, worked with surprising speed, laying his scissors flat on each head in turn and snipping the hair close to the scalp. Their beards, too, he gave a quick trim.

Led to his cell, Josh looked around it in dismay. In contrast to the plain but decently furnished room at Pentonville, this was a dingy iron kennel, barely two paces from wall to wall. It had no proper bed, just a plank with filthy blankets and a pillow of coarse sacking stuffed with coconut fibre. In one corner was an open tin waste bucket; in another, a lidded pail and a broom. On the table sat a wooden platter, a spoon, a tin pint-mug, and a handful of books.

'What are these for?' Josh pointed to the books.

'Bible, prayer book, rule book.'

'No good to me. Can't read much. So don't expect me to learn the prison rules.'

'Ah, but when you break any of them you'll be punished. Not hard to remember a rule after that.'

It didn't take long for Josh to become accustomed to the daily routine. A strident bell woke them all at five every morning. Soon afterwards buckets of water were brought, cell doors opened. After washing themselves briskly they had to sweep the floor, fold their bedding, then set to work on hands and knees, scrubbing the slate flags of the landing outside the cells. No amount of washing and cleaning dispelled the foul smells that always hung in the air, even after their waste buckets were emptied. It was as if they were living in the midst of a cesspool.

Many of the prisoners spent long hours every day segregated in their cells, shivering and shuffling: frequent movement was the only way to deflect the sharp blade of cold that stabbed at their ribs, their backs, their limbs, their joints. While they limped in small circles or rocked from one numb foot to another they had to go on picking and pulling the matted oakum, the lumps of wiry old tarred ships' ropes, to meet their daily target of three pounds of parted strands made ready for re-use. Their fingers became blackened and sticky, knuckles bloody, nails jagged. They kept at it, knowing that if they didn't complete the required amount their food ration would be reduced.

To Josh the tedium of oakum picking was familiar. In the strictly confined and regimented world of Pentonville it had occupied every prisoner day after day. But here at Princetown there were many other kinds of chore, new to him. Some of the men worked in the prison laundry, boiling and rinsing the dirty linen, cranking the wringer handle, hanging out wet sheets and cloths to dry. Others sewed canvas coal-sacks, mats and mailbags, or emptied dustbins and slop buckets. The strongest prisoners were usually given more strenuous duties beyond the dark walls. Assigned to working parties that took him outdoors, Josh thought himself lucky at first. The discomfort of wind and rain seemed a small price for getting away from stale air and cramped quarters for a few hours a day. Whether cutting peat, toiling on the prison farm, lugging quarry boulders or being harnessed with others to pull laden carts, he was glad simply to be able to move his body, feel the blood coursing through it, and breathe deeply.

After a fortnight of hard labour he complained loudly to a warder that there wasn't enough good food to sustain men like himself. 'We can't keep doing this kind of heavy work on a rumbling belly. We need more meat, better meat, not just this miserable little serve of stringy mutton. Most of the potatoes you give us here are rotten, and the bread's like sawdust.'

'Be grateful for what you get. The honest poor make do with less than you felons have here. Plenty of nourishment in prison fare. Good oatmeal skilly every day. Cocoa with molasses to warm the cockles.'

'I'm a big man. I've got a big appetite. I can't work hard when I'm empty.'

'Your size is *your* problem, F13. Not ours. Let's see what the Duke has to say about your complaint.'

That evening Josh heard heavy footfalls on the landing outside his cell, and the rattle of keys. The door was flung open and Duke Starkey came in, flanked by a pair of warders. 'I hear you don't like the food you're getting, F13. That so?'

'Some of it's not bad but there's never enough of it. Some of it's just putrid.'

'Well, I intend to change your diet immediately,' sneered the Chief Warder. 'You'll be put on bread and water for three days, back to ordinary prison food for a day, and then another three days on bread and water. After that, perhaps you'll feel more grateful for the meals you've been getting.'

Josh gave a sniff of disgust. 'You're a cruel bugger.'

'Any more insolence, F13, and you'll be flogged.' Turning his head as he left the cell, the Duke added over his shoulder, 'Meanwhile, don't think reduced rations entitle you to any reduced labour. Same working party as before. If you slacken your efforts, expect a beating.'

During the next couple of days Josh bartered away his little stock of tobacco for a few oatmeal biscuits. As the week wore on, hunger sucked more and more vitality from him. He felt light-headed and feeble. His arms trembled as he tried to keep a firm grip on the handles of the barrow, pushing load after load of stinking manure from the pigsty to the vegetable patch. Whenever he saw a beetle or an earthworm he seized it and chewed it. One night he ate half a candle. Becoming so ravenous that he thought he could almost have bitten a chunk of flesh from his own arm, he threatened the other men in his labour gang with violence if they didn't keep a share of their bread and potatoes for him and hand it over unobtrusively.

'Rob your mates, would you?' one of them protested. 'We're half-starved ourselves. Where's your scruples?'

'Don't give me a bloody sermon about scruples!' Josh roared. 'The likes of us can't afford to have any. This place turns us into beasts. Every mongrel for himself, and the devil take the hindmost.'

Yet there were times when they would stand up for each other. One such time came just a few weeks later.

TWENTY-ONE

INSIDE OR OUTSIDE THE WALLS, TENSION ALWAYS SIMMERED between prisoners and the Civil Guard. Whenever the inmates left their cell blocks for periods of exercise within the enclosed yard, this armed group of officers watched them closely from the walls. Whenever working parties were labouring out on the moors, the Guard would be nearby, carbines at the ready. 'Any insubordination and you'll be punished without mercy,' the sergeant liked to remind them stridently as the gangs set out each morning.

On this particular day Josh and half a dozen others had spent long cold hours near Two Bridges, cutting peat in a squelchy corner of Roundhill field, trundling each barrow-load to the prison workshops, stacking it there for later use as fuel, pushing the empty barrow back to the boggy field and starting the process over again. It was hard enough to dig and lift the heavy slabs of peat, but the most arduous thing was pushing laden barrows along the rough road to the prison more than a mile and a half away, wrists and arms aching with the strain of keeping the heaped burden steady.

They had to take turns with the three barrows. While some

were transporting peat to the prison, others continued to cut fresh clods and pile them up ready for the next load. Not a moment's rest. By early afternoon the youngest of them, a bony stripling of fifteen called Sidney Sullock, was finding it a struggle to do his share of the work, so the other prisoners tried unobtrusively to cover for him as best they could. But the vigilant sergeant pointed to him, yelling, 'You! Your turn to take a barrow!' The youth grasped its handles, raised them and tried to push forward – but immediately began to stagger. The barrow tipped sideways and the slabs tumbled out. Stepping forward with a curse, the sergeant struck Sullock hard between the shoulder blades with the butt of his carbine.

'Shame!' one of the other prisoners called out, and the rest took up the cry of protest: 'Shame! Shame!'

Josh strode up, helped the boy to his feet, glared fiercely at the sergeant. 'You filthy piece of shit!' he shouted.

That evening, Josh was pinioned to the tall triangular flogging frame and whipped repeatedly across his shoulders with the cat until he looked like a gruesome canvas on a painter's easel. Though the three dozen lashes broke and bruised his skin, they also hardened his resolve never to be cowed into a submissive silence, whatever the penalties.

A few months later, concealed by early morning fog, he slipped away unnoticed from his work gang and bolted. Scrambling along the mottled flanks of hills and stumbling across patches of bog, he realised before long that he hadn't chosen his moment wisely. The fog soon dispersed to reveal one of those tremulous March days when the season, after beginning to turn forward, hesitates and then retreats. A sudden drop in temperature had followed a partial thaw, and in the sunlight the moors glittered with what Josh had heard local men call an ammil: frosted moisture had left a thin coating of ice over bushes, grasses, boulders, lichens, and every projecting thing. He kept moving as long as he could but the cold air made his lungs burn, and when he reached the cover of a large rocky outcrop he stopped to steady his breathing. There at his feet in a shallow frozen puddle fringed with moss and moorgrass he could see icebound frogspawn, a mass of jellied eggs eyeing him sightlessly. It seemed a dispiriting sign of bad timing. The weather gave him little chance of eluding pursuit for long; he knew his defiance would probably be unavailing. Hungry, ashiver, after a day and a night of skulking among boulders and under clapper bridges, he was caught by four officers, who gave him a few vigorous kicks before marching him back in manacles to the prison, where the Duke enjoyed imposing rations of bread and water for three weeks. Famished, Josh could supplement his diet only by gnawing tallow candles and lumps of acrid oakum.

There was one warder who took pity on him. Disregarding the rules and risking his position, moon-faced Walter Gurrey twice managed quietly to bring him a bottle of beef tea with a biscuit.

Punishment didn't lessen Josh's obduracy. As the months crawled on into a year, two years, three, he became the most frequent ringleader in mutinous episodes. From time to time he assaulted warders, broke the no-speaking rule, refused to carry out assigned chores, hurled hymnbooks in the chapel. Each offence met with implacable retribution from the Duke. 'Enjoy being flogged, do you, F13?' he said on one of these occasions, his voice like the hiss of a lash. 'A pastime, is it, for a nigger too ignorant to read or write? That's good, that's good, because I'll be testing your endurance. Testing your fortitude. Know those words, do you, F13? They spell trouble.'

Every prisoner knew that this big black man and the Chief Warder were locked in bitter conflict, and none could see it ending well for F13. A shackled brawler had no chance of staying on his feet.

Tommy Hibbins from the next cell whispered a warning one

night when the duty warder was out of earshot. 'That bloody Duke, he'll do his best to break you, matey. He's got all the power.'

'No he hasn't. I've got the power to defy him, whatever he does to me. That's my way of keeping a grip on who I am.' Josh spat.

'He won't stop making you suffer.'

'And I won't let that humble me. He hates me for not flinching. If I refuse to bow my head, his power means nothing.'

Many of the men had privately devised some personal method of asserting partial independence from the abject condition to which the strict rules consigned them, but these silent attempts to avoid being merely passive prisoners usually didn't last long.

Sid Sullock sought a kind of companionship by caring tenderly for a spider, kept in a soapbox and fed with hand-caught flies, until a warder took pleasure in squashing the puny pet. Tommy Hibbins, put to work in the fetid bone shed beside the prison cesspool, pulverising bones from the prison's meat supply to be mixed into manure for the vegetable patch, hid one piece of bone and whittled it secretly into the shape of a key to his locked cell, only to be foiled and punished when the pains-taking labour was almost finished. A few others contrived loud and lengthy fits of coughing at chapel services, and substituted obscenities for official words in hymns, but officers soon put a stop to any of that.

These rebellious gestures were trifling compared with Josh Dunn's overt show of resistance, but the alternative was to yield to utter despondency, as some did. Through the empty hours of the night, the mandatory silence would often be broken by groans and sometimes by demented shrieking and raving.

'Hell itself can be no worse than this,' whispered Hibbins.

❖

The chaplain knocked at the Chief Warder's open office door and inclined his head deferentially.

'Good afternoon, sir. Might I speak to you about the behaviour of some of the prisoners, if this is a convenient moment?'

'Come in, Mr Grundy, come in. New problems, are there?'

'Not new, exactly, but during chapel worship a few men have become more unruly than ever.'

'Who?'

'The burly black fellow, especially.'

'Ah. F13. No surprise there. Seems determined to bring trouble on himself, that one. What's Sootyface been up to now?'

'Threw a pair of boots at me this morning during the scripture lesson. I think he was vexed by the passage in St Matthew's gospel about not resisting evil. Turning the other cheek instead. That's what I was reading when he bellowed out a string of filthy words and flung both his boots towards the lectern. And then, of course, others began to join in the clamour. Impossible for me to continue until some of your officers had wielded their cudgels to good effect and taken that darky off to his cell.'

'I'll see he gets another heavy dose of the cat. Not that it seems to deter him. It's like flogging a boulder.'

The chaplain produced a diffident cough. 'Solitary confinement for a week or two may have a more lasting effect, don't you think, sir?'

'Doubtful. In his case it hasn't worked before. No sign of change in him. But yes, we'll isolate him after he's been whipped. If nothing else, it will stop him for a while from infecting others with his defiant attitude. Like quarantine for a leper.'

'Well, perhaps it will chasten him eventually. Make him remorseful. A violent man can benefit from being alone with God and a wounded conscience.'

'Ever hopeful, eh, Mr Grundy? Well, I confess I can't share your optimism. These prisoners are stupid blockheads, all of them. Wouldn't be here otherwise. Experience fails to teach them anything, so it's futile to look for a reformed spirit. Especially in that black brute.'

'Yet in God's eyes no soul is wholly lost. No matter how difficult some of these men are, we must surely try to be compassionate towards them. *Parcere subjectis.* Their plight, after all, is dreadful. They must feel despair, immured in a tomb of the living.'

'Tomb? More like a kennel. That's why small things make them pettish. A cooped-up dog barks at its fleas. A hunting dog doesn't feel them.'

Slowly the seasons swung around. Painful years came and went. New prisoners steadily replaced those who reached the date of their release, or died in custody. Knowing that the term of his sentence could be prolonged arbitrarily, Josh made no effort to keep count of passing time. Few things differentiated one month from another, except for periods when the weather became extreme. There was a great freeze one winter, beginning with the most severe frosts anyone could remember and then a week of thunderstorms with heavy hail. Blizzards followed, blocking roads and cutting off supplies of coal and meat – even of water: the prison leat was so choked that two hundred men had to work for two days to clear its flow. Snowdrifts thickened to a depth of five feet. The visiting schoolmaster disappeared between his house and the prison, and only when the thaw came was he found kneeling in the snow, a frozen corpse.

On the day of his discharge, 8th January 1889, Prisoner F13 was accompanied to the Princetown railway station by the only officer who had treated him humanely during the eight years of confinement. Now Gurrey's task was just to purchase for the released man a special ticket that would take him by way of Yelverton junction to Tavistock, and from there to whatever further destination he might choose.

'After all that time to think about your freedom, I suppose you've made definite plans,' said Gurrey as they walked together.

Dunn scratched his head, stuck out his lower lip. 'Nothing much. Don't quite know what kind of work I might get, if any. Hard to dodge questions about what I've been doing. People don't want to hire a gaolbird.'

'Family?'

'Only a sister, if she's still alive. I turned up on her doorstep years ago but I just added to her troubles. Wouldn't do that to her again.'

'Where will you go, then?'

'Oh, London. I'll try London again. Not saying I won't be back in Princetown. Later on.'

'Back here? If I were you, I'd keep right away from this place. Why would you ever think of returning?'

Josh looked back over his shoulder. 'Got reasons.'

TWENTY-TWO

E HAD TIED ONE END OF A THIN ROPE TO THE TOP EDGE of a railing that separated churchyard from street; and now, stepping back across the footpath as far as the kerb, he pulled the other end taut so that it was about four feet above the ground. On his forearm rested the small white bundle of canine fluff. As the rope brought pedestrians to a halt, Josh lifted his dog onto it and gently stroked the silky ears. At once this creature, balancing precariously, began to move along the tightrope to an accompaniment of supportive murmurs from the gathering crowd of onlookers. When it reached the midway point it slowly lifted the front of its body and teetered on its hind paws for a few moments before continuing its unsteady crossing.

It came to the end of the rope and stepped daintily onto the railing. Applause broke out. As it jumped down it turned a full somersault. People cheered.

'Ladies and gents!' Josh shouted, holding out his hat, 'Kindly show your appreciation. Madame Caroline and her humble trainer need to eat.' Coins clinked into the hat. The dog leapt into the air for another somersault, and more of the smiling bystanders contributed.

'Thank you, one and all!' said Josh, tipping the money into his hand and lifting his hat to the crowd. 'Good day to you.' He drew the rope aside to let the foot traffic flow again.

Patchy and weak though the sunshine was, there had been enough summer warmth in it for the last few weeks to enable Josh to survive on the streets with the help of this performing pet, the bichon bitch. A useful earner, she was an affectionate companion as well. Little white dog and big black man kept each other warm in the dank alley nooks at night. He cradled her snugly, she nuzzled into his ribs, and they snored in unison.

Acquiring her had been a happy accident, just when he'd thought he was utterly out of luck.

On reaching London he'd gone straight to the wharves in search of work, but soon found that conditions for dockhands were no better than he'd encountered years before in Liverpool. Hungry men, exuding desperation, jostled each other in the crowd waiting for foremen to hire a handful of them. Among the hum of simmering resentments and muttered oaths, Josh heard half-formed plans about striking for the right to a fair minimum pay rate of a tanner an hour. Small chance of winning that battle, he thought – and less chance, anyhow, of regular employment for himself here. Even if he did get a day or two as a barrow-man shifting heavy cargo, he couldn't feel confident of coping with strenuous labour, not being as robust as he once was.

So then he began to sniff around what people were now calling 'the East End' – the slums of Whitechapel and Spitalfields. But there, disconcertingly, every second person looked and sounded strange to him.

'Who are these people?' he asked someone, gesturing towards the forlorn groups of oddly dressed men, their eyes dark and sunken, who clustered outside shabby shops and lodging-houses.

'Jews from Russia,' he was told. 'Refugees.'

'Refugees? Meaning what?'

'They've been driven out of their homeland. Miserable wretches. Can't get work here, most of them, so God only knows what's to become of them.'

In Josh's heart there was scant room now for compassion. The plight of Jews? Not his affair. What about the plight of a black Englishman who'd belonged to this country all his life and whose father had fought under the Union Jack? Josh should be ahead of these newcomers in the line for a job, he had no doubt of that. For a week, grim and weary, he trudged the East End streets enquiring about work. Any work. People looked away and shook their heads. There was nothing for him.

He thought back glumly to his days as a circus fist-fighter. Weakened since then by time in prison, by injury and maltreatment and poor food, he knew there was no prospect of returning to the bareknuckle ring; but perhaps there yet might be, somewhere in that gaudy little world of fairground hoopla, a few odd chores he could do in return for his keep? Although he no longer had any personal connection with showmen – Pablo Fanque had died years ago – he could still try to push his way into their attention.

Hearing that Sanger's Circus was about to open in Covent Garden, Josh walked to the site and loitered for hours around the cages. 'Need someone to help feed your beasts?' he asked the minders and tamers. No chance.

'Already costin us too much to tend em all,' said one, a morose-looking youth with a grimy clay pipe jutting from the corner of his thin mouth. 'Price o feed keeps going up. We're avin to get rid of some poor brutes. Like vis little lady.' He pointed to a ball of curly white fluff tethered to a post. 'Clever fing, fulla tricks, but most folks want to see big animals now. Besides, she was part of an act, paira dancing dogs, and it can't continue. Her little matey took sick, died a few days ago. So vis one, she's gotta go.'

Josh tickled the creature's ears. 'Dances, does she?'

The morose minder nodded. 'Look at vis!' He drew a piece of rope from his pocket, quickly fixed one end of it to the post and drew the other end towards himself. Letting her off the leash, he lifted her up and placed her on the tightened rope. She rose on her hind legs and minced to and fro before leaping down with a somersault. Josh felt his face soften into an unaccustomed grin.

'How much to take her off your hands?' he asked.

'Nuffin, matey. You're welcome to take her. But if you do, mind you treat her well. She's a sweet girl. Keep her meself if I could afford it.'

So Josh picked her up, tickled the creamy patches around her ears, gave her a few reassuring pats, and carried her away. He'd already decided to call her Madame Caroline.

Feeding her turned out to be easier than feeding himself, for Madame Caroline was adept at finding edible morsels in gutters and pavement corners. When Josh had enough money from her performances to buy the occasional titbit from street vendors – a jellied eel, an onion wrapped in a piece of boiled tripe, a few whelks, some buttered pea pods – he shared whatever he could with her.

It was a tolerable way of getting by, and he thought it would last a good while, even after the weather began to sour; but the end of it was sudden. As Madame Caroline leapt down from one of her tightrope acts, a fearsome mastiff came bounding towards her out of nowhere. Terrified, the bichon fled into the roadway. The wheels of a box-laden waggon instantly crushed the life from her.

Josh's sorrow expressed itself as anger. All the aggrieved feelings from his years in prison, every grudge and bitter resentment, came surging back now in a swollen flood until his heart was awash with obsessive urges to wreak revenge for all his suffering on his chief tormentor, Starkey. He became resolute:

he would go back to Princetown and confront the Duke. Being almost penniless, he would have to walk there, hoping to find enough food and shelter along the way to keep him going.

It was much more difficult than he'd imagined. Before leaving London he asked a few people how far they thought it would be to Dartmoor. Most shrugged, but one old fellow who said he'd spent a couple of years in Devon as a boy told him the distance was probably 250 miles or more, depending on the chosen route. So Josh reckoned a steady pace ought to get him there within a fortnight. But the wet days slowed him down, and the gusty winds in his face, and the aching hunger, and his bruised bleeding feet. He slept beneath hedges or in the lee of walls, or in barns when he was lucky. The problem of finding anything much to eat preoccupied him constantly. After three days there were no coins left in his pocket. He soon found that his idea of doing odd chores in wayside alehouses in return for a meal was unrealistic. 'Eh? Chop wood? Wash dishes? Nah. We do it ourselves. No help needed.' So he cadged and begged, always keeping a sharp lookout for any food he could steal. In different places along the way, dogs or owners chased him from a butcher's yard, a henhouse and a couple of kitchen gardens.

More than three weary weeks after setting out, he made his way quietly at nightfall into Chagford and slept in a church porch there until first light. Then, watchful and wary, he set off in a southwesterly direction, keeping roughly parallel with the Postbridge road but far enough away from it to avoid encountering other travellers. If he came too close to Princetown in daylight he might attract inquisitive attention. So he moved nearer to the higher rolling moorland, skirting the range with its clitter-strewn slopes and lofty tors.

A bitter wind had come up now, strengthening by the minute, and the going was hard. He had seen nothing edible all day except for a few whortleberries, and the hunger made him light-headed. Hearing the thud of approaching hoofs, he crouched behind a cluster of tall boulders and peered cautiously into the distance. A dozen wild ponies came galloping over a curve of hillside and on past him, tossing their small heads as they disappeared along a westward track. Josh decided to follow them towards the sinking sun, knowing that the Merrivale quarry and hamlet must be close in that direction and hoping to find something to eat around there.

Within a few minutes he came upon a small circular stone enclosure – part of the prison farm, he guessed – where half a dozen sheep huddled. As he climbed into their pen, all but one of them ran bleating to the far side of it. Walking up to the single creature that remained on the ground, its legs folded underneath, its shoulders twitching, he drew out his knife. 'Too sick to move, are you?' he murmured. 'Anyhow your days are done.' Swiftly he cut its throat and began to hack at its flank, stuffing warm flesh into his mouth.

As he carved off more chunks of meat, windblasts pummelled and flailed him. A pelting rain arrived and before long his clothes were soaked through, his limbs chilled. Water streaming down his face mingled with the blood around his chin. The sheepfold walls were too low to give him any protection from the worsening weather. Intent on finding better shelter somewhere nearby, he staggered off into the darkness, clutching a large strip of fatty mutton.

Time itself went numb and Josh was beginning to think he would die in this desolate place when, just ahead of him on a low ridge sloping to the southwest, he glimpsed a long row of stones jutting up from the ground like frozen tongues. Walking alongside this row, a few yards to the south of it, he came to a strange sunken box-like structure of thick granite, with a large split lid that gleamed in the rain. This, he thought, must be the cist that a prisoner from a Merrivale Quarry workgang had once described to him. An ancient grave, they reckoned, its tenant's bones long since crumbled away. Josh peered into it but could see nothing. He lay atop the stone, reached down through the cleft, and felt around. A large empty space. His hand touched damp soil but there seemed to be no water lying there; most of the rain was blowing across the split capstone. He swung his feet into the hole and gingerly lowered himself into it. As his eyes slowly adjusted to the darkness he could see that there was just enough room for him to lie down, curled tight, knees against his chest. With his wet jacket bunched beneath his head, he listened to the wildness hissing above him for a long while, until suddenly everything was quiet. Wind and rain had stopped together. Lifting his head through the gap in the gravestone lid, he saw that the clouds had parted and the moon was illuminating the sodden land.

Climbing shakily out of his burial chamber, blood on his chin and on his mind, he began to move towards the prison.

Dartmoor, Perth & London

2015

TWENTY-THREE

IT HADN'T TAKEN TIM LONG TO SEE THAT OLD ROBBIE, THE benign local historian who gave him access to Hilda Moss's letters, was hardly exaggerating when he'd characterised them as full of gossip about half the folk in the Chagford district. Hilda, a well-off widow with no children and ample leisure time, had lived alone near the Three Crowns Hotel from 1922 until her death in 1938, corresponding frequently throughout that time with her younger sister Rhoda in Tavistock. Having grown up together in Chagford, these two shared an avid interest in all the goings-on in the town and its surroundings. Hilda apparently revelled in her role as a self-described 'busybody reporter.' Every Sunday evening, without fail, she wrote down for Rhoda's delectation another breathless instalment in her serial reportage of recent neighbourhood happenings or current rumours that had come to her attention. Her prose was not so much a stream of consciousness as a babbling brook. To Tim's eye much of it seemed tedious and trivial, though he could recognise amidst the blathering some signs of intelligent curiosity. Hilda occasionally showed herself to be a sharp observer of certain changes taking shape in this miniature version of English society between the wars, and capable of shrewd insights into its inhabitants as well. Quirks, foibles, discrepancies between public and private selves – she didn't miss much in the personalities around her.

Some individuals recurred often in these pages, especially from the most prominent families in the vicinity. Rhoda was kept up to date with little bulletins about the Reeds of Rushford Mill Farm, the growth of their engineering business and especially the glimpsed comings and goings at their Teign View lodging-house with its numerous guests – 'I hear that a *renowned Author* called Mr Eden Phillpotts is visiting there at present, a man of *distinguished* bearing according to Ethel Crump, perhaps you may have heard about him, Rhoda? I'm not much of a reader myself as you know but apparently he's written many novels about Dartmoor, and I suppose I should try to find one or two of his books somewhere, there's even a story set here in Chagford, Ethel says.' Hilda also wrote in serpentine detail about the McIlwraiths' ambitious project of building an elegant house at Gidleigh Park 'in the very *grandest* Arts and Crafts style, so people tell me, with extravagantly large and graceful gardens, all sorts of quite unusual plants, *No Expense Spared* is the watchword! Nobody in town can say for certain where all the McIlwraith money comes from, for they're not true landed gentry, in fact they're *Australian*, so you do have to wonder, but I've heard tell their wealth is inherited from to the head of a *shipping* company, which could mean anything at all, even *piracy* perhaps!'

Rhoda had kept all of Hilda's letters, which then stayed in her family's possession until donated recently to the Chagford Historical Society by one of the grandchildren. What a treasure trove! Although none of these many items – nearly 800 in all – could be considered a masterpiece of epistolary art, together they comprised an important documentary resource. But while appreciating their potential value for some of his fellow-historians, Tim had bracketed off that thought as he skimmed through page after page with his mother's specialised question as his filter: was there any trace here of the mysterious forebear Phyllis Hardy?

In his quick scan of the whole boxed set of correspondence, Tim had found nothing that looked relevant. No mention of any Hardy, as far as he could see. Despondent, he was leafing back idly through a pile that dated from 1933 when something he'd missed caught his attention. 'It's nearly a year ago now that young Philomena disappeared all of a sudden, and nobody has heard from her since as far as I can discover, so it seems she has shaken Chagford's dust from her shoes, and I doubt we'll see her around these parts ever again. She will be trying, surely, to put her *scandalous* behaviour behind her and make a *fresh start* somewhere far from here, perhaps even with a change of name to cover her tracks, I wouldn't be surprised. Well, people always said she was reckless!'

Tim drew in a long breath. What if the 'Phyl' his mother hoped to find was actually a 'Phil'? Not a Phyllis but a Philomena? And what if the surname Hardy was acquired after she left this district – whether simply by marriage or, as Hilda Moss speculated, to disguise her identity? But this 'scandalous behaviour' preceding her departure – what might it have been?

He went back slowly through the letters, alert for any previous mentions of this Philomena, and found several dispersed passages that hadn't struck him as potentially significant until now. He made a note of names, dates, scraps of hearsay, likely facts. Bit by bit and inference by inference he began to compile the outline of a story.

Philomena, sole child of David and Margaret Starkey of Chagford, had been born in 1915, a few months after her father enlisted and sallied forth across the channel with an infantry battalion. Badly affected by mustard gas during the third battle of Ypres, hospitalised, deemed unfit for further military service, he eventually returned to Chagford to face an interminable convalescence. For his family the homecoming must have been all the more harrowing because shrapnel had killed his only brother in that same battle. David Starkey remained incapacitated, his wife struggled to look after the family until her death from 'heart problems' in 1930, and their neglected daughter became 'a flighty thing,' according to Hilda Moss's prim account. 'I've heard her called *high-spirited*, rather too charitably if you ask me! To my mind little Miss Phil is a *downright troublesome hoyden*. At the age of 16 no decent girl would be lingering at dusk outside the Three Crowns, *cheek by jowl* with farm labourers and such, laughing raucously and carrying on like a *junior Jezebel*.'

There was something further, and Tim almost missed it: a final reference to this rebellious young woman who incurred Hilda Moss's stern disapproval. It came as a postscript to one of the letters written less than a year before Hilda's death, when her handwriting had become spidery and almost illegible – which was why he'd overlooked a crucial name when first hastily scanning the correspondence. Slowly he deciphered the scrawled sentences. 'Well! I've just heard *in strictest confidence* an intriguing whisper about what happened to Philomena Starkey. Lorna Whitton was in Exeter recently for a cousin's funeral, and she says (never being one to keep secrets for long) that she saw her in the street there with a *child in tow*, and spoke with them at length. It turns out she is now living in Exeter as Mrs Philomena Hardy, and the child of course is her daughter. No husband in the picture, the story being that he – presumably Mr Hardy – went off to the Spanish War with the International Brigade and was killed there. But I can't help *wondering*…! Lorna says the daughter, Joan, looks to be fully five years old, so Miss Phil can't have wasted any time finding a husband after she left here – if indeed Mr Hardy *ever existed*!'

❖

Back in Princetown that evening, reviewing the notes spread over the bed in his room at the Plume of Feathers Inn, Tim suddenly saw that the sketchy shape of a family tree, discernible behind the incomplete narrative of Philomena Starkey, might be more remarkable than he had recognised at first.

Dominating the foreground was this wayward and seemingly wanton figure who probably became pregnant as a teenager to some local man and therefore moved away from Dartmoor. Whether or not she did really marry a person surnamed Hardy, only to be widowed by the Spanish Civil War, it was apparently as a single mother that she brought up her daughter – who must have been his own maternal great-grandmother Joan: a birth date in 1933 certainly did fit. And it occurred to him that something his mum mentioned in her email, to the effect that Phil Hardy said her husband liked to call her Foolhardy, could actually have been a twist of the truth, her own bitter private joke: perhaps 'foolhardy' was a term she applied ironically to herself, and then on that basis invented a new surname and husband.

But what now stirred a conjectural possibility in Tim's mind was not the Hardy surname that Philomena had acquired or adopted; it was her original family name, Starkey. It struck him that he'd met this name recently in another context: it had cropped up in the report about the trial of Joshua Dunn. The allegedly cruel prison officer who'd been the target of a vengeful scheme that led to Dunn's re-arrest was called Chief Warder Starkey. So could he be a relative of Philomena – and therefore part of Tim's own family lineage?

He checked his watch: half past ten – so it would be 6.30a.m. in Western Australia. His parents were always early to rise. He'd send an email now to tell his mother what he'd discovered, and with those leads she'd probably be able to check out the Starkey links through her ancestry.com account. If Philomena's father David had a connection to the man who was Chief Warder at Dartmoor Prison in the late 19th century, surely one of the online databases would tell her.

Tomorrow he would travel back to London. There was just over a fortnight left before he'd have to return to Perth, and he was keen to spend some of that time pursuing enquiries through the extensive repositories of First World War files at the National Archives in Kew. What he wanted to locate there was the service record and pension discharge for David Starkey, the man who was, in all likelihood, his great-great-grandfather. Crippled by mustard gas at Ypres – but what else could the archives reveal of his war experiences? And David's brother, the one killed on the same battlefront: there must be details for him too.

Before undertaking that work, he would still be able to spend two or three days with the circus records in Sheffield, just a couple of hours away by train from St Pancras Station. He knew from online information about the collections held there that he'd have plenty of stuff to browse through – thousands of photos along with posters, programs, file cards and much more.

If time permitted before he left London there were a few other things to fit in as well, such as getting to Tavistock Square to have a look at the memorial to conscientious objectors. He'd like to take a couple of photos of it for Valerie.

The day after he reached London a long email arrived from his mother, setting out excitedly a summary of the genealogical facts that his information had enabled her to trace.

Their family tree, she announced, now included this line:

Arthur Wellesley Starkey (b. Tavistock 1841, d. Princetown 1906), Chief Warder at Dartmoor Prison for many years. Married Anne Brown in 1864.

Their son *Albert* (1866-1929), lived and died in Princetown, also an officer at the Prison. Married Charlotte Flegg in 1890.

Their son *David* (b. Princetown 1894, d. Chagford 1935) married Maud Hill in 1914, served in the war and was sent home badly wounded. David had an older brother, Frederick (b. Princetown 1890, d. in combat, Ypres 1917).

David's daughter *Philomena* (b. Chagford 1915, d. Exeter 1968) claimed to have married a Mr Hardy c. 1933 who supposedly died c. 1937, though these matters remain unverified.

Philomena's daughter *Joan* (b. Exeter 1933, no father listed on birth certificate; d. London 2004). Married Paul Vercoe in 1958, migrated with him to Fremantle.

Joan's daughter *Vera* (b. 1961). Married Jeremy Holmes in 1982.

Sons Paul (b. 1983) and *Timothy* (b. 1991).

'So what do you think of all that, Tim?' his mother's message asked. 'Should we describe our pedigree as colourful rather than entirely respectable? If only we knew more about the individuals behind those names! That Arthur Starkey, for instance, the gaol boss, your 4xG grandfather: was he in truth an extremely cruel man, as the black prisoner claimed at that strange trial you were telling me about? If so, did he feel any pang of remorse at mistreating men in his charge, or couldn't a person in that position afford to have such scruples? And the 'foolhardy' Philomena – what was she really like? What were her feelings about getting pregnant, abruptly abandoning her crippled father, and bringing up a daughter alone? Was there resentment or defiant self-reliance or what? While there's some satisfaction in knowing a bit about these ancestors of ours, the facts just don't take us far enough, do they?'

TWENTY-FOUR

Hᵢ Tɪᴍ

I'd been expecting the police would get in contact to ask about Kemal, but it's taken them a lot longer than it should have. The day before yesterday a couple of detectives came at last to see me, by arrangement, at St Cat's. Just a 'routine' informal interview, they assured me. Predictable questions. I'd been helping Mr Kaleli with his studies, hadn't I? – So what were my impressions? Had I noticed anything unusual about his behavior or mood before his death? Did I know of any conflicts he'd been involved in? Any suspicious-looking people hanging around the campus at that time? I said no to all of that.

I didn't mention what I'd overheard near the Winthrop Hall undercroft, because I'd have felt like an idiot saying I couldn't be sure who it was with Kemal, or exactly what they were arguing over. Probably you think I should have told them something about it? But imagine their raised eyebrows: I could only say that I MAY have caught a few words of a disagreement that MAY have involved an African guy called Omar and MAY have had something to do with sex. What would that sort of witness statement be worth? What false paths could it lead investigators down (or up)? I don't want to cause trouble for any innocent person.

Instead, what I did tell them was that I'd been trying to think logically about possible explanations for his murder – and I showed them a list I'd made, summarising several scenarios, ranging from a scapegoating payback for the old Armenian genocide (which Turkey still won't acknowledge) to some explosive personal quarrel (but who with?). They glanced at my jottings, said they were already 'actively pursuing some of these lines of enquiry,' and took the notepaper away with them.

I guess you've followed a fair bit of Oz news while you've been away – e.g. you'll know there's been more Canberra chatter about a looming challenge to Abbott's leadership. So I won't try to update you with a digest of headlines. But thinking of your research topic, I wonder whether you're aware of the latest hoo-haa about Oz policy on refugees – or at least, the way it's implemented – essentially racist, so some say, in contrast to 'more inclusive' countries like the UK. (Is this being reported over there?) What's provoked fresh debate is that the government announced it will provide 12,000 additional visas in response to the chaos in Syria and Iraq. Some media commentators still aren't happy because they suspect that non-Muslims will be favoured. Others reckon those critics are confusing racial origin with cultural compatibility, and besides, official international figures for the year show that Australia's refugee intake through resettlement programs is three times larger than the UK's, with only Canada and the US taking in more – and Australia's per capita ranking is first. I don't pretend I've grasped the issues fully but you'll want to catch up on all of this when you're back.

Best

Valerie

As he read the last paragraph of Valerie's message, what came to Tim's mind was the Rally for Refugees that he'd attended in Kings Park earlier that year, in the heat of summer. He could picture it all clearly.

Waiting for the applause to subside, clasping the microphone with both hands as if in supplication, the slim tall young man peered around at the expectant throng and ran the tip of his tongue over his lips.

'I am grateful,' he began hesitantly. 'Very grateful for the welcome.' His husky voice hardly carried to the back of the crowd. He cleared his throat. There was a long pause. To convey encouragement, heads tilted towards him with nods and smiles. He seemed to take heart.

'Nobody among you, I think, has skin as dark as mine,' he went on. 'But I'm sure our hearts are the same colour.' More clapping, more nodding. Some called out a fervent yes. This was what they wanted to hear. He wiped sweat from his forehead with the back of a hand.

'The good people who organised today's rally have asked me to tell you what it feels like to come here as a refugee. Difficult question! Even if I could speak English language better, it would not be easy for me to describe experiences of every person who seeks for asylum in Australia. Not even possible. But I can say this: what brought me here from Somalia was a desire for freedom. Freedom from conflict. Freedom from oppression. Freedom to be educated. And there are many others like me. I have a good friend here in Perth, Ahmad is his name. His parents paid a people smuggler to take him to Australia because his life in Afghanistan was full of pains and fears. Australian navy men stopped his boat in the sea and he was put in detention centre for two years before he got asylum. Now both of us are university students here in Perth, working hard, happy to be living in this country. Some of his story is different from mine but one simple thing is the same for both of us: we wanted very much to become Australian citizens. Why? To have better life and contribute to this society. But now it is more difficult for others like us. A policy much more harsh. The Australian government is dumping its responsibilities for refugee welfare onto poorer neighbour countries. This is cruel. This is shameful. Where is the government conscience? Where? I ask you: does this Prime Minister have a pure heart?'

'No!' shouted dozens of the protesters, faces glowing with indignation. Others clapped vigorously.

Standing near the back of the crowd, Tim felt a nudge in the ribs. 'Eloquent, isn't he?' whispered his flatmate Pete. 'I've heard Omar speak before. Now you know why I wanted you to come to the rally.'

'Mmm.' Tim pursed his lips.

'You don't sound enthusiastic.'

'Oh it's just that…Well, let's wait till the speeches are over. Then we can talk about this. Meanwhile I'm going to stand under that big tree, where it's cooler.'

A camera crew wearing Channel 9 T-shirts distracted everyone by moving their equipment nearer the speaker. He'll sound good on tonight's TV news, Tim thought. And look good too – tall, personable, exotically handsome. A poster boy for the refugee cause.

Sidling a short distance away, Tim joined a dozen people in the shade cast by an enormous gnarled peppermint gum. It seemed immeasurably ancient, its dark fibrous trunk a thick hank of twisted rope. From where he now stood, Tim could look down the slope towards the tall obelisk that surmounted the State War Memorial. Beyond it there were glimpses of the broad river, and around to his left the tall buildings of the city centre.

The Somali student soon finished his address, and acclamation thickened the air. Pete, ablaze with ardour, seemed to be trying to out-clap everyone else. Then a series of other men and women with identically coloured hearts on their sleeves took turns at the podium, but Tim paid them little attention, letting his mind drift.

When Pete had urged him to attend this demonstration he'd readily agreed. He'd never been unsympathetic towards displaced ethnic minorities, and now his own research project was confirming with historical evidence how harmful it could be to push people away from a society's benefits just because of their racial background. Yet the rhetoric of today's event was making him slightly uneasy. There was something a bit confused, he thought, in what these speakers were saying – something indiscriminate in the conflation of refugees with any people trying to move into another country, and in the earnest advocacy of generalised human rights. For his own part, though he'd have said his leanings had always been leftward, he was beginning to form a view that the basic moral principle of respecting human equality shouldn't entail identical obligations to everyone regardless of their cultural affiliations and attitudes. Wanting one's community to have a core of basic shared values: was that necessarily racist? Wanting to protect social cohesion? Wanting to prevent national borders from being thrown open to all comers, regardless of what they believed and how they intended to act?

Surely it was a stark fact that some of those paying to come here didn't wish to respect certain principles enshrined in Australia's legal institutions – had no intention, for example, of treating women as men's equals. He doubted that Pete, though a law student, would concede the importance of that point. Pete liked to bang on about upholding individual rights as if these were so absolute that no larger consideration could complicate them.

The speeches had come to an end now. In preparation for their march to the parliament buildings, a florid man with a megaphone was marshalling the crowd of protesters into lines, and those with the most forcefully worded placards he beckoned to the front. 'Hold them up towards the photographers!' he shouted. Tim could read some of the signs:

LET THEM LAND! LET THEM STAY!

LIBERAL P.M. = ILLIBERAL DEMOCRACY

AUSTRALIA DAY CELEBRATES ILLEGAL
IMMIGRANTS OF 1788

OUR BORDER PROTECTION POLICY SHAMES US ALL

With jutting chin, Pete strolled over to Tim. 'So you don't agree with what you were hearing?'

'Not entirely, to be frank. Not with everything the speakers said. Hardly analytical, were they, Dr Bigwig and Rev Wotnot and company? A bit too indiscriminately zealous for my liking.'

'But what about young Omar?' Pete scratched his earlobe.

'Oh, he's quite an impressive orator, no doubt about that. All the same, I thought he didn't acknowledge the real difficulties of formulating a balanced refugee policy.'

'Balanced?' A quizzical eyebrow.

'What we need, I reckon, is a policy that would respect humanitarian principles but also get to grips with a few inconvenient truths.'

'Such as?'

'Such as the fact that some people – some – who've migrated here on stealthy boats after destroying their own identity papers turn out not to be victims of religious or political oppression.'

Pete looked at him askance. 'Holy shit! That sounds like a statement from a Murdoch newspaper editorial.'

'Maybe so. Does that necessarily invalidate it?'

Pete shrugged. 'Moot point, mate, moot point. To be continued later, eh? Come on, the march is setting off.'

'I'll need to give it a miss,' said Tim. 'I really must get back to the campus. Still plenty of work to do on my seminar paper, and only a couple of weeks left.'

'OK. See you at the flat this evening.' Pete hurried off to catch up with the marchers as they made their way along Fraser Avenue.

Walking slowly in the opposite direction, cap pulled low to shield the birthmark on his forehead from the sunlight, Tim looked out southerly over the wide expanse of Melville Water. He imagined countless generations of Nyoongar people standing on this very spot, eons before the successive appearance of Dutch, French and English navigators. Nearer to the present time, some of their tribal descendants would have watched Vlamingh's boat as it sailed up the river in the late 17th century. Others probably saw Baudin's party charting these waters at the beginning of the 19th century, and Stirling's prospective settlers a generation later. Those European explorers were all seeking prosperity, not asylum. But in Tim's mind the distinction was no longer clear-cut. He wondered how many of the ostensible refugees making their way here nowadays were also motivated mainly by a desire to improve their material prospects. You couldn't blame them for that, but where should the policy line be drawn? There seemed to be plenty of evidence that quite a few of the boat arrivals in recent years were from Iran's middle class, sufficiently well off to pay for their illegal passage, and were not fleeing persecution – just wanting to lift their standard of living further, with a generous welfare safety net for good measure.

He also thought it likely that Pete's admiration of Omar's speech had more to do with the young man's physical glamour than with his political message. Pete had never made any secret of his predilections.

The sun was high now, and Tim couldn't find many patches of shade alongside the curving road that sloped gradually down towards the university campus. Tall eucalypts lined both sides of the drive but their foliage was too meagre to provide much protection for anyone walking underneath. At the foot of each tree a memorial plaque carried the name of a soldier from Western Australia with the date and place of his death overseas. There were hundreds of them along this stretch of roadway alone. Some had died in New Guinea or Timor, defending their homeland against the threat of Japanese invasion. Others had lost their lives on battlefields in the Middle East or Europe. Others didn't survive imprisonment as POWs. Wouldn't they turn in their graves if they knew that thousands of foreigners, some of them scorning Australia's value consensus but wanting a big helping of its goods and services and opportunities, would come to this country many years later, some surreptitiously without visas, expecting to live here in comfort?

The question troubled Tim, stirring something in him. A yeasty lump of prejudice, was it? Warmed by privilege? Or simply his conscience?

Conscience. Few words were as loaded as this one. Omar had used it as a rallying cry. But conscience didn't mean the same thing to everyone in every situation. Should it?

No doubt Pete would have a few vehement things to say on the subject, and over the coming days the pair of them would debate it with their usual vigour. Tim could anticipate all the steps in the argument. Having gone to the same secondary school and then shared a flat since the end of their second year as undergraduates, they were pretty familiar by now with each other's habits of thinking. Despite a friendly mutual regard, Tim saw Pete as a chronically sentimental ideologue and knew that Pete saw him as an inveterate sceptic in whom the milk of human kindness had started to go sour.

He could predict this evening's pattern. Pete, seemingly good-humoured at first but slightly edgy, would insist that Tim account for his resistance to the sentiments of speechmakers at the rally. Tim would respond by trying to set out his views logically, and would then be accused of a robotic failure of compassion. And so on, to and fro, more and more fractiously. At any point Pete could fly off the handle, incandescent with anger. There was sure to be a lot of wrangling ahead.

TWENTY-FIVE

T HOUGH HE'D BEEN ABLE TO RECALL IT VIVIDLY, THAT RALLY in King's Park seven months ago on the other side of the world soon slipped to the back of Tim's mind as he came towards the limit of his extended leave and of his scrimping travel budget. With barely a couple of weeks left until the scheduled return flight to Perth, there were two lines of research to pursue intensively during that time. He would get a train north, hoping that something or other in those fairground history collections might happen to shed light on Joshua Dunn's life before prison. Only an outside chance of finding any mention of him, but worth a try. Then back to London after two or three days to see what military records in the National Archives in Kew could reveal about the war service of Tim's new-found great-great-grandfather Davy.

In Sheffield he turned up only a single relevant reference, a brief one: 'Mr J. Dunn, up-and-coming young negro pugilist' appeared in a poster advertising George Wombwell's animal show at the Knott Mill Fair for Easter 1866. From other sources in the circus archives there, he found that Knott Mill Fair was a hugely popular event held annually on the outskirts of

Manchester, a carnival that always attracted boisterous crowds to see the assorted performers, human and animal, go through their entertaining paces beneath the candy-striped canopies. The poster told Tim a couple of things about this early phase of Dunn's fairground career. First, though his act was a sparring match, it featured a demeaning peculiarity: his antagonist in the ring was a big buck kangaroo, its lethal claws covered with boxing gloves. Second, the venue had been shared on this occasion between two celebrated shows: Wombwell's and Fanque's. The famous George Wombwell himself had died many years earlier, and since then his wife had run his 'No. 1 Menagerie,' so she was presumably the person who recruited the youthful Joshua Dunn for mock gladiatorial combat with an exotic beast. It may well have been here at Knott Mill Fair, at this very time, that Dunn came to the attention of Pablo Fanque, his subsequent employer.

On the train back to London Tim tried to imagine what Josh Dunn's life as a fringe circus performer had felt like. Always restlessly mobile: might that become tiresome, or would he relish being so often on the move, gypsy-like, experiencing it as a kind of freedom? Would there have been much sense of companionship with other performers, or would his blackness have stood in the way? Why did he eventually leave the fairground world? Was it just that he lapsed into crime while employed by Fanque, and so lost the security of that work? Or did he turn away from it by choice, later finding himself on the wrong side of the law?

Whatever the sequence, it seemed clear from the later trial report that Dunn had spent many of his adult years in prison. No doubt this had meant harsh treatment, though some contemporary pontificators made light of the privations suffered by inmates. In Princetown's little library Tim had copied down these words published just a decade after Dunn breached the prison wall: 'The criminal is the spoiled child of the age, to be petted and pampered and excused.' The statement came from a history of the Dartmoor region by Sabine Baring-Gould, and underneath the copied quotation Tim added a snappish comment: 'This opinion, supercilious and ignorant, comes from the man who wrote that hymn Onward Christian Soldiers, with its naïve dream of a "happy throng" that is "not divided"! Rev. SBG, unfeeling parson of a parish near Tavistock – a classic case of empathy bypass!'

How might things have turned out for Joshua Dunn following the judicial sequel to his Princetown prison break-in? Eventually released after a further period of incarceration, did he manage at last to stay out of trouble? There seemed to be no way of knowing.

The small room Tim had managed to get in William Goodenough House, at the heart of Bloomsbury, would serve as a useful base for his final week-and-a-half in London. Nearby in Tavistock Square was the memorial to conscientious objectors, and with Valerie in his thoughts he went there first, taking photos of the massive stone to send to her. Inscribed on it three-quarters of a century after the end of World War 1 was a dedication 'To all those who have established and are maintaining the right to refuse to kill,' and an acknowledgement of their 'foresight and courage.' Foresight? If those who were reviled as cowards for resisting military service could have have known that this monument would be erected to honour them in 1994, what would be uppermost in their minds – gladness at being vindicated, or disappointment that the vindication took so long to arrive?

Each morning for nearly a week he took a trip on the tube to the Kew Gardens station, then a short stroll further on to the National Archives. Most of his first day there was spent acquainting himelf with the necessary procedures, completing a preliminary check of relevant research guide documents and getting a clear sense of where to locate what he sought. Military records extended voluminously across diverse collections, from regimental files and war diaries to service records. Of these, the best source of details about an individual soldier was in most cases his service record – if still intact, which it often wasn't because many such records from the Great War had been destroyed or damaged by bombing in 1940. Tim was in luck: the papers for soldiers discharged on medical grounds had generally survived unburnt, including casualty and disability statements, physical descriptions and discharge proceedings. With this set of microfilm files as a starting point, gradually he began to piece together further scraps of information on his ancestor David Starkey.

Then a visit to the Imperial War Museum, south of the Thames, enabled him to fill in more of the picture. He went there for a specific purpose, knowing it had comprehensive files on the wartime use of mustard gas; but the repository's holdings, he discovered, were vast and various. He lingered in the First World War Galleries and ambled through a couple of other special exhibitions. The range of resources amazed him. He made a memo note about one of them: *IWM has compiled an online register of nearly 70,000 UK War Memorials – let Val know in case she isn't aware of this.*

Back in Bloomsbury that evening, sitting quietly in a wood-panelled corner of the North Sea Restaurant as he worked his way through a generous serve of fish and chips, Tim pulled out his laptop and reviewed the main findings that had so far come to light. In sombre outline, David Starkey's story of lasting wounds spoke for many soldiers' tales from that war. His battle-front experience had been brief and brutal. In July 1917, as a prelude to the Third Battle of Ypres, German artillery bombarded the British positions night after night with shells that released mustard gas on impact. Davy was among the first to be affected by this new chemical weapon: a shell detonated close to him, spraying poisonous liquid and releasing vapours. Tim had read enough at the Imperial War Museum to know what form his forebear's suffering was likely to have taken. After about an hour his eyelids would be inflamed and sticky. He would be vomiting uncontrollably as his skin began to blister. Exposed out there under fire, he must have felt hopelessly vulnerable, probably stumbling, disoriented, terrified, wheezing painfully, going blind, trying to suck in enough breath to call for help. Someone – and now Tim knew who this was – had responded, leading Private Starkey to a Casualty Clearing Station. Then came the long sojourn in hospital and eventually his discharge. Perhaps it was only after what must have been a wretched homecoming that he learned about the death of his brother Fred at Passchendaele within weeks of his own incapacitating injury – drowned, reportedly, in a shell crater filled with glutinous mud and the rotting corpses of men and horses.

Beyond the gruesome details there was one startling discovery, something that changed in Tim's eyes the whole complexion of this narrative. Most of what he'd found in the military records over the previous few days, moving though it was, did little more than amplify the simple facts already gleaned by his mother from ancestry.com: one of the enlisted brothers dead, the other permanently injured – an all too common family tale of those distressing times. But when he came across a particular piece of additional information he felt as if a surge of electricity had struck him.

The prelude to this revelation had itself been surprising enough. Enclosed with David Starkey's service record was an old blurred photograph. On the verso, someone had scrawled 'Private

Starkey and his rescuer.' The image showed two men outside what seemed to be a makeshift medical shelter. One of them had his eyes closed, and swollen blisters were visible on his neck and beside his mouth. He was sagging against the other man, whose arm supported him – and whose skin was plainly black.

Tim stared at the creased and yellowed photo, willing it to tell him more. A black man in the King's uniform? Surely that must have been extremely rare back then? But no – the archives told him otherwise, and he felt a pang of chagrin at this gap in his knowledge: an apprentice historian researching blacks in Victorian Britain, yet he'd been ignorant of what some of them had experienced in the cataclysm that came not long after the turn of the century. A few hours of online reading sufficed for a conspectus of recent research on black soldiers in the British army during the Great War. Thousands of them, he learnt, served in the West Indies Regiment, comprising several battalions of Caribbean volunteers. Recruits from Nigeria, Sierra Leone and other colonies defended the borders of African countries adjacent to German territory. Black soldiers in British units were not numerous but they included some remarkable individuals, the most illustrious being Walter Tull, whose racial origin and orphanage background hadn't prevented him from shaping a successful pre-war career as a professional footballer. Enlisting early, he rose through the ranks and eventually became a commissioned officer (against the rules, which restricted officer status to men of 'pure European descent') and was recommended for the Military Cross before being killed in action. Reading that Tull had fought in the Third Battle of Ypres, Tim momentarily surmised he was probably the man who gave succour to the stricken David Starkey. But no, it wasn't so: photographs of Tull pictured someone who clearly didn't resemble, except in skin colour, that anonymous soldier with his comradely arm around Starkey's shoulders.

Then who was the rescuer? Finding the answer to that question proved straightforward when, having taken the belated step of using Starkey's regiment name as a search engine keyword, Tim came across references to a recent historical study called *The 2nd Devons War Diary: The 2nd Battalion Devonshire Regiment and its Lost Men 1914-1919*. Although its focus, according to the online summary, was on soldiers from the 2nd Devons who died during that war, it might also mention some who were grievously wounded, perhaps including Starkey. Tim hurried into the National Archives bookshop next door, picked up a copy of the publication and thumbed impatiently through the list of names in its final pages. Yes! David Starkey was in the index…and there, as Tim turned to the cited page, was a reproduction of the very same photograph he'd seen among the service record papers. Wounded white man leaning on steadfast black man.

But the thing that shocked Tim to the core in the accompanying passage of text was its account of what happened to the Good Samaritan not long after this incident. The man who, disregarding his own safety, had half-carried Tim's drooping ancestor away from the gas-fouled battlefield and brought him to a casualty station for emergency treatment was executed a couple of months later 'for abetting a deserter.'

There on the page were stark excerpts from the court-martial record. Asked to explain why, having previously shown courage under fire by going to the aid of an injured man, he had now committed such a dishonourable transgression as actively helping a coward to escape from battlefront duties, this black soldier had stood his ground, giving a cool rejoinder that sealed his fate. It was his firm belief, he said, that both of his actions had the same justification. Those two unfortunate men whom he had assisted, the first by leading him to a medical shelter and the second by facilitating his desperate abandonment of his post, were alike in having been rendered incapable of continuing to fight. One was physically damaged, the other mentally. War had inflicted anguish on both, and both deserved to be removed from harm's way. If treating them humanely was to be deemed a crime, he took personal responsibility for the consequence of his actions. One of the presiding officers then put it to him that if other men were to adopt his stubborn attitude, with its failure to acknowledge the extreme seriousness of abetting desertion, the morale of the troops would be swiftly sabotaged and the war lost. Didn't that weigh heavily on his conscience?

In the arraigned man's further response there was not a whit of self-protectiveness. His conscience was clear, he told the court. In fact, in deciding to help the deserter to escape he had been mindful of the example of a resolute conscientious objector named Gavin Staines, a quiet fellow he'd come across briefly the previous year, when several men who opposed the war were hauled illegally to the Normandy battlefront and treated with shameful cruelty by military authorities. Staines, he said, had shown admirable courage during his court-martial at Henriville.

After that intransigent declaration, the black man was found guilty and summarily condemned to death by firing squad. There was no delay in carrying out the sentence on Private Jem Dunn.

Dunn! The uncannily familiar surname seized Tim's attention. Dunn. A black man, enlisted in a regiment from Devon. Could there be a link to the hapless Joshua?

As the National Archives provided ready microfilm access to census books, it didn't take Tim long to find a record for 1901 of a Dunn family living in Tavistock. It listed one child: a son, Jeremiah (Jem would be his nick-name), born in 1894 to 28-year-old Martha Dunn. The father's name was Joshua: aged 55, place of birth Liverpool, occupation assistant butcher. That must be him!

TWENTY-SIX

D ESPITE OBVIOUS DIFFERENCES, TIM SAW THE LABORIOUS oakum-picking work once allotted to prisoners as an emblem of the painstaking research activity he'd recently undertaken himself. His tasks were self-imposed, of course, and physically comfortable, and satisfyingly productive; but what they had in common with the daily chore of gaol inmates in Victorian times was the slow process of teasing out separate strands from the thick of a matted tangle. For weeks he'd been plucking at the sticky filaments of family memory, tracing their twisted braids and prising them carefully apart.

Since coming to England he had followed these fibrous lines of enquiry as one coiled intricately into another and then another, with surprises at every turn. A casual remark in discussion after his conference paper on Fanque's circus had led him to episodes in the story of Joshua Dunn, providing incidental glimpses of Dartmoor prison life in the late nineteenth century. With a separate purpose he had gone looking on his mother's behalf for genealogical information, thinking it would probably be a bootless errand, only to discover that the prison officer targeted in Dunn's vengeful scheme, Duke Starkey, was among his own forebears, and then, in a further intertwining, that Starkey's grandson – Tim's great-great-grandfather – had crossed paths at a crucial moment with Dunn's son.

This convergent set of findings took him far beyond the questions he'd initially posed. Searching for one elusive individual, he'd uncovered a bunch of missing persons, their lives unpredictably plaited together in ways that brought his personal bloodline narrative into view. Astonished at his luck, exhilarated by such a rich reward for the doggedness of his investigations, he saw this research trip as immeasurably more successful than he could ever have imagined.

Yet there remained another thread, a loose end that he was now keen to trace. Jem Dunn, the young black soldier who saved two comrades only to be judicially robbed of his own life, had by his own account drawn defiant courage from his passing encounter in France with a conscientious objector called Gavin Staines. The dangling detail piqued Tim's curiosity. Who was this Staines, this staunch pacifist whose example had such unconsciously significant consequences, including the battlefield rescue of Tim's own ancestor?

Three days before Tim's scheduled Qantas flight home, he began in a flurry of detective work to uncover miscellaneous facts about Gavin Staines and sketch his movements during the war years. That reference to Henriville in Private Dunn's court-martial summary was a useful starting-point, and from there he went to the files of the No-Conscription Fellowship kept by the Peace Pledge Union in their Kentish Town repository. In the Imperial War Museum he listened to oral interviews with a handful of elderly surviving COs, recorded in the 1970s on reel-to-reel tapes. He hastily scanned a few pacifist memoirs, too, and several other relevant publications. These different sources yielded details about a number of things that Staines would have experienced in 1916, first while imprisoned in the grim Harwich Redoubt, then after being shipped to France to undergo a barbarous 'field punishment,' the Henriville court-martial and its menacingly theatrical parade-ground sequel, incarceration in a crowded stinking pit near Boulogne – and later, through his solitary confinement in Pentonville prison under a rule of total silence, and his succumbing to a serious illness while held there. Subsequently there had been a long period of partial convalescence and then in mid-1917 came his transfer to the Princetown Work Centre, Dartmoor, where he was kept until three months after the war was over.

That outline soon became clear, though Staines himself remained a shadowy figure flitting across the various scenes and situations. Even a group photograph showing him with other members of a Dartmoor hard-labour gang beside a high stone wall didn't reveal much apart from their names on the back: he was the tallest among them, and looked thinner than the rest; most of them were grinning under their cloth caps but his expression was guarded and his head bare; the image conveyed nothing else. What kind of man was he? What was his line of work before he became a prisoner of conscience? The tribunal that dismissed his case for exemption from military service would have noted his occupation – but most tribunal records had been destroyed long since. What had shaped his political convictions? And what about his family background: did parents or siblings support his stand? In the prisons at Harwich, Pentonville, Princetown, what did his fellow conchies think of him? What was it about his demeanour that exerted such a profound influ-ence on a person like Jem Dunn, who would probably have had only the briefest casual contact with him? His character seemed opaque, enigmatic, beyond the reach of a historian's delving.

Yet there was still something Tim hoped to find out before the time until departure ticked away: what had Staines done after his eventual release from Dartmoor? Did the postwar world treat him more gently? Did he return to whatever work he had done before the war?

With a mounting sense of urgency Tim went back over some of the documentary sources he'd looked at previously and checked a few additional repositories as well, including a collection of antiwar pamphlets in the University of London's Senate House archives and assorted papers from Quaker conchies in the Library of the Society of Friends opposite Euston Station. All this fossicking yielded nothing apart from a brief inconclusive passing reference in files of the Peace Pledge Union, which seemed to imply that for at least a few months in 1919 Staines had been employed, probably part-time, by the Society of Friends.

Then at the last moment, to Tim's amazement, he happened upon something that Staines himself had written: an article in a Quaker periodical called *The Ploughshare*. Appearing in October 1919, bearing the title 'War and Peace: Shakespearean Voices,' it turned out to be a strange piece in its blend of different genres – part literary essay and part pacifist testimony, but also with a hint of something more obliquely personal.

The article began by remarking that during the recent war some British militarists had tried to conscript the nation's greatest poet-dramatist as an ally in their zealous pursuit of bloody conflict on foreign soil. It continued in these trenchant terms:

Holding up *Henry V* as their favourite exemplary text, they take the patriotic belligerence of King Harry's battle-eve speeches to his men in France as a direct, definitive expression of the playwright's own views. But surely it is not. When I read the words given to this royal character at the beginning of Act 3, urging on his men at the siege of Harfleur, I am conscious of three factors that moderate the aggressive tone. First, Shakespeare provides within that speech a discreet counterbalance to the language of martial stridency: even the warrior king himself concedes that 'In peace there's nothing so becomes a man / As modest stillness and humility.' Second, this is merely a single speech by a single character in a single play; it should be placed alongside contrasting depictions of warfare elsewhere in Shakespeare's work – in *Troilus*, in *Coriolanus* and other plays where the dreadful futility of violent actions is plainly on display. Third, I see Harry's rabid rabble-rousing speech in that particular scene through the lens of my own wretched personal experience at the same place, Harfleur, half a millennium after the legendary battle: I was dragged there in chains by army bullies and subjected to vile treatment merely because I refused to contribute to the pointless slaughter of my fellow men.

Staines went on in this vein, not only contemptuous towards military and political leaders but also hinting at bitterness towards some whom he had once regarded as intellectually eminent men of letters.

Passionate advocacy of military force even invaded our universities, corrupting the attitudes of some who were once thought wise. It was, for example, disgraceful that the formerly respected Shakespearean critic A.C. Bradley took it into his head to contribute a preface to that war-mongering book by J.A. Cramb, *Germany and England*.

Reading passages such as that, almost shrill in the way they denounced certain academic scholars, Tim thought he could discern a sense of personal grievance, even betrayal, behind the words.

Then, as if to confirm this self-referential implication, the essay took an odd turn inwards. It resumed the argument that a wide range of Shakespearean characters, through their dialogue on diverse aspects of peace and war, give collective voice to the variety of conflicting thoughts and feelings 'astir within the soul of any sensitive person.' Staines proceeded to quote a line from *Richard III* in which 'the tormented king cries out, "My conscience hath a thousand several tongues" – and doubtless many among us have heard that internal clamour.' He continued:

> Although we can hardly claim Shakespeare as a fellow pacifist, his plays (and poems too, with their recurrent motif of 'wasteful war') do show that he could express eloquently what anyone sickened by the violence of warfare has felt. Moreover, he well knew what self-wounding creatures we are, though not everyone recognises the damage inflicted by inner strife. To some, conscience is simply the cautionary prompter of ethical principles, rehearsing that which is right and spurning that which is wrong. Others, however, less firm in their sense of rectitude, are mindful that the knowledge of good and evil came to humanity after the eating of forbidden fruit. At its most acute, conscience may take the form of a remorseful awareness of one's own transgression and the pain to which it can lead.

Tim rubbed at the birthmark on his forehead as he tried to identify what exactly could be detected between the lines of Staines's prose. Something fretful, even troubled by guilt? Impossible to tell. The man's character was as elusive as ever.

What had become of him? He seemed to have disappeared from the historical record by 1920. Census data for 1921 might contain relevant details but wouldn't be accessible for several years yet.

Tim called to mind the photograph he'd seen, showing Staines and other members of his Dartmoor work gang beside a long high wall. Now that the image had come back to him he was pretty sure he knew this wall with its unusual dimensions. He remembered his own last day in that region, walking around the field and tracks just to the north of Princetown under a surly sky and seeing the remains of a stone wall enclosing a large rectangular space. On returning to the prison museum he'd asked a staff member what the wall was and whether it once protected or even contained something inside it. He was told it had always been empty. Parts of it, said the museum officer, were dismantled a few years ago so that the stone could be used elsewhere. Conscientious objectors constructed it during the First World War, and the area it surrounded was still known locally as Conchies' Field. Regarding its purpose, there had been disagreement about that among Princetown folk. Some old-timers reckoned it just served as a solid boundary wall around one of the prison farm fields. No, said others; it looked too big, even in its dilapidated state, to have been no more than that. In their opinion it was intended to be a pointless task, a futile form of hard labour to keep the conchies busy, and only later did it get used as an enclosure for sheep.

'There's also a road that the conchies built,' the museum man added. 'It's paved with chips of granite. Begins a little east of Princetown, where the Devonport Leat passes near Bullpark, just beyond Tor Royal. The road goes across the moor as if heading towards Swincombe Bridge, but then stops in the middle of nowhere. Conchies' Road, people call it.'

What meaning do those stony structures have now for a historian, Tim asked himself as he finished packing his bags ready for the journey to Heathrow and on homewards. Are they just sad residual symbols of pointless effort, or more than that? After

all, he thought, those men did build things that have lasted –
and their labour, while relatively modest in scale, was hardly
more futile than that of the construction gangs who worked on
Egypt's pyramids or the Great Wall of China. Doesn't the space
enclosed by Conchies' Field signify *something*, if only because
of the human cost of that arduous shaping process? As for
Conchies' Road, although it doesn't lead to any physical destination, it's still a kind of memorial, isn't it? Not a memorial to war,
but to the stand taken by men opposed to war. These things,
embodying a melancholy legacy, may well endure for centuries
yet, perhaps as long as other structures built from moorland
stone – the kistvaens and tram tracks and the prison itself.

But did they mean anything positive to the men who built
them? Did the toil of manhandling the unyielding granite fortify
their belief in the rightness of the stand they had taken? Or did
those labours gradually weaken and diminish them, perhaps to
the point where they began to see conscience itself as no more
than a sturdy wall surrounding a vacancy, or a route that was
petering out into nothingness?

All such musings evaporated when he checked his email and
read Valerie's astounding message.

TWENTY-SEVEN

ON HER WAY BACK THROUGH THE CAMPUS TOWARDS ST Cat's after several fruitless hours in the library, Valerie walked beneath the dark extravagant ramifications of the giant Moreton Bay fig tree, on around the rear end of Winthrop Hall, where a few weeks ago she'd overheard that bit of argument involving Kemal, and then alongside the large Reflection Pond. The lambent light of late afternoon flickered lazily on the surface of the water, but as she paused to peer into it she could see it was turbid with duck droppings and slimy strands of algae.

Going up up the broad stone steps that separated the pond and adjacent lawns from the walkway in front of the administration building, she almost bumped into someone hurrying down in her direction. Startled, she squinted up at him, hand raised against the westering sun. He was tall, his face hard to read, with an expression that may have been half-quizzical, half-flinching.

'Whoa! Nearly collided with you, Valerie.'

A moment's hesitation before she recognised him. Tim's friend. 'Oh, sorry, Peter. Daydreaming.'

They stopped for a moment to chat, and she moved to a higher step so that the sun wouldn't be in her eyes and Pete wouldn't be towering over her.

'Tim been in contact with you recently?' he asked. 'I got an email from him two or three weeks ago, after his London conference. Said he was about to head for Dartmoor, of all places, following some line of research, but I haven't heard anything since. Lost forever on the misty moors, probably.'

Yes, she'd exchanged a few messages with Tim, she said, and yes – he'd been making the most of his time, busily pursuing his research enquiries, but was due to return to Perth very soon. Definitely not lost. He'd found out lots of things over there, including things about himself.

There was a pause. 'By the way,' said Peter, moistening his lips with his tongue-tip, 'have police been talking to you about the death of that Turkish guy? Tim told me you were friendly with him.'

She replied briefly, distracted by something she had just noticed: Peter was scratching his earlobe in a fidgety way. This odd mannerism seemed vaguely familiar, though for the moment she couldn't think why.

Back in her college room that evening, it suddenly came to her: she had seen that nervy repetitive little movement before, and she now thought she knew where. The implications were alarming but couldn't be ignored. Immediately she sent an email. It should reach Tim just before he leaves London, she thought.

There's something troubling me. I've remembered a detail that might shed light on Kemal's death. It's about the third man in that little scene I witnessed outside the back of the under-croft of Winthrop Hall. I told you that just a day or so before Kemal died there was a sort of barney going on between Kemal and Omar, and someone else was there with them, maybe also involved in the argument. This third guy had his back to me and I didn't get a look at him, and anyway you know me – hopeless at recognising individuals. But he was tallish and kept scratching his ear lobe in a jittery sort of motion, nervy and repetitive.

This afternoon I was talking with your flatmate Peter and noticed that same distinctive mannerism. I now believe he was the person I saw with Kemal and Omar. Peter asked me, a bit anxiously, whether police have been talking to me about 'that Turkish guy'. My impression was that he knows what happened, and may even have been the person responsible.

From what you've told me about his inclinations, and particularly about his attitude during that rally a few months ago, isn't it likely he was lusting after Omar? And I'm fairly sure sexual practices were what the heated exchange I overheard was really about. Kemal may have been expressing some sort of disapproval. He could be quite blunt at times, you know. So perhaps Peter blamed Kemal for trying to turn Omar away from him?

OK, that's getting very hypothetical, but still I now think I ought to get in contact with police and tell them about the incident, even though it may be trivial and irrelevant. I'll need to give the detectives Peter's name, but with the rider that I can't be 100 percent certain it was him.

Tim, about to leave for the airport, sent a hasty answer. He was shocked by her message, he said. Pete could be pretty crazy but he wouldn't have any part in a violent crime, no way. Hadn't Valerie been reading too many novels? If she felt determined to report what she imagined she'd seen and heard, that was up to her. But Tim was going to text Pete immediately to let him know police would soon come knocking on his door. Only fair he should be able to prepare for being interviewed, and anyhow Tim thought Pete kept a little drug stash somewhere in their flat and would need time to dispose of it.

Then Tim sent a tip-off to his flatmate, adding he was confident that Pete would have no trouble convincing the police to cross him off their 'persons of interest' list, but if there was anything he wanted to talk about privately he could count on a sympathetic ear when Tim got back to Perth the next day.

Things moved too suddenly for that. Pete's abrupt reply reached Tim as he was waiting to board his plane.

> Appreciate yr words of support but now that everything's closing in on me I've decided on a pre-emptive move. Sorry, mate. See Facebook. Bye!

Quickly Tim checked Pete's Facebook page. Under the heading 'Last Post' there was a long statement that left Tim feeling ill.

> Just been told police want to question me about death of Kemal Kaleli. Fact is, they're on the right track. I didn't mean to kill him, swung a punch that knocked the guy backwards and his head struck a concrete verge. I'd challenged him over what he said the day before when I was talking with my friend Omar and Kemal happened to be standing nearby. Omar called out to him something about Kemal's friendship with a kafir woman. Kemal retorted that attraction is natural between a man and a woman but 'a man who ensnares other men's love is an abomination.' I knew this was directed at me. I've never made a secret of being gay and I'd been trying to cultivate Omar, who seemed receptive to my overtures. But he must have been stung by K's comment because later that day when I tried to hit on him he turned me down flat. That's why I got really steamed up when I came across K in

the carpark the next evening. I had some meth in my system, and I've got quite a temper anyway. I lashed out and knocked him down.

No point in trying to express how sorry I am. Nothing can undo what I did. I've been lying low, hoping the whole thing would settle down but it seems I've been rumbled. I don't have the stomach for an arraignment and all the shaming that would go with it. For years it's been my goal to become a lawyer, but getting convicted for such a violent offence, plus my use of ice being uncovered too, rules out any possibility of that. Hopeless situation. So I've decided to act as my own judge and executioner. My body will be in my flat.

Tim's boarding call was on the PA system, but he sent a hasty text to his father, blurting out the news and imploring him to go at once to the flat. If Pete had carried out his intention, the police and his family would need to know urgently.

The flight seemed interminable. When his plane at last touched down in Perth and Tim switched on his phone, there was a burst of beeping messages from Valerie, his father, several friends. All carried the same grim confirmation. One of them mentioned the local newspaper, so while waiting for his baggage to arrive on the carousel he went to the kiosk and bought that day's *West*. It was there – a short item on page three.

The mystery surrounding the death five weeks ago of Turkish student Kemal Kaleli seems to have been tragically dispelled. Peter Fleming, a postgraduate Law student at UWA, has posted a full confession on his Facebook account, which led to the discovery of his body in his shared Claremont apartment late yesterday. His flatmate is believed to be overseas. Police say there appear to be no suspicious circumstances.

Tim pulled his bag off the carousel and found a place to sit down. Overwhelmed by a flux of feelings, he needed to calm down before he could face the taxi journey to Claremont, let alone the difficult conversations that lay ahead. His parents had told him they couldn't meet him at the airport because their car had a faulty alternator and was in for repairs. That was a relief. It gave him a bit more time to himself, time to mull things over in silence.

So many different things were swirling in his head, or heart, or gut. It might help to be analytical. What exactly were they? Grief, obviously, but mingled with guilt at the fact that his own well-meant message had precipitated Pete's suicide. There was a further rush of self-blame for not having been a more supportive friend to Pete in the past. And an equally irrational resentment towards Valerie because she had intuited the truth and brought it to light. Mixed up with those things were other thoughts, other feelings: his heavy sense of duty to speak to Pete's parents despite being unable to imagine what words he could use, and his discomfort, too, at needing to discuss self-ishly practical things with his own parents such as whether he could move back home for a while rather than stay in the flat where Pete had killed himself…

Such a tumult of emotions, all clamouring for attention, as if voiced by a thousand several tongues. He thought of that essay by Gavin Staines in the Quaker magazine, seeming to express a wounded conscience.

TWENTY-EIGHT

Valerie checked her watch again. Shouldn't have been so typically prepunctual; might have guessed he'd be running late. For her, the Tiamo café was only a five-minute stroll up Hampden Road from the highway corner just along from St Cat's, but she'd wanted to be sure of getting there before Tim, leaving time to compose herself for this first rendezvous since his return to Perth. Although they'd agreed, when exchanging text messages for the dinner arrangement, not to talk about Pete or Kemal this evening – too painful – there could still be some tension in the air.

Nearly ten past six. Ah – there he was now, waving from the doorway, grinning sheepishly, moving towards her. A shy hug, a boyish blush.

'Sorry I'm late, Valerie. Weary brain, still on Greenwich time.' He rubbed at the discoloured patch on his forehead, as if to remove any residual jet lag.

Hungrily she picked up the menu. 'Let's get our dinner decisions out of the way, then we can talk.'

After ordering their pasta dishes they picked their way carefully through conversational preliminaries until he had a stubby in his hand. Why did guys insist on swigging straight from their beer bottle at a meal table? What would be unmanly about using a glass?

'So…' she said with an enquiring look, and paused to sip her water. An obvious question should start to relax him. 'Your big trip was well worth the effort?'

'Oh, definitely. Surpassed expectations.' He wiped his mouth with the back of his hand. 'I mean, it's certainly given my research project a boost, but the time in England was hugely important in personal ways too. Given me a new way of looking at the world.'

'How so?'

'Maybe I'll tell you about some of that later on,' Tim said. 'But it's partly just that I've just become more conscious of the value of friends. I know we don't want to discuss Pete tonight. But leaving aside what the loss of him makes me feel…' – he cleared his throat, drank quickly from the stubby – 'there's the simple fact that while I've been away I've really missed you, Valerie.'

Trying not to frown, she inspected her glass of water and took a dilatory sip. He'd brought up the subject sooner than she'd anticipated. Not that companionable sentiment was a problem in itself, but she sensed he was moving towards a bid for something more intimate. Before he went overseas she'd been aware of his growing attraction towards her, and had studiously avoided the tacit appeal he was making. And then came that flare of argument over the essay-writing help she'd given to Kemal. While blaming Tim for starting it, she knew she'd inflamed the row as a way of keeping amorous developments at bay. She liked his company, yes, and was glad he was back in Perth, but had there ever been in her own mind any prospect of something physical with him? If so it had faded.

Now, as he leant forward in that earnest way of his, waiting for her to respond, she made an effort to reframe what he was surely implying.

'Well, all right, let's make a point of meeting for a friendly chat over coffee now and then,' she said, glancing up in time to catch the flicker of hurt in his eyes.

'That sounds rather tepid,' he said. 'Couldn't we have a closer connection that that? Look, I've been thinking. I'll need to rent a different apartment. Can't stay on in the pad where Pete… you know. And I'm hoping…I'd be really glad if you and I could share a place. Live together. I mean, as a couple.'

Looking down, she shook her head slowly. 'It just wouldn't work, Tim.'

'Why not? Before I went away we'd built a pretty strong rapport. OK, I got a bit tetchy about the kind of help you were giving to Kemal, but that was just a hiccup. I still feel a lot of affection towards you, and I thought it was a reciprocal thing. Have I been deluding myself?' '

'No, you're not delusional, Tim.' She offered a placatory smile. 'We do have a good friendship, and I'd like it to continue. Getting to know you this year, having some great conversations, it's been one of the positive things about coming to Perth. It's just that I'm not ready for anything deeper. That's not a comment about you. It's about me.'

'Meaning what?'

'I don't want to see myself as defined by having a woman's body. I've begun to think – this is getting embarrassingly confessional now! – to think I'm probably not, as the saying goes, "highly sexed." Compared with what seems to be common for other people. A friend at St Cat's told me she's preoccupied with sexual images, like being fondled by strangers, men and women. That's so not me!'

He finished his bottle in one gulp. 'So where does that leave me? Maybe just a kind of brother? That's what you're saying?'

She tried not to be irked by an edge of bitterness in his voice. 'As I said, Tim, it's not any deficiency in you. It's because of what I'm starting to recognise about what I need and don't need. I haven't actually got any siblings, remember? And I suppose that's been a missing role in my peculiar life. So you might see a sort of compliment in the fact that – from my point of view – you do fill a brotherly gap.'

He looked rueful, but she continued, hoping to repair the incipient breach. 'You know, Tim, I reckon that being an only child explains quite a few things about me. My stubborn independence. An unsociable tendency to turn inwards. But I wonder, too, whether there might be some general link between only-child status and a slower development of sexual identity. What do you think?'

Shrugging, he pushed his empty plate aside.

'Who knows?' she said, making an effort to lighten the tone, 'Maybe I'm going to be a late developer. Like a Greenland shark.'

'Eh? Like a what?'

'I read a magazine article about some amazingly elderly animals. Greenland sharks have the longest lifespan of any creature. More than four times the age of humans! So imagine a facts-of-life conversation between mother shark and her teenage daughter: "The bad news first, dear: you'll take 150 years to reach sexual maturity. The good news: you'll have a further 250 years after that to enjoy it."'

He did his best to laugh. Their coffee came and she changed the subject.

'What did you mean, saying your recent trip has changed how you look at the world?'

'Ah. Hard to explain. This research project of mine on blacks in Victorian England…I've come to recognise that I'd been treating the topic, unconsciously, as exotic. Disregarding the fact that if I really want to get into the history of race relations there's plenty right here on my doorstep, throwing a big shadow over the way we live now in Western Australia. Black experience as an object of scholarly curiosity – that was my attitude, to be frank. As if I could peer into otherness from what I assumed was a comfortable distance. But then to discover, quite suddenly, how Joshua Dunn's family intersected with past generations of my own family – well, it brought that supposedly "other" social world home to me. Home in a literal sense. The whole thing has become less academic in my mind now, more personal. And in a way, more political as well. You know?'

She nodded encouragingly.

'I used to imagine,' he went on, fiddling with his sugar spoon, 'that I was heading for a university career. But on the flight back here I had time to turn over a lot of things in my mind. Although I'm not sure now what I'd like to do once I've finished my doctoral thesis, not exactly, I do know I won't be continuing along the scholarly path. I don't want to see myself as cultivating the detachment of a professional historian. A sceptical stance has been my default position, and it's become too much of a habit.'

'Keeping emotion at arm's length, you mean?'

'That's it. On the plane I was looking through my notes about things I've read recently, and it struck me that a harsh comment I made on a certain Victorian writer, a parson who said something priggish about criminals, could apply to me as well. I'd remarked in my haughty way that he must have had an empathy bypass. Classic case of the pot calling the kettle black. I've often tended to stand back in the name of rational objectivity and make judgments about people at a remove from what they experience, rather than put myself in their shoes. Getting emotionally involved in the unfolding story of Joshua Dunn, even though many factual details remain out of my reach, has made a big difference to the way I see things. I don't think I have it in me to become politically active in any direct way, but if I can find some other means of working towards better cultural understanding, social justice…That sounds too abstract. Anyhow, some means of engaging with what ordinary people feel…'

As his voice trailed off, her smile came spontaneously. 'Much the same for me, actually,' she said. 'Not a political path, or anything in a public space. Incurable introvert, moi. But like you, I've been coming to the conclusion that the academic study of history just isn't congenial. In fact, I've made so little progress with my research that I think I'll probably withdraw from candidature. Partly because I feel I'm not personally cut out to be a scholarly apprentice, and partly because the idea of pursuing that role doesn't seem right anyway. Being supported by a taxpayer-funded scholarship to pursue a specialised research project culminating in a learned thesis that only a handful of people will ever read – hard to justify when I'm no longer convinced about the value of pure history.'

'That sounds like a more fundamental disenchantment than what I feel.'

'Perhaps it is. Of course I may only be rationalising my inability to shape an original argument on the topic I chose – which isn't your case: you're well along the way to completing a substantial thesis, and good on you. But whether this is a just an excuse for my failings or not, I've started to think that pure historical investigation is inherently limited.'

'Limited?'

'I mean, too often the strict discipline of adhering diligently to evidence produces a meagre result, don't you think? Sometimes inconclusive, sometimes inconsequential. In the last month or two I've found it more and more difficult to keep my thinking within a framework of what can be verified by laborious methodical investigation. I'm still really interested in how people have commemorated World War 1, but for an Australian angle on wartime events and experiences I'd rather pick up a work of fiction than a historian's sober monograph.'

'You've always been drawn more to creative writing than to archives, haven't you? A novelist manqué, perhaps?'

'Very perceptive, Tim. As a matter of fact, while you were away I wrote a short story based on what happened to my grandfather but fictionalising a few details. I've entered it in a competition. Regardless of the outcome, I've got more satisfaction from working on that little story than from any academic research. So I'm now inclined to drop my PhD enrolment and turn my hand instead to journalistic articles on historical subjects for popular consumption, or better still, if I'm up to the task, writing historical fiction. Especially about people who lurk on the shadowy fringes of the factual record and then disappear from it. For instance I'd like to imagine the inner lives of some of those blokes who are merely names listed on war memorials. Tell their secret stories, inventing motives and circumstances and complications.'

'Not only soldiers' tales, I hope,' said Tim. 'What about those who refused to fight? Heroic in a different way, I'd say. The nameless conscientious objectors honoured in that photo I emailed to you from London, showing the memorial stone in Tavistock Square – they deserve a novelist's attention too.'

'Fair enough. Plenty of narrative potential in what some of them experienced, I guess. Not Australian stories, though, because there was no conscription here. Not until half a century later. Vietnam.'

'But you've been thinking about British forms of commemoration back then as well as Australian. What the conchies went through, and how the Brits have remembered them, or forgotten them – isn't that worth exploring? In fiction you'd have scope to portray the nuances of conscience.'

'Maybe. I'd have to do a lot of delving into the background of it all. I haven't had your first-hand contact with Dartmoor and all of that.'

'But research wouldn't feel like a chore if it was in the service of fiction. You'd enjoy it.'

'Nice idea. Nothing would come of it, though, unless I started to imagine distinctive characters and their voices.'

'Well, I could probably help with details that might bring some of those people back to life. Point you towards sources I uncovered. I'd like to do that.'

Seeing that he'd aroused her interest, he went on with more animation than he'd shown since their conversation began. 'Here's a specific possibility for you to think about. Right towards the end of my stay in England I found a few tantalising snippets of information about a conscientious objector called Gavin Staines. Badly treated by military authorities, and then shunted off to Dartmoor. He'd crossed paths briefly with the soldier son of that black prisoner I told you about, Josh Dunn, and their passing encounter had fateful consequences for the young soldier. I could tell you more about that, but here's the gist of it: the principled stand this guy Staines took against the war did produce ripples of influence, though he probably wasn't ever aware of them. Anyway, I read an article that Staines wrote just after the war, a highly literary piece, and it seemed to hint at a mind under strain. So what happened to him next? I couldn't get an answer. He seems to have vanished suddenly from recorded history. Elusive as a will o the wisp flickering in the darkness over those bogs and mires of Dartmoor. The mysterious Gavin Staines is a perfect example of the countless untold stories hidden in the past and waiting to be imagined. There's a creative challenge for you, Valerie.'

'It does sound enticing, I admit. But *you* should be the one to tell his story, Tim! You've already immersed yourself in so much of it. You've got a really strong sense of place, too, not only physical features but the feelings they generate as well. That came through powerfully in your emails from Dartmoor.

And what about the fascinating Josh Dunn? You were saying you've become more empathetic through imagining what his life was like. You're perfectly equipped to write a historical novel about someone like him! Wouldn't that be an ideal answer to the question you were chewing over – how to find a way of engaging more closely with what ordinary people feel?'

'I don't have your literary skills. You read a lot of fiction, and you've started to write your own stories. You certainly have a way with words.'

She laughed. 'You can manage a nice turn of phrase yourself. Perhaps what's needed is someone who could combine your knowledge and attributes with mine.'

His face lit up. 'Better still,' he said, 'you and I could have a go at writing this kind of novel together. Seriously, I mean it! We'd bring different things to the task, complementary things. It's commonplace for non-fiction books to be co-authored. Why not historical fiction? Doesn't that ever happen?'

'Occasionally. I can think of a pair of mid-20th-century Australian writers who wrote successful novels jointly under a pseudonym that blended their names – M. Barnard Eldershaw. But do *you* really think we could collaborate in that way?'

'Worth a try. We might even enjoy it. A different sort of partnership from what I had in mind, but maybe a satisfying one.'

They smiled at each other with renewed warmth.

London

1919–1920

TWENTY-NINE

I COULDN'T HAVE KNOWN THIS WOULD HAPPEN, GAVIN STAINES thought afterwards. Couldn't have prevented it anyway. And the calamitous consequences are no more than I deserved.

Back in June 1918 most of the men held in the Princetown Work Centre had seethed with outrage when Parliament enacted a law to disenfranchise all conscientious objectors for five years beyond the war's end. Gavin Staines was inclined to shrug. Unjust legislation, yes, and spiteful and petty, but not a surprise. To be deprived like this of one's electoral rights, debarred from polling booths, was in keeping with officialdom's punitive attitude throughout the war towards those who refused to fight. It didn't matter much, he thought. Voting could wait; there would be other ways of participating in political action once peacetime arrived. He might even turn to journalism, using his skills as a writer to contribute articles to left-leaning publications. Anyway there was surely a good prospect of some form of teaching, perhaps through the Workers' Educational Association or university extension lecturing.

That confidence, he now recognised with a year's hindsight, had been naïve. The expected opportunities didn't materialise, and as 1919 moved into its drab autumn phase he was increasingly anxious about making ends meet. Repeatedly, sometimes rudely, he had been rejected for teaching positions, including private tutoring. At interviews, one of the first regular questions was about wartime service, and usually his candid answer brought things to a swift cold conclusion. The antiquarian bookshop where he had once been an assistant gave him short shrift. He applied unsuccessfully for many jobs around the city, gradually lowering his sights when it became clear that returned soldiers were always being given priority. Except for a few temporary spells of lowly clerical work, almost any kind of employment seemed to be closed to him at every turn.

Then a happy stroke of luck brought him an outlet for occasional publication and soon afterwards allayed temporarily his worries about finding paid work. It came about because he chanced to attend a public meeting in the first week of November at Caxton Hall, Westminster, held under the auspices of the Quaker-led Fight the Famine Council. A pamphlet handed to him in the street provided information about the newly formed FFC with its Save the Children Fund subcommittee, and drew him along to this Caxton Hall discussion. The meeting's clear purpose was to consider and publicise a commissioned report by an eminent international group of economists – Professor Lujo Brentano, Maynard Keynes, Sir George Paish and several others – on the devastating social and economic effects of the blockade that Britain was continuing to impose mercilessly on Germany and its allies. Hundreds of thousands of families, especially their milk-deprived babies, were suffering and starving. Countless numbers had already died. Many more were displaced, shuffling along the bleak byways of Europe as emaciated refugees.

Moving out of the crowded hall at this meeting's close, he felt a tap on his shoulder and turned to see a face that looked familiar, though he couldn't put a name to it. A smiling fellow, slim, long-necked, bespectacled, about his own age, spoke to him.

'Gavin Staines, isn't it?'

He nodded, rummaging in his memory.

'Arnold Morecroft. We met briefly three years ago, in France. I was the...'

'Ah! The journalist who came to interview us when we were about to be court-martialled!'

'Exactly.'

'Astonishing that you wangled permission to do that. I suppose they thought you'd keep your reporting meek and mild, being a Quaker, eh? Anyhow it was a boon for us, the fact that your urgent bulletin so quickly caught the attention of politicians. May have saved our necks. So thank you, belatedly, Mr Morecroft.'

'Arnold, please. I still remember things you told me in Henriville. Your remarkably stoical attitude. You didn't say a lot, but every word was well chosen and I wasn't surprised to find you'd been a university teacher. Then I heard that after they sent you back from France you were in Pentonville, like my friend Stephen Hobhouse. And later in Dartmoor, with Douglas Lindsay, the artist.'

'A very decent man, Doug Lindsay. It seems you know my movements nearly as well as I do. The Quaker grapevine must have been efficient. And what about you? – I'd guess your uncompromising reportage didn't give you an easy time during the war.'

'My freedom didn't last long after I wrote that piece about the treatment of absolutists like you. I was imprisoned for nearly three years. Hard labour, and the usual unpleasantness. Wormwood Scrubbs first, Pentonville later – you'd been moved on from there by then.'

Outside on the street they continued to talk with a comfortable sense of rapport. After a while Morecroft asked about Staines's current situation, and frowned with concern on hearing he was unemployed. He took a notebook from his pocket, asked Staines for his address and wrote it down. Then from another pocket he produced a copy of a small magazine and presented it to him.

'Something for you to read,' he said. 'And to write for, I hope. It would be good to have an article from you. I'm one of the editors, you see. Expect a letter from me soon.'

They parted with an exchange of smiles. As he walked slowly towards his lodgings, Staines turned the pages of the journal he'd been given, *The Ploughshare*, a monthly published by the Socialist Quaker Society. He liked the look of it, with its inclusion of poetry and book reviews alongside reflective pieces by such notable writers as the philosopher Bertrand Russell on public health policy and the experimental novelist Dorothy Richardson on feminism and class.

That evening he began to make notes for a little essay of his own.

In trying his hand at casual journalism he knew it could not be a ready source of income. No payment would be forthcoming for anything he might place in pacifist publications such as this. All the same, it was reasonable to hope that if he managed to get into print with a few well-written pieces on topics that went beyond the narrowly political, these could eventually pave the way to paid work for one of the larger magazines or newspapers. So he felt a surge of relief when *The Ploughshare* accepted his article on voices of war and peace in Shakespeare's plays. He was pleased with the scope and style of it, with the manner in which he had brought together his literary training with his personal thinking on questions of conscience.

The essay, seemingly, was only part of an upturn in his fortunes. By the time it appeared in print, a fortnight into the new year, he had a regular job. That a note printed underneath the article would bring serious trouble did not cross his mind. It simply stated: 'The author was interned as a conscientious objector during the war, having previously lectured in English literature at Queen's College London. He now works in the bookshop of the Society of Friends.'

He owed this part-time position with the Friends' bookshop at Devonshire House in Bishopsgate to Arnold Morecroft, who spotted the opening and recommended him strongly to Norman Penney, the man in charge.

'You'll find Norman can be a bit eccentric,' said Morecroft with one of his quick grins. 'Fond of flamboyant clothes, an unusual penchant for a Quaker, but he's ethically scrupulous to the point of primness. He runs our library next door and edits the journal of our historical society, those are his quiet passions. A shy reclusive scholar, is Norman. He's looking for someone to handle the bookshop transactions and deal with the public. Not onerous work, and only three days a week, so you'd have time for writing. Payment is very modest, of course, but it would keep body and soul together.'

Body and soul together, yes: for the first time in years, Gavin Staines began to feel physically secure, and with that came the unfamiliar sensation of a kind of peacefulness soothing his spirits. The bookshop work, though unexciting, was agreeable; his wages were sufficient to cover rent and food; his health appeared to have improved; and he had the prospective satisfaction of getting a few essays published from time to time. Above all, there was the growing friendship with Arnold Morecroft, the first person he'd felt close to for a long time. Despite a pardonable tendency towards self-righteous postures, Arnold showed himself to be an amiable companion, warmly inviting his new friend into the Morecroft family home on several occasions for dinner and relaxed conversation.

Yet Gavin Staines's mood of calm wellbeing proved to be as fleeting as a snowflake. One bitterly cold afternoon in early February, Norman Penney appeared unexpectedly at the bookshop's rear door, a stern expression on his face. In an abrupt manner he asked Staines to close the shop and come at once to the library office. Puzzled, Staines followed him into the room. Penney moved to his seat behind the desk. A whiskered stranger, a well-dressed ruddy-faced man of late middle age, sat in an armchair, glaring as Staines entered. As there was nowhere for Staines to sit, he stood with his hands clasped behind him, as if they were bound tight.

'A complaint has been made about you, Mr Staines,' said Penney, looking extremely uncomfortable. 'A very serious complaint. A matter of…character.' He paused uncertainly. 'I think it best that you should hear about it directly from our visitor. This is Mr Remington.'

Remington! To Gavin Staines that name was like a sudden fierce blow to the head. He flinched.

'I will come straight to the point,' said Remington, his words sounding as if they were being dragged over gravel. 'For several years I have been unable to trace your whereabouts, but someone recently drew to my attention a note attached to a published article of yours – a note which simultaneously gave this as your place of work and confirmed that you used to teach at Queen's College before the war. My only daughter was one of your students there. You know the dreadful circumstances of her death. You also know that you caused it, having taken advantage of her youthful innocence. Seduced her. I discovered your role only some while after Lavinia's death, and after your departure from the college, when I went through a few of her belongings – papers, notebooks and such. There was an intimate diary in which she wrote about you at length. With sickening frankness.'

Taking out a large handkerchief, Remington wiped his face. Staines stood motionless, clenching hands and teeth. His head throbbed, and it was like the nauseous sensation he'd once felt as a child after a moth crawled into his ear, every flutter of its flimsy wings a thunderous drumroll that could not be silenced.

'I'm sure you won't dare to defend yourself, Staines,' he went on. 'I have told Mr Penney in the plainest terms that I expect him to share my view of the matter. In short, it is this: your disgustingly immoral conduct, which had such fatal consequences for my beautiful daughter, disqualifies you from any further employment here. If you were to continue with this organisation you would bring disgrace upon the Society of Friends. Indeed I would exert all my considerable influence to ensure that it did. I have nothing more to say except that if I find you have taken up paid work somewhere else I intend to hound you there as well.'

He stood, nodded curtly to Penney, and strode off.

Losing so suddenly the financial security of his job filled him with dismay, but other grievous feelings intensified his consternation. Ashamed at the public disgrace, guilt-stricken at the stark reminder of half-buried transgressions, he was also bereft of Arnold Morecroft's friendship. A letter arrived a few days after his dismissal.

Mr Staines

I have just heard the startling news about your permanent departure from the bookshop position and the reason for it. I must say that Mabel and I are deeply troubled at the revelation of your improper conduct at Queen's College, with its tragic consequences, and of your evasion of personal responsibility for it. We would no longer feel comfortable having you as a guest in our home. Harsh though this attitude may seem, I trust you will understand that safeguarding the moral environment of our children is a natural priority for us.

I regret having to sever our connection in this abrupt way. That you have much goodness in you I do not doubt, but it is evidently intermixed with darker qualities, which can only be repugnant to a devout Christian family such as ours. *Strait is the gate, and narrow is the way, which leadeth unto life, and few there be that find it.*

I shall remember you in my prayers.

With sincerest good wishes for your spiritual welfare,

I am, etc.

Arnold Morecroft

THIRTY

S THE WEEKS SLID BY LIKE SLUGGARDS AND HIS PALTRY
savings dwindled, Staines moved from one short-
term rental arrangement to another, each room
shabbier and chillier than the last. For most of the time after
leaving Dartmoor he had been inured to niggardly habits and
surreptitious scrimping, to genteel pretence amidst board-
ing-house frugality, to threadbare furnishings and transient
fellow-lodgers, to insipid teashop sandwiches as a substitute
for decent meals. Then the brief period of employment in the
Devonshire House bookshop brought some relief from those
penny-pinchings. But now, cast abruptly out of work, stupefied
by the upending of temporary stability and by the rapid ebbing
of hopes, he recognised how much more desperately depleted
his situation had become.

His latest refuge was a mere attic, cramped, dank and grubby,
in a hostel near Blackfriars Bridge. It provided no more than
the barest shelter against the worst of the winter squalls. Rain
fell incessantly, sometimes frozen into sleet, feeding a constant
leak in a corner of the ceiling. He seldom exchanged words with
others who were staying there. They went slinking past, shame-

faced, on the unlit stairs. Most of the time he stayed in his room, lying on the narrow lumpy bed with his coat around him, reading intermittently by dim candlelight from the one book he still owned, a well-thumbed volume of Shakespeare's *Complete Works*. There was no reason to venture out into the raw weather, but even indoors he could hardly escape the cold hiss of winds that came twisting at him through every crevice. His crackling bronchial cough kept him awake through long passages of the night. He was acutely conscious of being only a step away from a dosshouse for the homeless.

The question pressing on his mind was no longer the one that had occupied his thoughts when he emerged for the last time through the arched gateway of Princetown's Work Centre. Back then, less than a year ago, he was asking himself 'How shall I live?' – an openly optative query, contemplating possibilities for the kind of life he might wish to shape for himself. It had seemed a straightforward matter of choosing his path into the future, deciding on a satisfactory line of work and a *modus vivendi* in the postwar world. Then, as his circumstances grew more difficult, the question had changed, not in form but in significance. 'How shall I live?' acquired a simpler point with an apprehensive edge, expressing concern about the very means of subsistence. And now, although physical survival was still an urgent challenge, he had become more preoccupied with a painfully moral version of the question: it was 'How do I live *with myself?*'

Again and again during this protracted self-interrogation he found himself brooding over the letter that discarded a short-lived friendship. When he had first read Morecroft's words it was momentarily difficult to recognise himself in them, as if facing his deceptive double in a smudged mirror. Yet the truth of the letter's severe rebuke couldn't be denied: Staines had never confessed that he was largely to blame for Lavinia's terrible death. It had been easier to tell himself that little purpose would be served by a public acknowledgement of his role. Wrapping it in silence, he had kept the whole episode hidden for years, and in doing so had implicitly demeaned the memory of her even while it continued to haunt him. This concealment was, he could now admit, a lapse of probity – masked, ironically, by the uncompromising stance he had taken against the war.

Lying back on his comfortless bed, hands clasped behind his head as he stared with vacant eyes at the ugly ceiling, he recognised for the first time how he had let a fatal rift open up between inner and outer layers of his conscience. It had not struck him before that an effort to live a conscientious life could become equivocal in this way, bifurcating into the voice within and the voice audible to others. There was the private struggle in one's own heart, an effort to discern the right pathway and try to follow it, as exhorted by those inward-facing medieval treatises seen five years before at the antiquarian bookshop, *The Pricke of Conscience* and *Ayenbite of Inwyt*. Separable from that fervent and often remorseful absorption in oneself there was what it seemed proper to declare publicly as a matter of principle. No doubt it could tend to be smug, this outward-looking witness-bearing social conscience; it could be just a display of exemplary rectitude; yet if some brave moral sentinels, like William Wilberforce or Bertrand Russell, had not insisted on openly championing certain causes despite opprobrium, many arrant injustices would have persisted and vital reforms been postponed indefinitely.

But boldly taking a public stand on something unpopular, as he himself and his fellow conchies had done – what virtue could such a proud action really have if there was duplicity at the core of an individual's being? He remembered the damning biblical metaphor for hypocrites: whited sepulchres, outwardly handsome but full of dead men's bones.

Night closed in. Sleep kept its distance. To quell the disorder in his spirit he turned to a resource that had brought composure at difficult times in the past, murmuring to himself long passages of poetry memorised as a student, mainly from Shakespeare's sonnets and plays. The measured rhythms paced his pumping blood until two lines swelled in a harsh refrain: *Love is too young to know what conscience is…My conscience hath a thousand several tongues…* And each with its insistent tale to tell.

At last, exhausted, he began to drowse, and drifted into an uneasy sleep where darkening phrases took on twisted shapes. Those thousand several tongues turned into *severed* tongues, deathly grey, a grotesque row of them that began where he stood and stretched far away like pointed tombstones sticking up starkly from the muted ground. Waking, sweating, shuddering, he felt condemned by the nightmare's accusation. Lavinia's death had silenced her as surely as if he had cut out her tongue. What story would she relate if she could speak? And the creature that would have been her child – their child – but never drew breath: perpetually the mere shadow of an infant, it remained wordless too.

By the time morning came, he had made his decision. As a whited sepulchre, he now knew where he belonged. He would go to his long home.

Finally resolute, Gavin Staines left the hostel and began to walk.

He had not gone there before, but knew that the place he sought lay northward beyond Kentish Town and assumed that if he became uncertain of his whereabouts there would be helpful landmarks. Yet along the way he took little notice of what went on around him, hardly conscious of the bustling footpaths or the hubbub of omnibuses and locomotives, horse-drawn carts and motorcars. Though it happened to be a rainless day, the biting cold still penetrated his coat but he paid no attention to it, head down, almost oblivious to the here and now. His thoughts were engrossed in fragmentary residues from the past. Lavinia's laughter, the staid library and lecture rooms at Queen's College, the lustful tigers in the Regent's Park zoo. His dead mother, his irrevocably estranged father, the unhappy house where he had grown up. The two bookshops where he had worked. Field punishment at Harfleur. The hell pit at Boulogne. The oddly diverse group of conchies in his Princetown work gang – Latimer, Lindsay, Bryce and the rest. The apparently pointless wall they had built together.

As if coming out of a trance, he shook his head, looked about and saw that he must be near his destination. For some while he had been moving steadily up Highgate Road, and there on his left now was part of the eastern boundary of Hampstead Heath. Coming soon to the right-hand corner he wanted, he turned into Swain's Lane, which took him directly to the entrance he had read and heard about.

He went on through the open Tudor-arched gateway of an imposing stone building. Where had those blocks been hewn, and by whose hard labour? Within the grounds, just ahead of him as he walked past the chapel precinct, was a crescent-shaped colonnade. Beyond that, a flight of broad stone steps led towards higher ground. Ascending half way up the hill, he found that the path gradually sloped down to a massive and ornate entrance portal, embellished with oriental motifs and flanked by obelisks. Further in, extending for a hundred feet or more in the gloom, he saw a narrow deep-cut passage lined with a series of grandiose stone vaults, symmetrical in shape and size, each having a large locked cast-iron door. At the end of the avenue he came to a circular road, resembling the avenue in being a kind of open-topped shadowy tunnel, also with vaults on either side of it. From the centre of the island of land in the midst of this circle rose a magnificent Lebanese cedar. Looking back, he could see how much this whole place resembled a sombre public park, with its scatter of dark shrubs, its dense yew trees and bare-branched weeping willows. It was tidier once, he guessed, probably receiving little attention from gardeners during the war years. Tangled undergrowth had spread around some neglected areas. A few stones were choking in ivy, and others had been tilted or split by expanding roots.

Light snow had begun to fall. His wanderings took him close to two separate clusters of people: one group standing in front of a grave marker, hats doffed and heads bowed; the other headed by a pair walking slowly side by side, an elderly man with his arm protectively around the shoulders of a young weeping woman, probably his daughter, with two solemn youths just behind them. Insulated in their grief, neither group took any notice of Staines. If they had looked at him they might have seen something of the vagrant in his manner as he shuffled hesitantly along the crepuscular pathways with no apparent purpose. They might have observed his lips moving silently as he recited under his breath King Lear's words to the homeless and friendless Edgar: *Why, thou wert better in thy grave than to answer with thy uncovered body this extremity of the skies… Unaccommodated man is no more but such a poor, bare, forked animal as thou art.*

Now, suddenly, there was a crouching animal high above him, huge, perfectly still. Muzzle resting on its snow-covered paws, the great stone lion slept untroubled by any compunctious thoughts. An inscription on the pedestal beneath read simply *To the memory of George Wombwell, menagerist.*

Weak with cold and hunger and thirst, Gavin Staines wended his way slowly back to the avenue of vaults. In the fading light he saw that the door on one of them was ajar. He went in. As his eyes adjusted to the darkness he could make out the shape of a brick-lined cubicle, furnished with stone shelves that rose one above the other on three sides of the enclosed space. Dusty coffins lay upon the shelves on two of the sides. He climbed into a vacant shelf-space and lay on his back. From the deep inside pocket of his coat he took the volume of Shakespeare's *Complete Works*, and put it beneath his head as a pillow.

During the last two hours he had read many names incised in stone, the names of the mighty and the obscure. Even allowing for the inflation of epitaphic language, it seemed obvious enough that most of these men and women had gone to their graves respected and probably loved for the benefits they had given to others during their lifetime. What of his own influence on others? Entirely harmful, as far as he could tell. There was nobody whose life had been touched positively by his own.

What's a life worth, he asked himself, if it leaves no beneficent legacy? No child to whom a torch of tenderness could pass, no edifying work of art or scholarship, no monument to stir remembrance, no honourable example of how to act. He and his fellow-conchies used to say that war wasted people's lives, but there was more than one way to waste a life. Without a single good thing, he believed, to show for his 33 years on this earth, he felt the unforgiving darkness seep into him. Soon all the clamorous tongues of his conscience would fall silent, and the severed tongues of those he had rendered mute would cease to haunt his inward eye. He would amount to nothing more than bones mouldering among the stones.

AFTERWORD

CHARACTERS IN THE PREVIOUS PAGES ARE CREATURES OF my imagination, and most of the action in which they take part is also entirely fictitious. No actual persons correspond directly to Valerie Morton, Tim Holmes and other university students in the narrative foreground, or to Gavin Staines and his fellow conscientious objectors from a century ago, or to the particular Dartmoor prisoners and gaolers from the Victorian period who figure in my work of fiction – except that some components of Joshua Dunn's invented career resemble episodes in the true tale of Joe Denny as recorded by Trevor James in his lively book *Over the Wall and Away* (mentioned below), which helped to shape my first thoughts about writing this novel. Although a few people on the story's periphery, such as Pablo Fanque and J.A. Cramb, do have real-life counterparts bearing the same names and attributes, I have concocted their interactions with my central characters.

On the other hand, many aspects of *A Thousand Tongues* reflect historical facts. I gratefully acknowledge here the use I have made of research by a large number of scholars.

Historians have documented and discussed extensively the experiences of British conscientious objectors during World War 1. In addition to valuable online records such as the material assembled by the Peace Pledge Union (for example, http://www.ppu.org.uk/learn/infodocs/cos/st_co_wwone4. html) I consulted numerous publications in printed form. The most useful for my purposes were these: David Boulton, *Objection Overruled* (MacGibbon and Kee, 1967); Peter Brock, *These Strange Criminals: an anthology of prison memoirs by conscientious objectors to military service from the Great War to the Cold War* (University of Toronto Press, 2004); Simon Dell, *The Dartmoor Conchies* (The Dartmoor Company, 2017); Will Ellsworth-Jones, *We will not fight: the untold story of the First World War's Conscientious Objectors* (Aurum, 2008); Martin Ceadel, *Pacifism in Britain 1914-1945* (Clarendon Press, 1980); Felicity Goodall, *We Will Not Go to War* (History Press, 2011); John W. Graham, *Conscription and Conscience: A History 1916-1919* (Allen and Unwin, 1922); Adam Hochschild, *To End All Wars: A Story of Protest and Patriotism in the First World War* (Pan Macmillan, 2011); Thomas C. Kennedy, *The Hound of Conscience: A History of the No-Conscription Fellowship* (University of Arkansas Press, 1981); and John Rae, *Conscience and Politics: The British Government and the Conscientious Objector to Military Service 1916-1919* (Oxford University Press, 1970). I also found pertinent information about the treatment of conscientious objectors in two fine books written from outside the British experience: *We Will Not Cease* by New Zealand pacifist Archibald Baxter (1939; 2nd edn Caxton Press, 1968), and *Peacemongers* by Australian historian Bobbie Oliver (Fremantle Arts Centre Press, 1997).

For the history of blacks in Britain, I drew on Stephen Bourne, *Black Poppies: Britain's Black Community and the Great War* (Stroud, 2013); Nigel File and Chris Power, *Black Settlers in Britain 1555–1958* (Heinemann, 1981); Kenneth Little, *Negroes in Britain: a Study of Racial Relations in English Society* (Routledge and Kegan Paul, 1948); Norma Myers,

Reconstructing the Black Past: Blacks in Britain c.1780–1830 (Routledge, 1996); Ron Ramdin, *The Making of the Black Working Class in Britain* (Gower, 1987); Edward Scobie, *Black Britannia: a History of Blacks in Britain* (Johnson, 1972); John M. Turner, 'Pablo Fanque, Black Circus Proprietor,' in *Black Victorians/Black Victoriana*, ed. Gretchen Gerzina (Rutgers University Press, 2003), pp. 20-39; and James Walvin, *Black and White: the Negro and English Society 1555-1945* (Allen Lane Penguin, 1973).

On geographical and historical features of Dartmoor – the region generally and its prison in Princetown – I found excellent information on the website of the Dartmoor National Park Authority (http://www.virtuallydartmoor.org.uk), on personal sites, notably Tim Sandles' *Legendary Dartmoor* (http://www. legendarydartmoor.co.uk) and David Worth's *Old Princetown* (http://oldprincetown.weebly.com), in displays at the Dartmoor Prison Museum, and in several books: Helen Harris, *The Industrial Archaeology of Dartmoor* (David and Charles, 1968); L.A. Harvey and D. St Leger-Gordon, *Dartmoor* (Collins, 1953); Eric Hemery, *High Dartmoor: Land and People* (Robert Hale, 1983); Trevor James, *Over the Wall and Away: More Escapes from Dartmoor Prison* (Orchard Publications, 2006); Giles Playfair, *The Punitive Obsession: An Unvarnished History of the English Prison System* (Gollancz, 1971); Philip Priestley, *Victorian Prison Lives: English Prison Biography 1830-1914* (Methuen, 1985); J.E. Thomas, *The English Prison Officer since 1850: A Study in Conflict* (Routledge and Kegan Paul, 1972); and Basil Thomson, *The Story of Dartmoor Prison* (Heinemann, 1907). Thanks also to Simon Dell, Director and Coordinator of Moorland Guides (http://simondell.co.uk), who kindly answered my questions about matters of local topography. As well, my own direct observations while staying in the Dartmoor region and walking around it have contributed to the creation of this novel.

My main sources for war memorials were K.S. Inglis, *Sacred Places: War Memorials in the Australian Landscape* (Miegunyah Press, 1988); Mark Quinlan, *British War Memorials* (New Generation, 2005); John Stephens and Graham Seal, *Remembering the Wars: Commemoration in Western Australian Communities* (Black Swan Press, 2015); John J. Taylor, *Between Duty and Design* (UWAP, 2014); and Jay Winter, *Sites of Memory, Sites of Mourning: the Great War in European cultural history* (Cambridge University Press, 1995).

On miscellaneous other topics relevant to parts of my story, I visited countless websites but the following books were especially rich in detail: Brenda Assael, *The Circus and Victorian Society* (University of Virginia Press, 2005); Felix Barker and John Gay, *Highgate Cemetery: Victorian Valhalla* (John Murray, 1984); Dennis Brailsford, *Bareknuckles: A Social History of Prize-Fighting* (Lutterworth Press, 1988); Robin Evans, *The Fabrication of Virtue: English Prison Architecture, 1750-1840* (Cambridge University Press, 1982); George Orwell, *Down and Out in Paris and London* (Victor Gollancz, 1933); for insights into Queen's College London in the early twentieth century, Claire Tomalin, *Katherine Mansfield: A Secret Life* (Viking, 1987); and, particularly stimulating on Shakespearean voices, R.S. White, *Pacifism and English Literature: Minstrels of Peace* (Palgrave Macmillan, 2008).

I am deeply indebted to the authors and publishers of all those works, and also to the Random House Group for kind permission to quote a passage from Julian Barnes, *The Noise of Time* (Jonathan Cape, 2016).

My warm thanks go to some astute readers who, amidst their own busy commitments, generously made time to look at this novel in draft form and give me their discerning comments: Ali Jaquet, Gale MacLachlan, Linda Martin, Clive Newman and David Whish-Wilson. Many others have encouraged me in my writing: critical friends, book reviewers, appreciative readers, members of responsive audiences and literary groups of various kinds. Without their interest and support the life of a fictioneer would be much less pleasurable for me.

Some of the work on this book was done during my tenure of the J.S. Battye Memorial Fellowship awarded by the State Library of Western Australia. For the privilege of that fortunate experience, enabling me to explore diverse holdings in the Battye Library research collections, I gladly record my gratitude to Susanna Iuliano, Kate Gregory and Margaret Allen.

www.ingramcontent.com/pod-product-compliance
Lightning Source LLC
Chambersburg PA
CBHW031958050726
47590CB00006B/1951